SHADOWBORN SORCERESS

SHADOWS OF THE LOESS HILLS

1

SHADOWBORN SORCERESS

SHADOWS OF THE LOESS HILLS

1

Visit Mandi Oyster online at
www.MandiOyster.com

Facebook: https://www.facebook.com/MandiOysterAuthor
Instagram: https://www.instagram.com/MandiOyster/

This book is dedicated to Bella, Galadriel, Merida, Westley, and all the other kitties who have shared my home throughout the years.

Thank you for the inspiration.
Schmendrick is a little bit of each of you.

Trigger Warnings

*This book contains themes and descriptions
of past child abuse, abusive parents,
encounters with demons,
and references to possible sacrifice.*

Reader discretion is advised.

Subtitles

There are many differences between dogs and cats,
but the main one is attitude.

Dogs worship their people.
Cats expect their people to worship them.

Schmendrick is a magical cat.
He has the typical cattitude times one million.

The chapter titles were his idea,
a reminder that he believes he is far superior.
And in all honesty, he's probably right.

Prologue

*"Only two things are infinite, the universe and human stupidity,
and I'm not sure about the former." -Albert Einstein*

$\mathcal{T}$here is no shortage of monsters in this world.

They come in all shapes and sizes, all colors and creeds. They live in cities and in rural areas. They even reside in lands people have declared uninhabitable.

They walk among humans, living their lives, hidden behind a magic shield.

Some people believe me to be a monster.

Probably even you.

Chapter 1

"Life is tough, but it's tougher when you're stupid." -John Wayne

$\mathcal{A}$fter four years of working there, Harvest Moon Coffee Shop had become a home away from home. Its rustic charm made me feel safe. The bricks sticking through the plaster on the walls reminded me that everything was more than it seemed at first glance. There was something hidden beneath the masks that all of us wore, not just me.

I finished making Kayla's iced caramel latte and handed it across the wooden counter to her. "Have a good day!"

"Thank you, Molly." She took a sip before reaching into her scrubs for her keys. "You're a lifesaver, you know."

I smiled, wondering how life would be if I were still part of the cabal.

"Hey!" the guy next in line barked to get my attention. Staring into his brown eyes, I searched my memory for his name to write on the sleeve.

Smiling at him, I grabbed a cup. "Caramel and white chocolate breve, isn't it?" It wasn't right to know someone only by their order, but for some reason, names had always eluded me.

"Yeah." His lips lifted in a lopsided smirk that told me he knew I couldn't remember his name and that he wasn't about to offer it up without me asking first.

Not wanting to, I held my pen in the air for another couple of seconds.

Jason. That was it.

While I scribbled it above the Harvest Moon logo, I wondered again how I'd ended up here of all places. I didn't even like the smell of coffee.

One order blended into another until finally, with my last 32-ounce caramel, chocolate, dark chocolate, white chocolate, pumpkin, Irish cream, caramel syrup, salted caramel, blue raspberry, banana, with one white, one dark, one ristretto, whip with matcha sprinkled on top made, I hung my apron on the hook, pulled my jacket on over my black uniform t-shirt, and stepped out into the cloud-covered day.

Pulling my phone out of my pocket, I watched cat videos while I strolled the two blocks home. The bite in the air hadn't been there when I'd stepped outside for a break, but the wind had changed, and the cold sank into my bones. Looking up at the sky, I realized the clouds were threatening to drop the first snow of the year. There was nothing like Midwest weather, where you could have all four seasons in one day.

Walking up the three steps to my front door, I noticed the weeds in the flowerbeds, the peeling ivory paint on the wood siding, and the cracks in the cement. It was far from perfect, but it was mine.

I stuck my key in the lock and sucked in a breath, trying to let go of the stress from the day, the handful of customers who complained their coffee was too hot or too cold or too wrong, hoping that when I stepped inside the negativity would be left on the stoop like an unwanted visitor.

"Schmendrick!" I called as I stuffed my tips into the vase by the front door, fluffing out the silk roses to make them look like they hadn't been disturbed. Enough light flooded through the windows that I didn't need to bother with flipping the switches.

"Here, kitty, kitty." I kicked my tennis shoes off, then traipsed through the house, glancing into the living room, kitchen, and bathroom on the main floor. The bare eggshell walls stared back at me, urging me to decorate them. Someday, though, there was a good chance I'd have to run again, and I needed to be ready.

I shook off the morose thought, hoping it wouldn't sink into my subconscious and turn up in my nightmares, and continued my search. When I didn't find him, I climbed the stairs. "Schmendrick, I'm home!" I peeked into the spare room, but he wasn't there either. "I know you can hear me."

Pushing my half-closed door all the way open, I found him sprawled across my queen-size bed in a full-on sploot. A beam of light broke through the purple curtains, shining on his sleek black fur. He slowly opened his bright green eyes and yawned, showing off a mouth filled with sharp teeth. "Of course, I heard you. I'm not deaf, you know?" His voice held all the velvety charm of a storyteller, one that you could listen to for hours without ever growing tired of hearing, with a hint of mischief and wisdom blended in. "Why are you interrupting my beauty sleep?" He stretched in that way that cats do. "It had better be worth it."

"You're already handsome enough." I lifted him, rocking him like he was a little baby. He acted like I had violated him, squirming and trying to get down until I scratched his head.

A purr rumbled through him, vibrating against my fingers. "Did you need something, Molly?"

Setting him back down, I turned to the dresser to gather my clothes and caught a glimpse of myself in the mirror. I hadn't planned on looking, but the dark circles under my eyes grabbed my attention.

I turned away from my reflection and tossed my clothes onto my bed. My socks bounced over the mattress, knocking into the only picture I'd brought with me when I escaped. The frame toppled over with a loud clack. I circled the bed to stand the picture up.

Schmendrick stared up at me from the photo. He looked exactly the same. His fur was as sleek as it had always been. His eyes held that same knowing look, but I had changed immensely.

When I was younger, I hated everything that made me stand out from the other sorcerers. I'd hidden my horns and tail, made my hair blonde—thinking it was the furthest from a demon's—changed my eyes to an icy blue, and my skin to porcelain. The glamour made me look like my mother's daughter, a powerful beauty, not a monster.

The night I left the cabal, I changed all of that. Even though some people looked at me like I was a freak, I decided my natural purple hair was unusual and gorgeous. It fell in waves to the middle of my back. Blue eyes didn't match my olive skin, so I changed them to gray.

That was how I looked now... but tired.

"If you're just going to stare at the old picture, I'm going back to sleep." Schmendrick fluffed the comforter on my bed, getting ready to lie back down.

I turned toward him. "Why did I think I could do this on my own?"

"Treats." He tipped his head to the side, and his ears flicked. Then he jumped down and wove through my legs. "Then talk." He trotted toward the steps, his tail straight up in the air, and I knew I would get no more out of him until I met his demands. I set my socks with the rest of my clothes and wondered if this was the first time he'd gotten off the bed today.

Schmendrick entered the kitchen ahead of me and watched as I unlocked the cabinet. As soon as I pulled the container of treats out, his whiskers curled forward, and his eyes dilated. By the time I put a handful on the silver platter that he insisted on eating from, he was practically drooling.

"Not enough." He sat, curling his tail around his legs. The tip of it twitched. "Not for this conversation." He lifted a paw and licked it nonchalantly, but I knew it was killing him not to scarf them down.

Shaking my head, I added another handful. "You're going to get fat."

"So." He snagged a treat in his claws, holding it in front of his mouth. "It's not like you ever take me out in public anyway."

I sat at the table, drumming my fingers on the surface. "We tried that. You wouldn't shut up."

"And, I still don't see why that mattered." He gobbled up a couple more morsels, trying to look dignified but failing miserably. "If you can talk, why can't I?"

Knowing it wouldn't do any good to explain it for the umpteenth time, I waited for him to finish. Once he did, he jumped onto the chair across from mine and stared at me over the table.

"I know this isn't what I'm supposed to be doing with my life." I sighed, and so did he. "Why didn't I stay in the cabal and learn how to be the next archon?"

Schmendrick rolled his eyes. If you've never seen a cat do that, you obviously don't have a magical cat. "You know why." He lifted his paw to his mouth and licked his claws. When I just kept looking at him, he said, "Because the cabal is filled with insensitive bastards who are utterly terrified of your magnificence, and frankly, you deserve far better than that."

He had a point.

The name-calling and ostracization were more than an insecure teen could handle. The abuse… I pinched my eyes shut, not wanting to fall down that rabbit hole again. It wasn't my fault I had a demon for a sperm donor.

When I'd asked Mom why he seduced her, she had straightened her shoulders, her stance regal and arrogant. "I am from the Ravenwood line. We are the strongest sorcerers still living. We have not diluted our blood by mixing with humans." She'd stared at me for a long time, and I'd known that she was looking through my glamour, seeing all the ways I reminded her of him. The spiraling horns, pointed ears, and fangs. "But you… you will be stronger than us all." She'd squeezed my shoulder. "One day, you will take my place, and no one will dare challenge the new archon."

Her normal, human-looking eyes had sparkled. Power meant the world to my mother, and even though she had it on her own, her hunger for more could not be satiated.

I stared out the window, looking at the maple tree in my backyard, but not really seeing it. I'd turned twenty-two on January 9th, and the niggling fear that had been my constant companion since fleeing the cabal had turned into a formidable beast that I couldn't conquer.

Mom had always emphasized how important my twenty-third birthday would be, how my training to become archon would begin in earnest after it. Even though I hadn't felt the slightest brush of magic, I knew they would come for me. I knew they would drag me back to the cabal.

"One of these days, fate will come knocking, and your path will be laid out in front of you." Schmendrick jumped down and strutted into the living room. "But for now, quit dwelling and go shower. You smell like you've been pumpkin spiced."

Chapter 2

"You can lead a human to knowledge, but you can't make him think."
-Mandi Oyster

Schmendrick had been cleaning himself since he sent me to shower, so I grabbed my coat and a handful of tips and stepped out into the night. Standing on the porch, I let my eyes adjust.

Staring up into the heavens, I felt my shoulders relax. Millions of stars shone down at me, twinkling against the velvety darkness. Living in a small town had its benefits. Growing up, I'd had no idea that the night sky could come alive like this.

As I walked along Locust Street and breathed in the cool, evening air, I was grateful I'd sought refuge in Glenwood, Iowa, where most, if not all, of the residents were blissfully unaware of magic. It was only about thirty minutes away from my cabal, but most sorcerers avoided sparsely populated areas. It was too difficult to hide what we were. Unless, like me, they had forsaken their magic. It had been months since I'd so much as bibbidied or bobbidied, let alone booed. (No, we don't actually say those things, but you catch my drift.)

I was going to have to soon. I could feel the power building inside of me, urging me to release it, but as soon as I let it go, it would be a beacon to my cabal, showing them exactly where they could find me.

That was why I had moved to a bedroom town. I could drive back into Council Bluffs and, with a bit of luck, avoid seeing anyone from my cabal, Bellevue, or Omaha to release my magic, and hopefully, nobody would think to come to Glenwood to look for me.

But, still, there was a risk, and I wasn't quite ready to take it just yet. Every time I had before, it'd been days before I'd felt safe stepping out of my door.

Maybe I should drive to St. Joe or Kansas City. It wasn't the first time the thought had crossed my mind. Both would be all-day trips there and back again—definitely not a hobbit's holiday, though—but they might be far enough away to keep me hidden.

Eventually, we'll find you. My stepfather's voice echoed inside my head.

Dread skittered up my spine, and my heart raced as I cautiously glanced over my shoulder.

Nothing. Just an empty stretch of sidewalk and a trailer filled with fall decorations in Jim Hughes Real Estate's parking lot.

Caius wasn't there. It was just his memory. Just the fear of him finding me.

I inhaled and held the fresh, evening air in my lungs. Then I released it, hoping all my anxiety would follow it out of my body.

I wanted to be brave, to walk the eight blocks to Parea, and let off a little steam, but I couldn't force my feet to take another step, not with the spirits hovering outside Peterson Mortuary. Sometimes ghosts followed their bodies before realizing they'd died. They lingered for a while before moving on to the afterlife or deciding to remain Earthbound.

I watched their transparent figures ambling about and debated crossing the street to get by them. Instead, I turned around and dashed back to my house, fumbling with my key and shutting the door harder than I meant to.

Glowing eyes peered down at me from the upstairs hallway. "How far'd you make it this time? To the sidewalk?" Schmendrick moved two steps closer. "Impressive, really."

"Who knew a talking cat would be so snarky?" I twisted the deadbolt and relaxed slightly when it slammed into place.

He rubbed against my leg, wrapping his tail around my calf. At one time, I would have been shocked that he could move so quickly and silently, but I was used to it after living with him for seventeen years. "My guess? Everyone but you, but don't worry, ignorance can sometimes be bliss, or so they say."

Frost clung to the blades of grass, edging them in white lace. The fresh, clean scent brought on by the cold air invigorated me. There was a spring in my step that had been missing since I didn't even know when. It hadn't been there before I left my cabal, and fear of being found had kept my spirits down ever since.

As soon as I opened the door to Harvest Moon, my nose was assaulted by the smell of coffee. My shoulders dropped as I trudged behind the counter. It wasn't that I didn't enjoy my job. If only there were a way to get rid of the scent that clung to the air in here and followed me home, trapped in the fibers of my clothes.

I traded my jacket for an apron, adjusted my name tag, and donned my smile just in time to greet the first customers of the day.

A steady stream of regulars filled the first hour. I knew most of their orders by heart but waited patiently as they perused the menu, finally deciding on the same drinks they had every other day.

Finally, with the early rush of customers taken care of, I had a moment to breathe. I grabbed a rag and mopped up spills. Then I refilled the napkin dispenser. I was rinsing my hands off when the bell above the door rang.

The hairs on my arms rose, and thousands of spiders skittered down my spine.

Never before had it sounded so ominous.

I turned slowly, fully expecting the devil himself to have entered.

A bear of a man stood silhouetted in the doorway. As he stepped forward, I moved back.

My magic surged, fighting for release, burning my fingertips, and pulsing in my chest. I clenched my fists at my sides, trapping it inside me, praying it didn't flare like a beacon.

This was the type of man my stepfather would send to retrieve me. Someone I wouldn't stand a chance of fighting against. Someone whose magic was a match for my own.

He strode beneath the light. His curly, salt-and-pepper hair fell to his shoulders, and his well-trimmed beard parted to reveal a nervous smile. His kind brown eyes met mine, and I relaxed instantly.

"Welcome to Harvest Moon." The words spilled from me automatically, and I was surprised to find that my voice didn't shake at all. "What's your order?"

"Well, I'd like a large cold brew. Three sugar in the raw. Light ice with oat milk."

I grabbed a cup and slid the collar on. "Name?"

"Chuck, but ah, please melt the sugar with a bit of hot coffee." His smile slipped out again. "If you don't melt it first, your first couple of drinks are unsweetened with sugar gravel."

I scrawled his name on the collar and set about making his coffee just as he'd asked, ensuring the sugar melted before adding the rest of the ingredients. As I went to hand him the cup, I stared at the name, wondering why I'd written it that way. Shrugging, I handed it over.

"Chuckles, huh? I like it." He grinned and took a sip, savoring it. Then he glanced at my name tag. "The coffee's good, too, Molly-cule." Laughter sparkled in his eyes.

Blushing, I turned away as he put a tip in the jar. "Thank you."

As soon as the door shut, Simone walked over from the drive-thru window. Her blonde ponytail bobbed from side to side with each step she took. Her black boots clacked across the tiled floor. "Flirtin' with the customers." She reached into the jar, and I envied the way she looked so put together when I felt like I was falling apart all of the time. "Get ya a good tip?"

"I-I wasn't." I shook my head. We'd worked together for the four years since I'd moved to Glenwood, but we never talked after hours. "I have no idea why I wrote that or how much he tipped."

"Well, he wasn't my type." She tapped a red fingernail against lips of the same color. "Not that any man is." Flashing me a smile, showing off her perfectly straight, bleached teeth, she added, "But I'm willing to flirt for tips, too. Use what God gave ya, right?"

I looked from her to the door, wondering what kind of tips I would get if I actually tried flirting. Did I even know how to?

Simone dropped the cash into the jar and sashayed to the window. With my back to her, I closed my eyes and focused on my breathing, flexing and releasing my fingers until I felt like my magic wasn't about to erupt. I was only two hours into my eight-hour shift, and I already felt like I'd run a marathon.

Thankfully, I didn't embarrass myself again before my shift ended. However, my magic burned inside me, searching for a way out. One more intense encounter would be the end of my time in Glenwood.

I clocked out and practically ran through the door, pulling my coat on as I went. The steel-gray clouds threatened to drop their snowy loads at any second, and as much as I hated the idea, I was going to have to go somewhere to release my magic. I was going to have to drive through the coming storm.

My hand shook as I tried to jam my key in the lock. I inhaled a huge gulp of air, hoping to steady myself. Then I tried again. When I pushed the door open, Schmendrick was sitting on the table next to the vase with my tips.

"Magic is oozing off of you." He casually licked his paw before rubbing it over his ear. Then he stared at me like I'd told him to clean his litterbox. "I've been able to sense you all day. I couldn't even get a decent nap in."

I pulled a handful of bills out of the vase and jogged up the stairs. "Why didn't you let me know?" I tapped my finger against my temple.

The first time I'd heard his voice in my mind, I'd been close to five. My magic was just coming in, and I couldn't control it at all. Most children that age might produce a sprinkle, but not me.

Rain poured from the ceiling, filling my bedroom. I climbed onto my dresser, but the water surged past my thighs.

As it rose, I screamed, "Mo-om! Da-ad!" Tears streamed from my eyes, mixing with the flood, and sobs choked me.

I tilted my head back, but the water climbed over my chin and poured down my throat. I thrashed, kicking and clawing, fighting to get the air my lungs so desperately craved.

Calm yourself, child. The unexpected voice startled me, halting my flailing. *Be still.*

My body responded to his command, and though fear held me in its clutches, the water receded, leaving me lying on the floor, sucking down oxygen. A cat had curled up on top of me. His eyes stared into mine. Their vibrant green reminded me of a forest after a spring rain.

I smiled at the kitty, and he bit my belly. "Ow!" *I jerked up, and the cat sprang off me.* "What was that for?"

"When a cat saves your life—" *he sat, curling his tail around his feet* "—then sits on you, the proper thing to do is to swear your eternal devotion to said cat… or at the very least, to pet him. It's common sense, really."

"You talk!" *I scooted back. The magic overload and nearly drowning were too much to deal with. But a talking cat! I thought I was going crazy.*

He lifted his lip, exposing a fang. "Aren't you familiar with familiars?"

"Dad"—*even though he never thought of me as his daughter, Caius insisted on being called 'Dad'*—"says familiars are just stories crazy cat ladies tell." *The air conditioner kicked on, and I shivered in my wet clothes. Pulling my legs up, I wrapped my arms around them. Then I let my voice take on Dad's imperious tone.* "They make those stories up so they don't look like weirdos conversing with stupid animals."

"Which is precisely why a familiar's dulcet tones have never graced your stepfather's ears." *His eyes glinted with mischief.*

"I believe I explained that." Schmendrick's voice brought me back to the moment.

I shook my head, clearing the memory and trying to figure out what Schmendrick was talking about. "You did?"

His ears flicked back as he sauntered to the end of the table and jumped to the floor. "I was trying to nap before our trip. I'm sure you'll yammer the entire way." He glanced over his shoulder at me before disappearing into the kitchen. "Or worse yet… sing."

"If you know we're leaving, why'd you go in there?" I looked up the stairs, wondering if I should shower or at least change my clothes. Would I be taking too long, risking too much?

He peeked around the corner, narrowing his eyes in mock disappointment. "Really, Molly?" He tsked. "I thought you were smarter than that." He turned and flicked his tail. "I won't be going anywhere without treats, and a quick shower would do you a latte good."

Chapter 3

"The two most common elements in the universe are hydrogen and stupidity." –Harlan Ellison

*G*inormous snowflakes splashed against my windshield in slushy explosions that left my view obstructed before my wipers had a chance to clear them. Ice clung to the edges of the blades, and frost crept across the bottom of my windows. The only good thing was that it wasn't covering the road yet, but if it snowed like this all the way to Kansas City, it was going to be a rough trip.

In the short time it took me to drive down Highway 34 to I-29, my hands were cramped, and my shoulders were stiff. I spent most of that stretch praying no deer would jump out in front of me, especially around Mile Hill Lake.

After I merged onto the interstate, I glanced at the passenger seat. Schmendrick was curled up, sleeping soundly. "In my next life, I'm going to be a cat," I mumbled.

"Only if the gods favor you." He peeked at me through a half-slitted eye. "Wake me up when we get there… but only if you have treats. Lots of treats."

"So much for listening to me yammer the whole way." I pried my fingers from the steering wheel, flexing them several times before turning the radio up loud enough to drown out the hum of the tires. Schmendrick was wrong about me singing the whole way. I was too focused on staying on the road to even register what was playing.

My headlights shone on the flakes, reminding me of traveling at light speed in the old Star Wars movies. By the time I crossed the Missouri border, the storm slowed, allowing me to relax a little.

"If only." My voice was louder than I'd intended, but Schmendrick didn't even twitch an ear. "I'm ready to be there."

Once I reached St. Joseph, the snow had stopped falling, leaving the roads slushy and wet. I took the first exit and pulled up to a Sinclair station. "Schmendrick." I petted his ear, rubbing the inside with my thumb and the outside with my index and middle fingers. I loved how soft and velvety it felt, but it wasn't something he let me do very often. If he had been awake, he would have jerked his head away.

He slowly blinked his eyes open and yawned, his gaze filled with languid disdain. Stretching his front legs and extending his claws, he purposefully dug them into the seat. Not for the first time, I was grateful I had opted for cloth interior. "Are we there?"

"We're here." I waved my hand at the window. "I need something to drink and maybe a candy bar."

His ears pulled back, and I swore he glared at me. "Why, pray tell, did you wake me then?"

"So I could listen to your beautiful voice." I petted his chin, and despite his grumpiness, he leaned into it. "Do you want anything?"

He opened one green eye to peer up at me. "Other than a nap?" He flicked his tail twice. "No, Molly."

As much as I wanted to, I didn't slam the door shut. I closed it as quietly as I could and made my way through the slush to the store. My first stop was the restroom. Then I stood in front of the candy bars, amazed by the variety. "How'm I supposed to choose?" I said aloud, earning a strange look from the man reaching for a Snickers.

I finally settled on a Salted Caramel Twix. You couldn't go wrong with caramel, right?

When I was searching the cooler for the perfect drink, magic rubbed up against me, just a slight brush, but it sent shivers racing down my spine. I glanced over my shoulder, wondering why there was familiarity in that touch. I knew I'd felt it before, but it was too little for me to place.

Striding in front of the coolers, I looked down each row, expecting to see a familiar face, but there was nobody around. I stood on my tiptoes and scanned the convenience store. The few people inside weren't paying any attention to me.

I walked back to the cooler, and as I reached inside, that same magic grazed against mine. Sparks danced on my fingertips, and Schmendrick's voice in my head nearly made me drop my pop. *Molly, get out here now!*

I raced to the front of the store, held up my drink and candy bar for the cashier to see, and threw a twenty on the counter. "Keep the change." I rushed outside and yanked my car door open. "What's going on?" I plopped down in my seat and yanked my seatbelt across me, fumbling with clicking it in place.

"Magic is spilling out of you worse than a tipped-over fishbowl." He brushed his cheek against my hand, and the tips of each strand of fur were highlighted in purple.

"Oh, God." I slammed the car into reverse.

He set his paw on top of my hand. "Calm down. You're bound to attract more attention if you're driving like a bat out of hell."

"Where do I go?" My voice trembled slightly.

"Stop somewhere between here and Kansas City." He circled the seat multiple times before finally lying down and curling his tail around himself. "Ideally, amidst the unending cornfields. Unleash your magic in one of those mouse-infested expanses, then head toward KC for a stretch before flipping a whooptakai."

I glanced at him through the corner of my eye.

"What?" He settled his head on his paws. "I like the way it rolls off my tongue. Whooptakai."

Shrugging my shoulder, I tapped my thumb against the steering wheel while waiting for the red light to turn. "Why go…" Schmendrick's soft snores, the ones he insisted he didn't make, sounded from the passenger seat before I had a chance to finish my question. "To be able to sleep like that." I shook my head, knowing it would never happen.

Heading south on I-29, my heart raced, and I gripped the steering wheel way too tightly. Every half second or so, I glanced at the rearview mirror. If anyone was following me, I couldn't tell. It was dark, and the headlights behind me caught in the water and frost on the back window, blurring them and making them all look the same, but that didn't keep me from looking again and again. I wanted to race away so that I would know if one of them was trying to keep pace with me, but I drove the speed limit, heeding Schmendrick's advice.

Tension hardened the muscles in my shoulders and made a pounding headache climb the back of my neck and up my skull. I rubbed my right arm, hoping to ease the pain that had settled there.

Schmendrick climbed onto my lap and made biscuits on my thigh. After a few minutes, he curled up and purred louder than I could ever remember. The sound reminded me of a tree frog croaking. (I know that sounds unbelievable, but you've gotta hear it to understand.)

With his purr rumbling against my body, I felt my blood pressure drop, making me relax my grip on the wheel, and I stopped fretting over whether or not I was being followed and just drove.

"When you reach the upcoming bend, switch off the headlights, and hit the accelerator with all your might." Schmendrick hadn't sat up or looked out the window, so I had no idea how he knew where we were. "Take the next exit." He stretched his front legs out before curling up again. "With a bit of luck, you might shake that fool off your tail."

The headlights behind me disappeared when I drove around the curve. I shut mine off, and panic set in. "How'm I supposed to do this?! I can't see a thing."

"Must I do everything myself?" Schmendrick stood on my lap with his front paws on the top of the steering wheel. He glanced back at me with that humans-are-pathetic look. "Gun it, or this won't work."

Against my best judgment, I pressed the pedal to the floor. My heart rate sped up along with my car, and after a few seconds, I realized I was holding my breath.

"Keep going straight. Okay, now slight left." His tail swung back and forth, hitting me with each pass.

I clenched the wheel and leaned forward, but it was no use. I couldn't see a thing in front of me. Out here, in the middle of nowhere with no streetlights and the moon blanketed in a thick layer of clouds, the night was darker than any I remembered.

Glancing in the mirror, the headlights were much smaller than they had been, but one set in the left lane was gaining. Trusting Schmendrick would help me get there safely, I sped up even more. Wondering the whole time why someone would trust a cat. Thankfully, I couldn't tell how fast I was going. Knowing would've probably given me a heart attack.

"The exit's coming up." Excitement oozed from Schmendrick's voice. He turned to look at me. His whiskers curled forward in eager anticipation. "Don't slow down. I'll tell you when to exit." He set his paw on top of mine. "Don't screw this up. I'm not ready to lose another one of my nine lives."

I wanted to remind him that at least he would live, but fear kept the words trapped inside me. There was a light at the end of the off-ramp where it met the road I would be turning onto. I hoped it would be enough to guide me so this wouldn't end up being a suicide mission.

"Ease off the gas," his voice was slow, drawing out each word, "but don't touch the brakes."

The air in the car felt thick. My heart pounded against my ribs, and sweat dotted my hairline, dripping from my temples. I couldn't let them find me. I couldn't go back. The life I'd made in Glenwood wasn't perfect, but it was mine. The choices I'd made were mine. In the cabal, I wouldn't have the luxury of making decisions. I would go back to being a tool and an outcast.

"Exit now." Purrs rumbled through his body. "When I say, crank the wheel to the right, and pray to the gods, or if you'd rather, me, that we make it."

A nervous laugh escaped my lips at that comment. I always knew Schmendrick had a god-complex—what cat didn't—but I was surprised to hear him say it out loud.

"Now!"

I cranked the wheel and closed my eyes. The tires squealed, and my heart lodged in my throat, making me suck in panicked gulps of air.

"Straighten it out," he mewed, the pitch of his voice hovering between fear and excitement. "Not bad for a demon sorceress."

I rolled my eyes at him and peeled my fingers off the steering wheel. My knuckles were sore from clenching it so tightly.

"I guess since you're the only one, I should just say, 'Not bad for you,' shouldn't I?" He curled up on the seat. "Turn on your daytime running lights, and don't slow down yet. Drive about ten miles, then pull into a cornfield and do your thing. Try not to make a mess of it. Cleaning up after you makes it hard to get a proper nap."

I did as he said, constantly checking my mirrors to see if anyone was following me, but it seemed I'd lost my tail for now.

At almost exactly ten miles, I found a pull-off into a field. "How—" I stopped before I could finish the question. Even if he was awake, he wouldn't tell me how he knew about the field. In all the time I had known Schmendrick, he'd told me very little about himself. He said his past didn't matter. All that mattered was that he was with me now. I half expected to wake up one morning and find that he'd moved on, but so far Mr. Snarky Bottom had stuck with me.

I got out of the car and pulled my jacket tighter as I walked toward the rows of corn that towered above me. My boots sank into the rain-softened earth beneath my feet.

The clouds parted, and the full Hunter's Moon shone down on me. I basked in its glow. Sure, the sun was nice, but its light was harsh and blinding. The moon, though, was made for creatures like me. Letting go of my glamour, I transformed into my true body. My tail swished behind me, and my horns spiraled through the air. My shadow stretched in front of me, terrifying and awesome. I rarely ever let the real me loose, not even when I was home alone, but at that moment, it felt right.

I lowered my gaze from the blue-edged clouds surrounding the moon and focused on my car. The person following me was still out there, assumedly searching for me. Not wanting whoever it was to find me, I concentrated on the filthy black paint. Slush and dirt had been kicked up off the road while I drove through the snowstorm, leaving my car a horrible mess.

Flicking my hand in its direction, magic flowed from my fingertips. Even though most people would call me a witch, I was half sorceress. Both used magic, but sorceresses were more like Liv Beaufont and less like Hermione Granger. We didn't use wands or cauldrons. We didn't ride brooms or play Quidditch. We were born with magic coursing through our bodies, and even though we looked human, we were as different from them as they were from apes.

As I called upon my magic, my muscles relaxed. It poured out of me, and the tension in my body eased, reminding me of lying on a massage table while a gifted masseuse worked the knots in my shoulders. I knew my body would ache later, but at that moment, it felt divine.

Silver spread over the hood and then down the sides of my SUV, changing it to look like so many others on the interstate. Then the license plates changed from Iowa to Missouri.

My magic hadn't dwindled, so I turned my attention to the crops. I couldn't create food, but I could expand what was already there. I lifted my hands, weaving them until a net of power hovered above the field. As it settled on the stalks, each ear of corn filled out until it was nearly bursting from its husk. Whoever this farmer was, he would have a record yield without any clue why.

Once finished, my arms dropped to my sides as if they were boneless, and my gaze inadvertently returned to the moon. A thin tendril of cloud covered the bottom of it. Magic danced in the air, its release leaving me spent. I closed my eyes and breathed deeply, feeling more like myself than I had in months. I needed to do this more often, but the fear of being caught held me back.

A wolf howled, and I snapped my eyes open.

Another answered its call, and I decided it was time for me to leave. There weren't timber wolves in this area anymore. There hadn't been since the 1800s.

That meant that these were werewolves, and I needed to get out of their territory.

I ran back to my car while donning my glamour. Schmendrick was still curled up on the passenger seat. "Feel better?"

"Much, but we gotta get outta here." I jerked my seatbelt on and drove toward the interstate.

He flicked his tail a couple of times before wrapping it around himself. "The full moon is the one time that they can't control their change. They're not concerned about you. They're out there running around, chasing their tails, like the stupid dogs they are."

"I'm sure, but that doesn't mean I want them to find me out here alone."

He jumped up, staring at me over the console. I glanced at him for a second before turning my attention back to the road. "Alone? You think you're alone?"

"I was when I was in that cornfield." I reached over to scratch his ears, but he jerked his head back.

He turned his back on me, walked in three circles, and settled on the seat facing away from me. "You, my dear, are never alone. Even if I'm sleeping on your bed and you're at work, you are not alone. I can sense you. I know when you need me, and I will be there in a heartbeat if need be."

"I didn't mean anything by it." I twisted my hands on the steering wheel, trying to figure out how I ended up in this predicament. "I know that you are always there for me, but to the wolves, I would have looked alone. That was all I meant, Schmen."

"Let me get some sleep." The annoyance drained from his voice, so I figured I was forgiven.

I drove to the interstate and headed south. If any magic was still leaking from me, I didn't want to lead my stalker to Glenwood. It would be best to let any residual power wear off before driving home.

It was three in the morning when I walked through the door. I trudged up the stairs, praying I'd led the stalker astray, and threw myself down on my bed, falling asleep before I remembered I hadn't changed my clothes.

Chapter 4

"In view of the fact that God limited the intelligence of man, it seems unfair that He did not also limit his stupidity." –Konrad Adenauer

Melissa wiped her feet on the rug as she walked to the counter. The snow had melted already, leaving a muddy mess behind. She looked worse than I felt. Her hair was pulled up in a messy bun, and by messy, I meant it was a total disaster. Twigs and leaves clung to the strands. Dirt smeared her cheeks, and dark rings surrounded her eyes.

"You, uh, you've got something in your hair." I reached over and pulled a stick out, holding it up for her to see.

Her cheeks reddened slightly, and she flashed a smile, showing elongated canines. "My dog got out, and I had to chase him through our timber."

"Hopefully, you found him." I grabbed a cup and waited for her to confirm her usual order.

Her eyes sparkled, and her voice took on a sultry tone that I probably wouldn't have picked up on if I didn't know what she was. "Oh, I caught him." She seemed lost in the memory for a few seconds before saying, "Let's go with a hot caramel macchiato."

"This one's on me." I set her drink on the counter and smiled. "I think you need this today." I turned around to grab a rag so she wouldn't feel obligated to drop a tip in the jar or to make it bigger in exchange for the free coffee.

I heard her cup slide toward her and turned back to wipe off the counter. "Aww, thank you, Molly." She took a sip. "You're sweet as can be."

As far as I knew, nobody in Glenwood had any idea that I was a sorceress, but over the last few years, I'd discovered that Melissa and her friends were all part of the Loess Hills Pack. When I'd settled here, I hadn't realized this was their territory. There were at least twenty werewolves in it, and they made mornings after full moons much more interesting.

Throughout the rest of my shift, several members of the pack staggered in. Some were a little more put together than Melissa, and others… well, it was amazing they could find the energy to push the door open.

I paid for each of their drinks. It wasn't going to be a profitable day, but there were things in life that were more important than money. Even though I wasn't great at making friends, I knew that having a pack of wolves on my side could be beneficial.

"Why do you do that?" Simone asked as I lifted my apron over my head.

The disgust in her voice made my eyes roll, and I was glad my back was turned so she didn't notice. "Do what?"

She huffed as she tossed the rag onto the counter. "If they can't afford to buy coffee, they shouldn't come in here."

"Who says they can't afford it?" I folded my arms over my chest and moved one foot back, widening my stance.

Her lip lifted, and she shuddered. "Didn't you see how dirty they were? It's too early for that to be from hard work. It's just downright filth."

"Haven't you ever had a bad day?" There had to be more to her than painted on, designer jeans and manicured fingernails, didn't there? "Or wanted to pay it forward? If you do good, good comes back to you." I clocked out for lunch, grabbing my coat but not putting it on. I needed to get away from her before I accidentally outed the wolves.

Maybe I'd tempted fate by saying that. Maybe I hadn't done enough good to cover the bad. Maybe it was just a coincidence, but when I stepped outside, the air felt charged.

The door to the coffee shop closed with an ominous thud before I could step back inside. I backed up against the building and looked around, searching for the source of the energy, but I didn't see anyone who wasn't from Glenwood.

"Maybe they were just passing through," I said, hoping I would believe it, but I didn't. It was too much of a coincidence after being followed last night. I opened the door and slipped through it. I threw my coat on the first table I came to and slumped into the chair. Holding my head in my hands, I tried to figure out what to do next. Moving seemed to be my only option.

I'd tried not to get attached. I'd kept from making friends. But the thought of leaving made tears well up in my eyes. I wiped them away, but more pooled.

"Oh, honey, are you okay?" Viv, my boss, pulled out a chair and sat across from me. Her warm, brown eyes were filled with sympathy. Since day one, she had felt more like a surrogate mother to me than a boss. She wanted the best for all of her employees, and even though she was in charge, we all knew that she truly cared about each of us.

I opened my mouth to answer, but knew if I did, the tears would fall faster, harder, so I covered it with my hand and lifted my shoulders.

"We're pretty slow." She looked around the seating area as if to emphasize her point. A couple people sat at tables, but most of them were empty. "Why don't you take the rest of the day off?"

Somehow, I was able to say, "Thank you," without breaking down.

She stood up and patted my shoulder. "Sit here as long as you want, dear, and if you need someone to talk to about it, my door is always open."

I stared out the window, watching the traffic drive by on Locust Street, wondering what the right move was, trying to figure out what to do next. Laying my head on the table, I breathed in through my nose for a few seconds, holding the oxygen in my lungs for five seconds before exhaling.

The bell above the door rang, and I turned ,expecting to see one of the regulars. My heart plummeted.

They'd found me.

Chapter 5

"Stupidity is also a gift of God, but one mustn't misuse it."
-Pope John Paul II

Caelan.

My one regret. The only friend I'd had besides Schmendrick, my cat. He probably would've run with me, but I hadn't been willing to risk it.

Instead, like a coward, I'd snuck away, hiding in the shadows, leaving behind years of abuse at the hands of my stepfather, years of bullying from the other sorcerers my age who could see through my glamour to the demon underneath, from a world filled with magic and monsters, and from Caelan.

He strode toward me. The light streaming in through the windows backlit him. When he took another step, the effect was gone, leaving him momentarily silhouetted between the tables and chairs.

As he walked closer, his boots clomped against the wood floor. His gaze roved across the room, taking everything in.

Except for the frown that pulled his completely kissable lips down—for the most part, they'd been off-limits since we'd only been friends, but there was that one time when he forgot—he looked just like I remembered him. Brown hair that curled at the ends. Hazel eyes curtained by thick, dark lashes. His charcoal sweater covered a body that, unless he had changed in the four years since I'd last seen him, was hardened by time spent at the gym.

His magic brushed up against me, and I realized it was him I had sensed last night. He'd been the one following me.

Of course, it was him.

Who else would they send to bring me back to the cabal? He'd been my only friend. The only one who hadn't cared that I was half demon, but the look in his eyes as he walked toward me was far from pleasant.

Hurt and anger darkened his irises. He stopped a few paces away from me and shoved his hands into his pockets. His eyebrows pinched together. "Molly?"

"Caelan." Now that he was here, there were so many things I wanted to say to him. I pushed against the table, scooting my chair back. "I'm sorry." I grabbed my coat, ready to dart out the door. "I just... I couldn't stay there."

He lifted his hand in a stop motion and shook his head. "Don't care." His worn cowboy boot tapped against the ground. A habit he'd always had when he was angry or worried. "The cabal sent me to tell you that Seraphina has been kidnapped."

My coat slipped from my fingers, falling over my feet. Caelan's eyes followed the motion, and his gaze lingered on my shoes for too long. Sorcerers didn't wear sneakers. The rubber soles were not a conduit for the universe's energy. Before leaving the cabal, I'd only worn them when I worked out, but since I'd been hiding my magic and trying not to use it, I wore them all of the time.

"When?" My voice came out in an undignified croak. "By who?" I couldn't believe someone was dumb enough to kidnap my mom.

He glanced around the room. "Let's go somewhere a little more private." He nodded over my shoulder, and I imagined Simone and Viv standing there.

"Sure." I picked up my coat and pulled it on. Then I turned around and tried to give Viv a reassuring smile. "See you tomorrow."

Following Caelan outside, I felt the heaviness of the air weighing on me. Everything was about to change, and I wasn't ready for it.

Caelan pulled keys out of his pocket as he strode toward a car. When he stopped beside it, I said, "I'm not getting in your car. I'm not going back."

"Fine." He shot me a look that let me know the feelings he'd once had for me had died a painful, tormented death. "Let's walk the two blocks to your house then."

My stomach plummeted, knocking me off balance, but somehow, I managed to remain on my feet. If he knew where I lived, what else did he know? And, how?

Chapter 6

"If Stupidity got us into this mess, then why can't it get us out?"
–Will Rogers

"Well, come on." Caelan glared at me. "I haven't slept in twenty-eight hours, thanks to you, so the least you could do is stop standing there looking like a damsel in distress."

How could this be the same person who used to chase after me and fight off the bullies when they beat me down? I'd known that leaving without saying goodbye would hurt him, but I honestly thought he would understand why I had to do it.

I walked to the corner and waited for an opening in traffic to cross the street. Before I had the chance, Melissa and Garrett pulled into the parking lot, stopping their truck near us.

Garrett rolled his window down. His dark hair was buzzed, and there was something in his eyes, a warning not to defy him. His shirt sleeves pulled so tightly over his muscles that I worried they would cut off his circulation. I'd always suspected he was the alpha, but I had no way of knowing for sure. "Are you okay with him, Molly?" His canines were longer than I'd ever seen them.

I glanced at Caelan. He had changed so much since the last time I'd seen him, but that good-hearted boy still had to be in there somewhere, didn't he? "I think so."

"She'll be fine." The muscles in Caelan's jaw clenched, and he stepped forward, placing his body slightly ahead of mine. When we were younger, I would have thought he was trying to protect me, but clearly, that was what Garrett was doing.

I turned my attention back to the truck in time to see Melissa nod at Garrett. I'd been told that werewolves could communicate telepathically, but I'd never seen it in action before. She opened her door and sauntered over to us. She seemed more put together than this morning. Her auburn hair hung past her shoulders with no twigs or leaves decorating it. "I guess I'm going with you."

"That's not necessary." I shoved my hands in my pockets.

Caelan tensed up beside me, and I could feel his magic so much stronger than four years ago. Strong enough that Mom would probably think he'd be a good match for me.

Garrett leaned out the window. "You have been kind to all of us." I started to object, but he shook his head. "We know who you are. We know that you know what we are. You have earned an honorary place in our pack." His bright blue eyes turned yellow when he narrowed them at Caelan. "And we take care of our own."

I watched him drive off, wondering how I'd gotten here. Once his truck disappeared, I smiled at Melissa. "So, uh, was he the 'dog' you were chasing this morning?" The three of us walked across the street.

"Technically, he was chasing me." She laughed. It was the kind of laugh that made you join in. When she stopped, she set her hand on my shoulder. "Is everything okay? We were under the impression that you were hiding from them."

Caelan looked back at me, his lip pulled up, and he shook his head. "Yeah." That one word held more sarcasm than I'd ever heard from him before. "Some thank you for protecting her for twelve years."

"Mom's been kidnapped." I would have to find some way to apologize to Caelan, to make him understand that he wasn't who I'd run from. "Caelan was about to fill me in on all the details."

"Not until we get to your house." He reached across me, holding his hand out. "Since Molly still has no manners, I'm Caelan, and you are?"

She slipped her hand into his as we walked along. "Melissa Hunt."

I strode up my steps and took a deep breath, trying to exhale the bad before going inside. With Caelan and Melissa beside me, it was harder than normal. I knew negative energy would follow me over the threshold.

Schmendrick stood on the table by the door. As soon as I stepped inside, he jumped up and draped himself over my shoulders. *What have you gotten yourself into, Molly?*

We're about to find out. I scratched behind his ear and led the others into the living room.

"Hello, Schmendrick." Without so much as an invitation, Caelan plopped down on my recliner.

After what seemed like an eternity, Schmendrick acknowledged him. "Caelan."

Melissa stared at the cat on my shoulder for a few seconds before turning to me. "Your cat talks?"

"Congratulations on your astute observation." Schmendrick shifted, and I reached up to scratch his chin, hoping it would keep him in line. "Don't let my eloquence intimidate you, though, dog. I'm sure your howls are equally impressive."

She shot him a smile that was more fang than grin. "I believe you mean wolf." She sat on one end of the couch, and I positioned myself on the other.

Schmendrick climbed down onto my lap, sitting with his paws hanging over my leg. Low growls rumbled through him. If I were with humans, I doubted they would have noticed, but I was sure Melissa and Caelan both heard his warning.

"Are we sitting in Molly's living room while the rest of the cabal gathers outside?" Schmendrick pinned his ears back. "Or are you the only one privy to her location?"

Caelan shook his head. "I told no one else where to find her."

"Then why don't you make yourself useful and conjure up a fire?" Schmendrick's tail flicked back and forth, the only outward sign of his agitation. "If Molly does it, she'll have to turn her back on the two of you, and I don't like that idea at all."

Caelan waved at the wood piled in the fireplace, and flames roared to life. "You used to trust me."

"Oh, Caelan…" Schmendrick paused and sighed dramatically. "Trust is such a fragile thing, isn't it? I trust you as much as any cat can trust an impudent mortal."

Caelan's mouth dropped open, but no words came out.

"In case you're too thick to figure it out, that means, not at all." Schmendrick set his paw on top of my hand, not caring how his words affected Caelan. "I trust that Molly will give me my treats daily, that the sun will shine, and that humans will always have the capacity to do good but the stupidity to keep them from achieving it. As for trusting you?" He pulled his ears back, flattening them against his head. "Let's say you're near the bottom of the list, somewhere between vacuum cleaners and vets."

I looked at the cat sitting on my lap, wondering what he knew about vets. With him being immortal and talkative, I'd never taken him to one. Imagine the vet's face if Schmendrick started answering the questions on his own. "Why don't you like vets?"

"Give them the chance and… snip." He shuddered. "When I meet the right girl, I want the decision to have children to be ours, not some sadistic vet's."

Melissa pinched her lips together and nodded. "Makes perfect sense to me."

"You used to trust me." Caelan shifted his gaze between me and Schmendrick. The pain in his hazel eyes made me want to go to him, to beg him to forgive me, but I hadn't seen him for four years. Maybe Schmendrick was right not to trust him. "I was your friend."

"That was before you chased us through Missouri. Neither Molly nor I is prey. We deserve more than to be hunted like mice." Schmendrick resituated himself so that he was sitting up, staring at Caelan.

"I wouldn't have had to chase you if I had recognized Molly." He stared at me longer than was comfortable. "Your glamour is stronger than when you left. I can't see you at all anymore."

He couldn't see me? Why? I sat there with my mouth hanging open, trying to figure out what had changed. Even though I'd glamoured myself with blonde hair and blue eyes, the other sorcerers had always been able to see the demon underneath, and except for Caelan, they'd never let me forget that I was a monster. My mouth floundered, searching for words, but nothing came out.

My mind wandered back to him walking into Harvest Moon and the way he'd acted. If he really couldn't see me, that explained the strange look he'd given me and the way he'd said my name like a question.

"So why are you here?" Schmendrick tilted his head so that he was giving me the side eye. "Why did you bring him here?"

"He showed up at Harvest Moon and told me Mom was kidnapped." I closed my eyes and sucked in a deep breath. "Then he told me he knew where I lived, so here we are."

Schmendrick focused on Melissa. "And why is the dog here?"

"Wolf," she snarled.

I stroked him from the top of his head to the tip of his tail over and over again. The motion helped release some of my stress. "He's just trying to get under your skin."

"Trying?" He fought to prevent his hiney from lifting into the air. "I don't try to do anything. I've succeeded." He sneered at her. "So, why are you here?"

Her irises were more yellow than the golden-brown color that I was used to seeing. I thought of Garrett's eyes changing from blue to yellow earlier and filed that away to think about later. "Garrett told me to make sure Molly was safe with Caelan, so I'm here."

"I wouldn't hurt her." Caelan clenched his teeth, making the muscles in his jaw bulge. "Seraphina disappeared five days ago. When she didn't return the next day, Caius started getting a little concerned. He went into her office and found that it had been ransacked."

I remembered hiding under the desk in Mom's office, playing with Schmendrick while she worked. Bookcases lined the walls, filled with the history of the cabal, spells, and relics. The windowless room was always dark; the only light allowed in there came from the flicker of candles. Mom insisted that artificial lights and the sun would damage the books and ruin the magic hidden within them.

More than once, Caelan had stayed in there with me, helping me hide from the rest of the cabal. He'd stolen a kiss from me there. My first ever.

I shook my head. I didn't need to be thinking about those things now. I needed to focus on Mom. I needed to find a way to get her back.

"Caius cast a spell to show the past twenty-four hours in that room." Caelan rubbed his hands down his face, then stared at the tan carpet in front of him instead of looking at me. "Someone with a black hooded cape entered the room and, after an intense fight with Seraphina, threw her over his shoulder and disappeared. Several members of the cabal have tried to track the spell to no avail."

His story didn't make any sense. I couldn't imagine anyone overpowering Mom. She was strong, resourceful, and the smartest woman I knew. How could this have happened?

"Whether you or any of the rest of us like it or not, you are next in line to lead." Caelan stood and walked to the fireplace. Bracing his hands on the mantel, he kept his back to me. "Seraphina never named another to replace her."

I laughed, and the sound lacked humor. "You'll find Mom. You don't need me to be archon."

His gaze darted toward Melissa before returning to me. His hazel eyes didn't quite meet mine. "I'm supposed to bring you back."

"I think not." Schmendrick shook my hand off his head.

Back. The thought of returning made my heart race. For a moment, I felt like the terrified little girl I'd been. "Why?"

"I was ordered to." Caelan's hands curled into fists, showing me that he expected a fight.

I sucked in a shocked breath and choked on the air. When I finished coughing, I pressed my hand to my chest. "You expect me to return to the cabal, to him? After the way he treated me?"

Caelan narrowed his hate-filled, hazel eyes on me. "I don't expect a damned thing from you. I did once. Then you walked out on me. Did you ever look back? Did you ever even think about me… about us?"

"I didn't want to leave you." Emotions clawed their way up my throat, but I pushed them down. "I left a hateful cabal that wanted nothing to do with me, a power-hungry mother that wanted my potential, and an abusive stepfather who wasn't afraid to beat me into submission when Mom's back was turned."

He stood and walked to the fireplace, grabbing hold of the mantel with both hands and leaning his head against it. "But you didn't care enough about me to even ask if I'd come along."

"Well," Melissa cleared her throat, "I think I may have missed my cue to leave. I'll let the two of you hash this out." When she stood in front of me, she handed me a business card with a holographic wolf on one side and Loess Hills Pack and a phone number on the other. "Don't hesitate to call if you need anything." She scratched Schmendrick's head. "Bye, *pussycat*."

When the door closed, I focused on Caelan. He stood by the fireplace with his back to me. "I'm sorry I hurt you. I wanted to ask you to come with me, but I knew your parents would search everywhere to find you, and I couldn't risk being taken back. I needed to get away, and I couldn't do that with you tagging along. I'm not going tonight." He spun around, looking ready to fight, but I picked Schmendrick up and headed into the kitchen to get him treats. "I have a guest room you can sleep in if you want to."

"I don't." Vitriol filled his words. "But I have no choice. Caius ordered me to stay with you until you return."

I narrowed my eyes. "I thought the council sent you."

"They did, but Caius wants you back."

Chapter 7

"$\mathcal{I}$ have to go back." I'd tossed and turned all night, sleeping only a few minutes at a time. "I have to find Mom."

Schmendrick stretched. "Indeed, you must return to rectify this situation."

"I won't be archon." I tossed the covers to the side. "I'll find Mom, then come home."

Caelan followed me to Harvest Moon, but I refused to let him behind the counter. I left him at one of the tables with a chocolate caramel cappuccino. His brown hair curled over his ears and at the nape of his neck. He leaned back in his chair, and the ire fled his eyes when he sipped his coffee. The way he looked reminded me of the Caelan I'd known. Maybe he was still in there.

Vivian's door was pulled most of the way closed, so I knocked on the wall next to it.

"Come in." She sounded frazzled, but she always did when dealing with paperwork.

The room was cramped with a desk, file cabinets, and one extra chair that was typically overflowing with papers. "Hey, Viv, I don't know if you or Simone heard Caelan yesterday, but my mom's been kidnapped."

She dragged her hand through her short hair, making a rooster tail stick out at the crown of her head. "Oh, my." She dropped her pen onto her desk and gave me her undivided attention. "Are you okay?" She shook her head, and her brown eyes glistened. "Oh, of course, you're not. What are you doing here?"

I chewed on my bottom lip and shrugged. I'd woken up numb. Mom was a force to be reckoned with, and I didn't understand how anybody would be able to walk into her house and snatch her. She had power and wards and the wrath of a thousand gods. "I need to go home." The word tasted as bitter as the coffee smell permeating the air. It wasn't my home anymore, but I didn't know what else to call it. "I don't know how long I'll be gone."

"You've got two weeks of vacation. Why don't you start with that, and if it's not enough, go ahead and take all the time you need." She stood and pulled me into a hug. She was the kind of mother I'd needed growing up. The kind who wouldn't turn a blind eye on the bruises that appeared from the time Caius entered our lives. "Just keep me informed, okay?"

Viv walked out with me and grabbed an apron, tugging it on over her long-sleeved tee. "I'll work your shift. You just take that handsome man and do what you need to do."

"That handsome man hates me." I glanced at Caelan, hoping he couldn't hear us. His hazel eyes tracked my every move.

She shook her head at me. "If he hates you, why'd he come here, and why's he looking at you like that?"

I couldn't answer her. She knew nothing about the magical world. She had no idea that my mom was the archon of a cabal. Hell, she probably didn't even know what a cabal was. She wouldn't understand that Caelan was acting under orders and that if he refused, he could lose his place among his people. Except for in the military, humans didn't live with the strictness of cabals and packs and all the other groups the monsters of this world lived in.

They were intended to keep us in check. To keep us from being found out. To keep us safe. But sometimes the things meant to protect us were the things that did the most harm. I shuddered and tried to push off the dread threatening to overcome me.

I walked past Caelan, and he immediately jumped to his feet, following me out the door. "No coffee for you?" He pointed at my empty hands as we stepped into the cold morning.

"No, yuck." I couldn't help the way my face scrunched up in disgust. "I can't stand the stuff."

"Then why do you work there?" He took a drink and looked at me, waiting for me to answer.

I checked for traffic before stepping into the street. "I had no skills when I came to Glenwood, no previous employment. Viv was kind enough to offer me a job, and I accepted it."

We walked the rest of the way to my house without any more conversation. Squirrels dug through piles of leaves, searching for more nuts to store for the coming winter. Large flocks of starlings filled the trees, gathering for their flight south.

I stood in front of my door, and Caelan stared at me while I breathed out the bad. I could do this. I could face the cabal, find Mom, and return to the life I'd chosen. Easy peasy, right? I sucked in another deep breath before turning the doorknob.

Schmendrick was perched at the top of the steps. "Are we leaving?"

"After I grab a few things." I trudged up the stairs, feeling like my life was about to end. In a way, it was. The life I'd worked so hard for was about to slip away. The cabal would know where I'd been. If I made it back here, things would be different. There was no way Caelan had used a spell to keep them from tracking him, and I couldn't keep him from telling them where he'd been if they ordered him to. Unlike me, he wasn't immune to their spells and oaths. That was one good thing about being half-demon. They couldn't control me the same way they could him.

When I reached the top, I realized I needed in my spare room. "Do you mind?" I waved at the door. "I need to get my bags out of the closet."

"It's your house." The snippy Caelan was back. I should have expected as much, but I was hoping we could move past his hatred of me.

His duffel sat on the end of the perfectly made bed. The denim-colored comforter didn't have a single wrinkle in it. You couldn't tell the room had been used. That was what the cabal expected from each of its members. After all, cleanliness was next to godliness. It was why my purple comforter was never perfect. I threw it over disheveled sheets and blankets, unable to completely break the habit of making my bed.

I had no intention of staying at Ravenwood Estates, but if the search for Mom started today, I wanted a change of clothes. I grabbed a bag before marching past Caelan. His arms were folded over his chest. While my back had been turned, he'd taken his coat off. His black button-down shirt was tucked into his khaki pants. Not a wrinkle on either.

Well, wouldn't they be surprised when they saw me? I wasn't about to follow their dress code. I planned on showing up in my blue jeans and t-shirt with a hoodie pulled over the top. I wanted to wear athletic shoes, but their rubber soles would put me at a disadvantage, and since I hadn't used much magic in the last four years, I was already at a big enough one.

Once I'd packed, I grabbed my keys and my tip money. Caelan trailed behind me every step of the way.

I reached for the doorknob, and Schmendrick growled. "I know that this trip is stressing you out, but you made a most grievous oversight."

"What?" I turned to him.

He strode into the kitchen and sat, looking up at the cabinet. "It seems that you neglected to pack my treats. I expect you to rectify this situation promptly."

"Sorry, Schmen." I stuck the jar of treats in my bag.

Caelan walked outside in front of me, swinging his keys around his finger, catching them, then repeating the motion with each step. "We'll take my car."

"I hope you mean that you'll take your car." I pulled the door closed and strode toward my car. The glamour had worn off of it by the time we hit the Iowa state line.

He grabbed my arm and jerked me to a stop. "No, Molly. You need to come with me. Caius' orders."

Chapter 8

"Stupidity combined with arrogance and a huge ego will get you a long way." -Chris Lowe

"I don't take orders from Caius." I ground my stepfather's name through my teeth. "And you would do well to remember that." I pulled my arm away from him, staring into his eyes. The anger I saw in his probably reflected what was in my own. "You have two choices. You can watch me disappear for good, or you can follow me, but I will not be stranded there, carless. It's not happening, Caelan!"

He stomped to his car and yanked the door open. "Don't try anything funny, Ravenwood."

"A blessing that he refrained from asking to ride with you," Schmendrick said as he curled up on the passenger seat. "I was not about to give up my seat or have him sitting behind you."

Tapping my hand on the steering wheel, I backed out of the driveway. "Do you think he's changed so much that I can't trust him?"

"I believe your escape from the cabal bruised his fragile ego, and now he's nursing a grudge." He yawned, showing a mouth filled with sharp teeth. "Prepare for retribution. I'm not sure what form it will take, but I believe he's set himself on a course of petty vengeance."

"Great." Since it was obvious that Schmendrick planned to nap the whole way to the cabal's property, I turned the music up, hoping to drown out my thoughts. I drove up I-29 to I-80, then exited on the Highway 6 ramp. I sat at the stop sign with my left blinker clicking obnoxiously while I tried to force myself to turn onto the road. I'd vowed to never return. For the first year and a half, nightmares of them finding me and dragging me back had plagued me. Every time the door had opened at Harvest Moon, my adrenaline shot up as panic tore through my body.

I'd finally figured out how to live without constant fear. Yeah, there were still occurrences here and there, but not like it had been. And now, I was going back.

I glanced in my rearview mirror and saw Caelan motioning me to turn. I lifted my foot, inching forward, before realizing I hadn't looked. A semi zipped past me, blaring its horn, and I slammed on the brakes. After I caught my breath and checked for traffic multiple times, I pulled out.

Thirty minutes after leaving home, I had to turn right onto Ravenwood Circle. There was only one road in or out, and if you weren't a sorcerer, you would never know this street existed. Most people saw a continuation of the surrounding forest. Anyone trying to enter the trees found themselves exiting further down the road. In the eighteen years I'd lived in The Mystic Ravenwood Estates, nobody had accidentally stumbled into the community.

Ravenwood Circle curved through The Mystic Ravenwood Estates in a giant oval with roughly fifty houses situated on either side of the street. The oval was bisected by Ravenwood Drive. I grew up in the center house on Ravenwood Drive with a church on one side of us and our town hall and community building on the other. (Guess what it's named. Go ahead. Just spit out the first thing that comes to your mind. Did you guess Ravenwood Hall or anything close? Ravenwood Citadel. Do you think my ancestors were a bit narcissistic?)

"Breathe, Molly."

Like when I was a little girl, I had no choice but to obey Schmendrick's command. Air filled my lungs, relaxing my body.

He slitted one green eye to look at me. "Remember that you are not just a mere mortal, but an intriguing blend of magic and darkness, both light and shadow. The cabal is only as powerful as you allow it to be. Don't grant them victory before the fight has even begun."

"You're right." I sucked in a deep breath as I turned down my road. The house I'd grown up in was the only thing I could see.

So maybe it was more than a house. It was a mansion, complete with statues and paintings and chandeliers and gardens, open staircases, marble floors, and the things you imagined an obnoxiously massive house to hold.

Everything else just blended into the background. It looked the same as it always had… perfect, but I knew the horrors the walls hid. I knew looks were deceptive. I blinked, forcing my gaze away from the monstrosity. "How did you get to be so smart anyway?"

"Wisdom is a feline forte." He didn't even bother opening his eyes. "Immortality grants me the luxury of perfecting it."

One of these days, I would get a straight answer from him about his past. As I parked in front of the town hall, I realized this was not going to be that day.

Caelan rapped his knuckles against my window, and I reluctantly rolled it down. "I'm going to gather the council members. Don't disappear."

His command made me realize I hadn't turned my car off, and my hands were on the steering wheel. I pushed the ignition button and folded my arms over my chest. Schmendrick was right; I couldn't let them win. I needed to stand up for myself, then get the hell out of here on my terms, not theirs.

Caelan spun on his heel, and I swore I heard him let out a relieved "thank you" as he walked away. He didn't have far to go. All the members lived on Ravenwood Drive, where Mom could keep an eye on them. I almost felt sorry for them and their lack of privacy, but then I remembered growing up here. I remembered that they'd all seen the way my stepfather treated me and that none of them had lifted a finger to help.

While Caelan went door to door, I stared at Ravenwood Citadel. The medieval castle belonged somewhere in Europe, not Iowa. It had everything you would expect: a massive, stone archway, huge, carved wooden doors, and towering spires. To me, though, its most impressive features were the guardians. Two black marble statues stood sentinel next to the entrance. Carved gryphons with the heads of ravens and the bodies of panthers, they were said to protect the castle from intruders. Even though they were stone, I always felt their gazes upon me.

"The council won't let me go in with you, Molly." Schmendrick followed my gaze. "Of course, I don't follow their orders, but I won't let them see me unless I need to." He shot me a toothy grin. "They don't realize the purrfectly good company they'll be missing out on."

I rubbed his head, the motion soothing. "No, Schmen. To be honest, they don't realize a lot of things." I closed my eyes and focused on my breathing. This was not going to be fun, and the last thing I needed was to explode on them.

A knock on my window broke me out of my meditation. Caelan glowered at me through the glass. "We're all waiting."

Chapter 9

"To forget one's purpose is the commonest form of stupidity."
-Friedrich Nietzsche

"*H*ere goes nothing." I unbuckled my seatbelt. As soon as I opened my door, Schmendrick jumped out.

I'll see you on the inside. He ran off. *But you won't see me.*

I stood on shaking legs and held onto my car door. Driving here was bad enough, but I was about to walk straight into the middle of the hornet's nest.

"Seriously," Caelan's voice was filled with annoyance, "that's the best you could dress to stand before the council."

I slammed the door shut and shoved my hands into my hoodie's pouch. "Seriously, it is, and if you're just now noticing, it must not be that bad." I strode up the stairs, passing under the archway and by the guardians that looked down on me, judging me just as Caelan had, to the massive double doors.

"No matter what I do, I'm not good enough, so I might as well be myself."

Reaching for the handle, I stopped. The Ravenwood crest—a raven with its wings spread wide and a shield emblazoned with an R on its chest—was carved into the dark wood, split by the slit in the doorway. This was my family. They cared about legacy, image, and power. I cared about none of that. Sure, I loved being magic, but I didn't need to be the strongest or the best. I just wanted to do good, to be good.

I grabbed the handle and felt its runes burn against my palm, recognizing my power and lineage. A blue light flashed at the top of the door, branching out like lightning to follow the veins in the wood. It traced the crest, illuminating the R on the shield. Light burst from the raven's talons, forming a new engraving. In it, I knelt in front of one of the gryphons. My glamour was gone. My tail curved in the air behind me. The gryphon's wings were opened wide, each feather was carved with intricate detail, and its taloned paw rested on my shoulder. Schmendrick stood next to me, looking up at the beast with awe in his eyes.

The door had shown me a lot of images throughout my life, but this was new.

As I stepped into the entry hall, I wondered what it meant. Many of the images I'd seen had changed my life in some way. The last one had been my cue to leave. I shook my head, refusing to let that image bother me. I needed to enter this meeting free from distractions.

The low heels of my boots clacked against the stone floor, echoing off the walls. The ceiling was four stories above me.

Straight in front of me, a doorway led into the great hall. Off to each side, marble staircases curved up to meet a balcony. Just out of sight, hidden by the steps, there were hallways leading to the other wings of the citadel.

On the outside, the building appeared to be the size of the rest of the houses in Ravenwood Estates. Once inside, it turned into a sprawling castle that should have taken up the entire neighborhood.

Caelan tried to step past me, to lead me to the great hall, but I was a Ravenwood, and no one here would guide me like a dog on a leash.

"I know the way." I walked in front of him with my shoulders back and my head held high.

He stayed behind me, but I heard him mumble, "You could make this easy on me."

I spun around, catching him by surprise. "I could, but if I do, the wolves will descend on me, thinking me prey. I will not give them that chance."

"Fine." His Adam's apple bobbed in his throat. "When you're ready." He waved his arm, motioning me to keep moving.

Even though I told Caelan I wouldn't be prey, when I stepped into the massive room and stared at Mom's empty throne on the raised dais, I felt like a lamb led to slaughter. The six chairs to either side of hers were vacant. The council members never waited for their subordinates to arrive. Tapestries adorned the wall behind the empty chairs. They all featured the raven gryphons or the Ravenwood crest.

Light streaked in through stained-glass windows, high-lighting my path as I strolled along the midnight runner. Keeping my focus forward, I tried not to look like I was about to flee. In my peripheral vision, I saw the massive archways that lined the room. On the other side of them were shadowed walkways where anyone could be hiding.

I stopped in front of the dais, where I would have to crane my neck to look into the faces of the council, another power trip that rubbed me the wrong way, and folded my hands in front of me, waiting as was expected.

What felt like hours later, the herald stepped out of the shadows beneath one of the arches, strode across the dais, and stopped directly in front of me. "Esteemed practitioners of the mystic arts, I beseech your attention!" His gray mustache danced above his lip as his shout reverberated through the room. "Behold, the distinguished Arcane Council." He slipped away as the council members filed in.

They were a mixture of men and women, all looking flawless, dressed in their designer clothing. The women had their hair smoothed into updos of one kind or another, and the men either had their trimmed hair perfectly combed or pulled into a low ponytail. They stood in front of their chairs, six on each side of the archon's seat. At some cue that I neither saw nor heard, they sat in unison.

It wasn't until that moment that I noticed Caius wasn't sitting in a council seat but on Mom's throne. If I didn't know him, I would say he looked dignified with the silver streaks scattered through his brown hair, but I did. I knew him better than most people. I knew the monster he hid from the rest of the cabal, and I saw the predator lurking behind his pale blue eyes. It sent dread skittering down my spine.

My stomach churned. I'd hoped I would never see him again, that whatever hold he had on Mom would diminish, and he would disappear. Instead, Mom had disappeared, and Caius was trying to take her place.

Suddenly, the nausea I'd felt turned into a fiery rage. How dare he try to supplant Mom! How dare he think that marriage gave him the right to wield her power. My jaw tightened so much that I wondered if I would crack my clenched teeth.

"Caius, please take *your* seat." Siobhan Thornheart, Caelan's mother, stood and glanced down at me. When her hazel eyes met mine, I realized where Caelan had inherited his from. Her auburn hair was pulled into a chignon, and her makeup was perfectly applied.

Caius glared at her but moved to the left-hand side of Mom's chair.

Siobhan lifted her hands and closed her eyes. "Let the ancient wisdom and energy of Ravenwood Citadel fill the Arcane Council and this chamber as we convene. Let us focus our hearts, minds, and spirits. May our deliberations be guided by the light of understanding and the strength of unity. This meeting of the Arcane Council is now officially in session." She returned to her seat, and Thaddeus Alder took his place in front of me.

His umber skin was a shade darker than the glamour I wore. His black hair and beard were close-cropped, and his thick muscles pressed against the seams of his suit. "Council members," he began, his voice resonating with a deep timbre that commanded attention, "we are gathered here today to determine Mahlia Seraphina Ravenwood's suitability to assume the role of archon in Seraphina Morgana Ravenwood's absence."

Chapter 10

"*W*hat?!" I covered my mouth with my hand to prevent anything else from escaping.

Movement beneath the dais caught my attention. Schmendrick sat with his back leg up in the air, licking the inside of his thigh. Just seeing him there helped give me the strength to look up again.

Caius sneered at me. "What did you believe you were here for, oh daughter of mine?"

"I came because Caelan," I waved my hand at him, "told me Mom had been kidnapped. I came to help find her, not to become archon."

He narrowed his brown eyes on me for several seconds as if assessing the truth of my statement. "My *daughter*," —the way he said that made it sound like the most vulgar curse word imaginable—"Mahlia, is not fit to lead this cabal."

Schmendrick quit bathing long enough to step out of the shadows and look at Caius. "Oh, please. You *wish* she were your daughter." After rolling his eyes—again, you really need an immortal kitty to adopt you so you can see this for yourself—he sat on his haunches and licked his paw.

"Which is precisely the problem." He pointed at Schmendrick. Then, realizing he was talking to a cat, he turned to the other council members. "Her father is a demon! Do we truly want the daughter of a demon running this cabal? Dark magic is against our laws."

Warmth spread through my body as my blood practically came to a boil. "First, my name is Molly. I would think you would know that by now, Cai." He hated that name almost as much as I hated Mahlia Seraphina. "Second, I don't dabble in dark magic!" My hands were tightly fisted at my sides to prevent the magic sparking across my knuckles from releasing. "I've barely used any magic at all in the last four years."

He narrowed his eyes at me, and if looks could kill, I wouldn't have to continue with this stupid meeting. "Do you truly believe that a half-demon wouldn't *dabble* in dark magic?"

Siobhan and the other council members looked up from their discussion. "We do not make assumptions without having facts to back them, Caius." Siobhan turned her attention to me. "Molly, I suggest that you take a deep breath or two. When you are calm, please dismiss your cat. Despite him being a familiar, we do not allow animals in here."

Schmendrick raised an eyebrow, flicking his tail in annoyance. "Oh, how utterly quaint. I believed sorcerers to be animals, too." He strode toward the shadows. "So, if you're not animals, are you plants or fungi, then? Hmmm… Perhaps, I'll join the ferns to discuss this for a spell. At least they know what they are." He shot me a Cheshire grin before disappearing.

Alden Whitman stood from the last chair on the dais and strode to the center with his hands behind his back. He looked like what most people thought of when they heard the word wizard. His long gray beard swayed as he walked. While some people had wrinkles that looked joyful, his were evidently formed by narrowing his eyes, puckering his lips, and searching for the worst in people. When he faced me, I could see his disgust as plain as day in his cold, slate eyes. "Seraphina obviously believed her daughter would care about the cabal. She believed her daughter would be something that she very clearly is not. Her decision to leave the fate of the Ravenwood Cabal in the hands of this," he waved his hand at me while he turned toward the other council members, "*creature* that stands before us was not a decision made while in her right mind. It is a mother's place to love her child from birth, but oftentimes, parents are blinded by that love. I believe that in this instance, that was most assuredly the case."

Every one of his words was a slap in the face, a reminder of why I'd left here and how I was better off far away from these people. I stood in front of the Arcane Council, though, and took each of his verbal punches without blinking an eye and, hopefully, without the hurt showing on my face.

"We, too, question Seraphina's choice in this regard." Siobhan gestured to the other five members who sat on the same side as she did, and I wondered if their opinions mattered more than the others, if they were the senior council or something. If I had stayed, I would've been privy to all of the inner workings of the council, but I'd run before Mom had started bringing me to meetings.

Siobhan stood, and Alden grinned at her like he'd won some major award. "However, we do not feel that matters."

Alden's face fell, and he spluttered, "H-how can it not matter?"

"Since we believe Seraphina will be back, we see no reason to replace her at this time." Siobhan wiggled her fingers in a shooing motion at Alden, and he slunk back to his chair, looking defeated.

Caius sprang up. His face was bright red, and a vein in his neck bulged. "Who will lead then?"

"The council will run things just as we do when Seraphina takes a vacation or leaves to meet with other cabals," Siobhan stated simply before turning her gaze on me. "Since you are not part of the council or the guardians, you are dismissed." She lifted her lips in a sad imitation of a smile, the kind that was meant to show how sorry she was that she couldn't break the rules. "We'll inform you when Seraphina is located."

I stared up at Siobhan, probably with my mouth hanging open and everything. "Why did you bother sending Caelan after me and bringing me back? Just to tell me I can't have a position that I don't want and then to dismiss me?" My eyes narrowed in on Siobhan and Caius. Everyone else in the room vanished behind a dark haze. I ground my teeth together, trying to quell the rage, but it wouldn't diminish. "What the hell? You could've left me to my peaceful life. Did you just want to show me that you can find me if you want to? Did you want me to know you're still in control of my life?"

Siobhan shook her head and pinched her lips together, apparently not appreciating my outburst. "If Seraphina does not return, the council will call upon you to take her place. You need to be prepared for that to happen."

"You can't—" Caius' face turned bright red. "She can't—"

"Caius!" Thaddeus jumped up. "If Seraphina does not return, Molly will be archon. If she chooses to abdicate her role, Siobhan will fill her place until the next archon is chosen."

The council argued amongst themselves, and Caelan took hold of my arm, trying to drag me out of the great hall. "Come on, Molly." He sighed heavily. "You know as well as I do that only council members and guardians are allowed access to evidence."

"Why did Caius order you to bring me back?" I gestured toward him. "He obviously doesn't want me here."

Caelan tipped his head to the side and looked at the dais. "Who knows?" He tugged on my arm again, but I braced myself.

I couldn't let him tear me away. I couldn't leave without knowing that Mom was safe. As badly as I wanted to return to Glenwood, I needed to stay, to find Mom.

Claim the right of Ancestral Guardianship. Schmendrick's voice was like a bucket of ice water being thrown over me, instantly pulling me out of my shock. *Molly, claim the right, and*

take your place. Help find your mother and bring her back. Once she's
back, you can disappear again.

I stood straighter, hopefully looking more confident than I felt. "I claim the right of Ancestral Guardianship."

Chapter 11

"Proper stupidity is fascinating." ~Ricky Gervais

The loudest silence I had ever heard filled the great hall. Caelan dropped his hand from my arm, and everyone else stared down at me from their seats on the dais. The hush pressed on me, a heavy weight that would crush me if the council had its choice.

I sucked in a deep breath and repeated the words that Schmendrick spoke through our bond. "Regardless of your prejudices, it is my right, bestowed upon me by the blood that courses through my veins and the lineage that predates even this esteemed council."

My entire body trembled, but I stood with my chin up and my back straight, daring them to refuse me. Growing up, I'd admired the Ancestral Guardians, but I'd never imagined becoming one of the sorcerers in their ranks. They were strong and brave, keeping non-humans in check and preventing magic from being revealed to the world.

"She can't do that." Caius stood up and pointed his crooked finger at me while looking at each of the council members, waiting for one of them to come up with a reason why.

Siobhan tipped her head in a gesture that seemed a lot like respect. An auburn strand slipped out of her chignon, and she tucked it behind her ear. "Actually, it is perfectly within her rights."

Until that moment, I'd believed Siobhan hated me. Why wouldn't she? Everyone in the cabal thought Caelan was psycho for hanging out with the daughter of a demon, the abomination. Some believed he was trying to get into Mom's good graces, but most were just disgusted by his actions.

Growing up, I rarely ever saw Siobhan, but I always assumed she felt the same way about me as everyone else, so I couldn't understand why she was siding with me, why she didn't find a reason to forbid me from claiming my right.

"Caelan, as the only Guardian here, please escort Molly to the dais." She stepped back and waited while Caelan held his arm out for me to take.

I slid my hand onto his bicep, and a flood of memories crashed over me. I clenched his arm tighter, trying to keep from stumbling. I saw us playing tag in the forest that surrounded the cabal, running through the trees, holding hands as we crossed a creek. I saw us lying under the stars, staring up at the sky and dreaming about getting away someday. I saw him steal that kiss from me and the pure joy that lit up his face when I kissed him back instead of pulling away. The memories flashed by as if I had been watching them from the outside instead of being part of them.

Apparently, my touch didn't have the same effect on him that his had on me. His muscles tightened, and he pulled away, but not far enough that the council would notice.

Instead of walking straight up to Siobhan, Caelan nudged me to the side. We walked under the arches before climbing the stairs. My legs shook with every step we took. My unsteadiness was a weakness that they would pounce on if I didn't get it under control. As I walked toward Caius, he whispered, "This changes nothing."

I may have accidentally kicked him on purpose.

Caelan stopped right in front of Siobhan and pulled his arm free from my grasp. I didn't know how to stand or what to do with my arms.

"Kneel." Command resonated in her voice, and I wasn't sure if I could have fought it if I wanted to.

Once I did, she placed the tip of a sword against my chest, just over my heart. I'd given up asking where things like that came from when I was only a few years old. Mom's answer was always, "We're magic, dear. Everything is at our beck and call. The very winds answer us."

"Mahlia Seraphina Ravenwood," magic filled the air and made the blade glow blue, "in the name of Ravenwood Cabal, I, Siobhan Aria Thornheart, induct you into the Ancestral Guardians. The responsibility you are undertaking is immense. Do you promise to protect, to serve, and to preserve the harmony of our world?"

This was not what I wanted at all. I wanted to go back to Glenwood, to make coffee for over-caffeinated, overworked people, and to mind my own business, but I needed to find out what had happened to my mother, and to do that, I needed access to Mom's study. I needed to know everything Caelan knew. I couldn't stand on the sidelines. I needed the help of the other guardians, so I needed to step up and accept the responsibilities of this position. "I do."

"Do you promise to safeguard both the magical and non-magical communities, ensuring that they coexist harmoniously?"

"I do."

"You must stand united, trust in your fellow guardians, and be vigilant, courageous, and unwavering in your commitment to justice and order. Can you do that?"

"I can." The sapphire glow shot from the sword into my heart, piercing me with a sharp pain that was gone almost as soon as I'd registered it. The magic spread through my veins, lighting them in a blue blaze. I held my hands up, watching it settle in me, an unbreakable promise.

But would it be? This felt binding, but they'd never been able to control me with magic before.

Siobhan reached down to me, helping me to my feet. "Welcome to the Ancestral Guardians. May you stand tall in the face of danger, may you bring justice to those who disrupt our world, and may you honor the legacy of our ancestors by ensuring our magical heritage endures. Only death or this council can release you from your vows."

"What?!"

Chapter 12

"In politics, stupidity is not a handicap." -Napoleon Bonaparte

$\mathcal{W}$ondering if I'd heard her correctly, I stared at Siobhan. With her heels on, she had to have been six inches taller than me, but right then, it felt like she towered over me.

Schmendrick. I needed to hear his voice. I needed him to reassure me that I hadn't made the worst mistake of my life.

Yes, Molly. He yawned.

I should've known that he was napping while I was panicking. *Did I just royally screw up?*

Well, you are a royal, so that's definitely conceivable. I could picture the smug expression that was surely covering his face. *It was the only way, Molly. Without joining the Ancestral Guardians, you wouldn't be able to find your mother. I'm sure they'll be more than happy to release you from your vows as soon as she's back.*

I sucked in a deep breath. I could do this. Find Mom, rescind my position, and go back to my life in Glenwood. The cabal would be happier without me, and I would be better off without them.

Molly, get out of your head and pay attention. Schmendrick's voice brought me back to the dais where I stood in front of the council.

"Mahlia, Caelan, take your places among your fellow guardians." Siobhan gestured behind us.

They'd come in without me noticing. I thought Caelan would continue across the dais, but he turned and walked back the way we'd come. I followed him, not even glancing at the others. I didn't want to see the hatred in their eyes, so instead, I focused on Caelan's back. (Okay, so maybe I looked at his derriere, but how could I not? It was right there in front of me, looking amazing in his tight pants.)

One second, I was admiring the view, and the next, I was falling. I landed face down in front of Caius. The toe of his boot pressed into my ribs harder than necessary.

"Oh, Mahlia, dear." Caius knelt next to me. The look on his face was a strange combination of malice and triumph. "You should try to remain upright." He helped me to my feet, giving the others quite a show as he brushed me off.

I wanted to shove him away, but with the council and guardians watching, I couldn't without making myself look worse. As soon as he let go, I stalked after Caelan. As he led me in front of the dais, I scanned the other guardians. Eight sorcerers roughly my age watched me take my place on the floor in front of the councilors.

"Ancestral Guardians," Siobhan spread her arms wide, "I stand before you to announce the newest protector." Her gaze settled on me. "Please step forward, Mahlia Seraphina Ravenwood."

I strode toward the dais, trying to ignore the whispers that followed me. They would have been indecipherable to anybody else, but my demon senses allowed them to reach my ears. "What is she doing here?" "How dare she come back?" "She's such a freak!" "She's hiding it well, but we all know what she is." "The archon's daughter?"

After all this time, they hadn't changed. They still saw me as a monster, an abomination. I knew that. I really did, but I'd dared to hope, and hope was a dangerous thing, especially when it was crushed.

"As the overseers of our mystical legacy," Siobhan continued as if she couldn't see their mouths moving, "I beseech you to extend your timeless guidance and blessings to Molly. May the wisdom that flows through the currents of magic be shared, and may Molly find harmony within the echoes of our storied past."

I turned to look at the rest of the guardians. Like Caelan, they were dressed in business casual attire. Not a hair was out of place on any of their heads. Five of the eight were familiar to me, and disgusted looks clung to each of those faces.

Ignoring them, I focused on the three new people, the ones who didn't know they should be afraid of me. There were two men and one woman. They must have assimilated into our cabal after I escaped.

"Thorn Wilder." A man with long hair, the color of freshly tilled soil, stepped forward, extending his callused hand to me. "So, Ravenwood, as in Ravenwood …"

"Everything." I couldn't help the eye roll that followed. "Yes." Clasping his hand in mine, I caught a glimpse of his powers. Every sorcerer had an element that they were more attuned to than others. For Thorn, that element was Earth. "Pleasure."

I stepped in front of the woman. "Nahvienne Del Mar." She brushed her cobalt curls over her shoulder before taking my hand. Water was her element. If I hadn't realized that from her name, the power surging through her would've been a dead giveaway. "I knew Archon Seraphina had a daughter, but I thought—" She looked away from me, catching the gaze of the man next to her.

"You thought what?"

"Crikey! We thought you were dead." The last guy's strong Australian accent caught me off guard. He patted my shoulder, and electricity shot through me, merging with my own. Part of me felt sorry for these people. They were telling me about themselves with a single touch, but they were getting nothing in return from me. "Michael Brisbane, at your service. Call me Storm."

I smiled. He, at least, wasn't concerned about me knowing his element.

I kept a pleasant expression on my face until I turned toward the council. "Dead. You let them believe I was dead."

"You left." Caius' lip pulled up, and he shrugged. "Nobody believed you'd return, and your disappearance would've reflected poorly upon your mother and me."

"Since you were abusing—"

Alden jumped to his feet, faster than I would've thought possible, making his gray beard sway. "Enough!" He narrowed his eyes at me. "You may have weaseled your way into the Ancestral Guardians, but you will not make a mockery of our meetings. You will not accuse the council members of wrongdoing. You will do your job. You will train. And, you will show us the respect we're due."

Power sizzled over my hands. I shoved them inside my pouch and glared at the council. "I am showing you the respect you deserve. Every one of you saw the bruises that man left behind."

Caelan slammed his hand down on my shoulder. "Stop." Power laced that single word, and though my anger still simmered just beneath the surface, the fight drained out of me. He nodded to the council. "Please proceed."

Siobhan nodded at her son. "Our priority needs to be finding and rescuing Seraphina. Those of you without missions will work with Caelan."

"But I have wraiths." Lorelei's arms were folded over her chest, and she had the same petulant look on her face that she'd worn the day I decided to leave.

"And, they say people change," I mumbled.

Caelan's lip curled on one side. "Well, unless you were always selfish, you did."

Guilt clawed at my insides. He was right. I had done what was best for me without letting him choose for himself. Since I hadn't asked him, I would have to deal with his ire. Maybe someday he would forgive me, but I couldn't really blame him if he didn't.

"Caelan, you will take Nahvienne with you to meet with the Loess Hills Wolves." Siobhan nodded at her son. "If we can get them to work with us, they may be able to track the entity that kidnapped Seraphina."

I stepped forward, receiving glares from most of the council members. "May I tag along with them?"

"You need to train before you start going on missions." Caius glared down at me. "By your own admission, you haven't used magic for four years."

I sucked in a deep breath. This man brought out the worst in me, but I needed to work with him to find Mom. "Yes, but since I'm a—"

"You will do as you're told!" Caius clutched the arms of his chair.

"Not this time, she won't." Caelan fighting on my side was the norm five years ago, but at that moment, it shocked the hell out of me. "Molly is an honorary member of their pack, and I can guarantee that without her help, Garrett will not work with us."

Thaddeus clapped his hands together. "Fantastic." He looked around but didn't find his excitement mirrored on any of the other councilors' faces. "Sorcerers haven't had an in with the wolves in ages. This could benefit us greatly."

"You're right." Siobhan strode across the dais until she stood directly in front of me. "You may accompany Caelan and Nahvienne."

I lifted my hand.

"Yes?" Siobhan's voice was edged with annoyance.

Everyone turned their focus on me, and my stomach rolled in response. "No offense to either of my fellow guardians," after the last outburst I'd received, I was a little more cautious, "but I think it would be better for me to approach them alone."

Caelan nodded, and Siobhan huffed. "Fine."

"However." Nadia Olmeda stood. As she glided to the front of the dais, she brushed the imaginary wrinkles out of her skirt. Her black hair shone blue where the light hit it. She stopped and looked down her nose at me. Her lip lifted as if the very idea of addressing me was detestable. "We fully expect you to train while you are gaining their support."

I nodded. "I do know how to use magic, you know?"

"Do you know how to use a sword, a bow, hand-to-hand combat, or any type of self-defense for that matter?" Caius grinned, and shivers ran down my spine.

Chapter 13

"Schmendrick!" I shouted as I stepped outside. The warm sun on my skin couldn't do anything to stop the chill that had settled on me. Caius knew I hadn't known how to protect myself from his attacks. He'd never allowed me to train with the others, always stating that it wouldn't be fair to them to have to defend themselves against a monster like me.

A rustle in the landscape focused my thoughts on the present. Schmendrick emerged from the ferns and stretched one leg as far forward as he could, then the other while yawning. "Yes, Molly. No need to yell." Yellow pollen clung to his midnight fur, making me think of a bumblebee.

"What do you mean there's no need to yell?" I threw my hands up in the air before dragging them down my face. "You could've told me that I was joining for life!"

He sat on his haunches and glared up at me. "If I remember right, you are the sorceress. You were raised in the cabal with their traditions." He tilted his head to the side. "Shouldn't you have known that?"

I sat on the cold stone stairs and rubbed Schmendrick's head. "Caius tripped me. In front of everyone." Some of my tension disappeared when he started purring. "And somehow, nobody noticed."

"Par for the course." He curled up on the step beside me. "Molly, you're about to percolate. What's brewing in that brain of yours?"

Shaking my head, I looked down at his smirking face. "Seriously? You know I probably have to quit that job, so you can give up on the coffee jokes."

"But they ground me." When I didn't snicker or comment, he butted his head against my hand, forcing me to pet him. Cats always knew how to get their way. "You know, like coffee grounds."

"Yeah, I got it, Schmen." A shadow fell over me, and I looked up to see a turkey vulture soaring across the bright blue sky. "So… the gryphons." I focused on him again.

His green eyes had just a sliver of pupil in them when he gazed up at me. "The future is full of possibilities, a million different ways each event may unfold, but in none of them was there even a hint that you wouldn't join the Ancestral Guardians. So, yes, they knew."

"Molly." I didn't need to look up to know who was talking; like the siren she was named after, her voice was capable of luring sailors to their deaths or, at least, making me want to jump off the nearest cliff.

"Lorelei." I couldn't help it. My lip curled up when I said her name. After four years, you would think I could get rid of the bad taste her name left in my mouth.

She stood in front of me, staring me in the eyes. "I would've never recognized you without your horns. How did you ever manage to get rid of them?" Everything from her bleached blonde hair to her six-inch heels screamed vanity.

I pasted on a phony smile and wiggled my fingers. "Probably the same way you'll get rid of that hairy wart on your nose."

She gasped, and her hand jerked toward her face, stopping just shy of it. "You didn't." She narrowed her hate-filled eyes at me. "You wouldn't."

"Wouldn't I?" I picked up Schmendrick and sashayed to my car, hoping I looked confident. "It sort of goes with the whole witchy attitude you've got going on." I opened the door, and Schmendrick jumped to his seat.

Sitting behind the steering wheel, I burst out laughing. "Did you see the size of that hideous thing?"

"Do you mean Lorelei or the wart?" Schmendrick licked one mussed spot of fur for a split second before moving on to another. "You'd better hope you never get sent on a mission with her. She'll have your back… with an arrow or a blade." He licked again, almost seeming possessed. "Whichever is most convenient."

I watched him clean himself like a madman—well, mad cat if you must. "What is going on?"

"Napped in cat mint." His tongue hung out of his mouth for a moment before he resumed his frantic behavior.

I chuckled as I pulled my seat belt over my shoulder and clicked it into place. "Well, stay out of it next time."

"Can't. It's too good." His manic behavior continued until we were halfway to Glenwood.

Once he fell asleep, everything that had happened the last couple of days crashed over me like a tidal wave, dredging up memories that I thought I'd buried deep enough they'd never again see the light of day.

I watched from above as Caius held me down, sawing my horns off. Each swipe of the blade was raw, excruciating agony.

He swaggered toward me, his axe thrown over his shoulder. "I promise it will only hurt for a second. Then your tail will be gone." His smile was menacing when he swung. "Now, you almost look like the rest of us."

Sharp, remembered pain sliced through my tail and tightened my chest, making it nearly impossible to breathe. I jerked. The rumble strips grumbled beneath my tires, pulling me back to the present.

Schmendrick had always been there for me at times like this, but this time his soft snores were his only offer of comfort. I stopped at Mile Hill Lake and walked to the water's edge. The oak and cottonwood trees surrounding me gazed at their stunning autumnal dresses in the mirror-like reflection on the water.

I breathed in deeply, closing my eyes while letting the sounds of nature calm me. I wasn't a child any longer. My tail and horns had grown back—much to Caius' dismay—and I wouldn't let him do anything like that to me ever again.

Once my heart stopped racing, I pulled the business card out of my pocket and called the Loess Hills Pack. With each ring, anxiety settled deeper into my stomach. Garrett had only just given me this number. Had he really meant what he said, or was it just to make Caelan play nice?

"Loess Hills Harley Davidson. How can I help you?"

I held my phone out and stared at the screen, wondering if I'd dialed the right number. "Hi, I was trying to reach Melissa Hunt."

"Speaking."

"Oh, hey, I didn't recognize your voice." I shook my head, realizing I probably sounded like an idiot. "Sorry. This is Molly."

"Is everything okay?" Genuine concern filled her voice, and I decided that maybe I was an honorary member of the pack.

The reflections rippled as a breeze caressed the water's surface. "Yeah, I, uh, need to meet with Garrett if I can."

"He's up at the castle." She made it sound like having a castle in Southwest Iowa was a normal thing. "I'll let him know you're on your way. Just give them your name at the gate."

Chapter 14

Castle Unicorn sat on the top of the bluffs. Unless you knew it was there, it was easy to miss through the surrounding forest. I'd never been up to it, but I'd heard stories about the massive dogs that guarded the property. As I pulled up to the gate, it all made sense.

I pushed the call button. "Can I help you?" A man's voice carried through the speaker.

"Molly Ravenwood to see Garrett Hunt."

"Come on up." The wrought iron gate pulled across the drive. "Take it slow."

The driveway wound through walnut, hickory, and cedar trees, among others, slowly climbing to the top of the bluff. Squirrels scurried across the rocky path in front of my car, then chattered at me from the branches where they took refuge.

The forest ended, and the castle that I hadn't been able to see the moment before loomed in front of me. Unlike Ravenwood Citadel, it was built from bricks. An iron archway with open gates was the only way I could see to get in.

I parked my car and patted Schmendrick's head. "Hey, Buddy, do you want to see Garrett with me?"

He showed no signs of waking, so I opened my door, then stood in front of the imposing gates, breathing in the heavy tang of iron. The fae would not be able to enter this way. I wondered if that was the intent when Castle Unicorn was built.

Something about the tranquility of the grounds brought back memories of life before Caius. They flashed through my mind as I strolled along the path. Catching fireflies that flashed around the pond. Smelling the heady aroma of all the flowers with Mom and chasing after frogs that inevitably found the water before I caught them. Listening to their songs as I drifted to sleep under the moon's watchful gaze while Mom combed her fingers through my hair.

Shaking off the past, I glanced around, hoping to find someone lingering about. I turned to continue to the door and nearly ran into a man. I had to look up, and up and up, to see that it was Garrett.

He chuckled, making his fangs peek out between his lips, and his sapphire eyes sparkled with mirth. "Good to know I can sneak up on demons still."

"At least half ones." I backed up a step, needing to keep my personal bubble clear. "Jeez, Louise! Are you half-giant and half-wolf?" I'd only ever seen him sitting in his truck. Standing in the massive shadow he cast, I felt more like half-pixie than half-demon.

He clapped his hand down on my shoulder. "Just the alpha genes. When it's time for a new one, those genes kick in, and it's a helluva growth spurt." He led me toward one of the patio tables and pulled out a chair for me. "Now… I didn't expect to see you so soon, so what can I do ya for?"

Not wanting to keep him for any longer than necessary, I started rehashing everything that had happened since Melissa left my house. I was in the middle of a sentence when my eyes widened, and my pulse ratcheted up about twelve notches. *What a dumbass!* I mentally slapped my forehead as I focused on the stained-glass window behind him. "I'm sorry. Is it okay that I was looking you in the eyes?"

With supreme gentleness, he grabbed my chin and guided it so I was facing him. "You are not a wolf, and I saw no threat in your eyes. So, yes, it is." He dropped his hand. "Please continue."

I finished my story, then sucked in a deep breath. Asking for help had always been nigh on impossible for me.

Don't you think nigh on is such an underused phrase, Schmendrick? I mean really. Think of some of the stupid things you hear in daily conversation. Wouldn't you rather hear that it was nigh on impossible? And why is it so hard to ask for help? Everyone needs it sometimes. Why do we fret over it?

I could practically hear Schmendrick shake his head. *Molly, just spit it out before the wolf eats you or something.*

"The Arcane Council wants me to ask for your help. They said a wolf may be able to pick up the trail."

"If they'd have sent anyone else..." For just a second, I thought a hint of gold flashed through his eyes, but if it did, it was gone before I could confirm it.

"Siobhan appointed Caelan and Nahvienne. Then they were going to allow me to tag along." I shrugged. "I told them they should let me come alone."

Garrett picked up his phone and sent a quick text. Then he leaned back with his hands behind his head. "It's been centuries since wolves and sorcerers have worked together. We stood side by side against many of the evils in this world."

"Really?" I'd never known the sorcerers had anything except for animosity for the wolves—actually, any other races at all. "What happened?"

His jaw worked, moving slightly as he clenched and unclenched his teeth several times. "Ask your people sometime, and then let me know what they say."

Interesting.

A young girl with curly black hair backed through the patio door holding a tray with a pitcher of lemonade and two glasses. A smile tugged at her lips as she set the tray down and filled the glasses.

Garrett grabbed one and nodded at me to take the other. "Thank you, Ariella."

"Yes, thank you." I intended to take a sip but ended up drinking much more. "This is really good."

Garrett lifted his glass. "Fresh squeezed from lemons grown in our greenhouse."

"Do you need anything else, sir?" Ariella's hazel eyes never met Garrett's.

"No, that'll be all for now." As soon as the door closed behind the retreating girl, he returned his focus to me. "There is no love lost between our species, but you were kind to us when you didn't need to be, and Seraphina is your mother."

I fidgeted before remembering he could decipher every movement I made, not just through sight but also smell and sound. You couldn't think of all the things wolves could smell without feeling at least a tad bit uncomfortable, so I dropped the thought as soon as I could. "First, I had motives."

He raised a thick eyebrow but didn't say a word.

"I knew you were wolves, and I wanted peace between us. Second, she is my mother." I rubbed my thumb on the outside of the glass, focusing my attention on it. I hadn't shared so much about myself in… forever (maybe?). "I would like to free her, save her, whatever she needs, but I have no intention of being one of them again. Once she's back, I plan to rescind my position and have her name someone else as heir to the throne."

"If you were archon," he rubbed his chin, and it sounded like sandpaper scraping against a rough cedar board, "the rift between our peoples could possibly be bridged."

"I—"

He held up his hand. "I'm not saying you have to. I'm saying think about the good that could come about before making such an important decision." He stood, and I followed suit. "Melissa will accompany you tomorrow, along with Jayden."

"Thank you for the lemonade and the help." I stood and pushed my chair in. "I'll think about what you said."

He waved toward the setting sun. "Now, unless you wish to be here for the change, you may want to leave."

"The ch—"

"Wolves." He grinned, and his teeth were longer than just a moment ago.

My heart pounded against my ribs. *What will happen if they change while I'm still here?* Fear held my feet in place, and I looked up into his eyes. Amber. No hint of blue remained.

"You're safe." His voice was gruff. "Don't run, and don't be surprised if some wolves chase your car to the road. It's a game they like to play."

Chapter 15

"Why God ever created canines is beyond me." Schmendrick stood with his paws on the window, watching the wolves chase my car through the forest between Castle Unicorn and the road. "I mean look at them. The mouth breathers." He shook his head and lay back down on the seat.

If it weren't for him, I would probably be panicking. Garrett told me to expect this, but it was surreal. Wolves rushed through the woods, running at the car. They growled and snipped, jumping on each other, rolling on the ground, then darting off again.

Instead of being scared, I kept thinking that Viv and Simone were going to have a busy day at the coffee shop tomor-

99

row. Unfortunately for the wolves, they wouldn't be getting free drinks.

When I pulled up to the gate, it opened automatically. I glanced in my rearview mirror and watched the wolves skid to a stop. They lifted their heads in unison and howled. The beautiful, mournful sound filled me with a longing for something more, but what, I didn't know.

"Hey, Kiddo." Schmendrick's paw rested on my leg. "You okay?"

I shook my head to snap myself out of the fog that had settled over me. "Yeah. You know tomorrow we're going to have to work with Melissa, so it would be good if you didn't piss her off too badly."

"I have heard that dogs have thin skin." He curled up on his seat. "I guess we'll see if it's true."

"How could you?" Caelan seethed. "You were my best friend. I always thought you would be more someday."

I stretched my hand out but let it fall shy of touching him. "Cae, I never meant to hurt you."

"Don't call me that! You lost that right the day you walked out without so much as a goodbye."

My tail drooped. How could I fix this? There had to be a way.

A cold nose touched my hand, and I jolted awake. "Molly, you can't dwell on his insecurities. He knew what was happening to you. He didn't try to stop it. He didn't try to save you."

"But I should've given him a choice." I grabbed my hugging pillow and buried my face in it.

Schmendrick curled up against my back. His soft purrs calmed me. "You couldn't, and you know it. Forgive yourself. You have to before he can forgive you."

"How'd you get to be so smart?" I closed my eyes, hoping sleep would find me quickly.

"I'm a cat."

"Hey." I peeked inside Viv's office. I hadn't planned on going to Harvest Moon, but I needed to do something besides sit and wait for Melissa to show up. "I can work a few hours this morning if it's okay with you."

She spun her chair around, and her brown eyes widened when she nearly fell out of it as she brought it to a stop. "Molly." Regaining her balance, she rushed over to me and pulled me into a tight hug. "Did they find your mom? Is she okay?"

"No." I stepped back. "But there's nothing I can do but sit and wait, so work will keep my mind off things."

She gave me one of those looks that said she didn't know what to say or how to respond. That not smile that said, "I'm sorry, honey," but there were only so many times you could say sorry before somebody wanted to throw something at you. Yeah, that was the look. "Well… I'm glad to have you here. Let me know when you need to go."

The regulars shuffled in half asleep, and I served drink after drink, dreading the moment I would have to return to Ravenwood Citadel and stand before the judgmental faces of the council and the other guardians. And Caelan…

Schmendrick had been right last night, but every time I saw the anger on Caelan's face, guilt welled up inside of me. How could I forgive myself for the hurt I'd caused him?

The wolves came in one at a time throughout my shift. Finn, a pack member who was probably in his early twenties, winked at me when he grabbed his cup. "Thanks for the run last night."

As he sauntered out the door, my chin dropped to my chest. Simone heard everything, and I was sure she picked up on that.

When the rush died down, she sashayed over. Her hips swung with each step. If I walked like that, I would topple over. "So, who was the hunk you went running with last night?"

"Oh, his dog got loose, and I helped him catch it." I pulled cups out of the cabinet and then moved onto lids, keeping my eyes off her while I told my lie.

She made herself a peppermint mocha latte, took a long sip, and assessed me through aqua eyes that were such an unusual shade that they had to be contacts. "Mmhmm. I'll bet that was what happened. A pretty thing like you doesn't spend every night alone with her cat."

"Oh, you'd be surprised to find out how boring my life is." I washed the counter and watched Garrett drop off Melissa and a beast of a man—I went out on a limb and guessed he was Jayden—at the front door. My heart leaped into my throat and lodged there for a moment before sinking into my stomach. I wasn't ready for this, but keeping the wolves waiting was out of the question.

Pulling off my apron, I walked back to Viv's office, hoping that Simone wasn't following. "I have to get going. I'm not sure when I'll be back again."

Viv stood and took my hands in hers. "Dearie, you do what you need to, and know that my prayers are with you." She squeezed my fingers gently before letting go.

As I strode to the door, I wondered if God would listen to prayers concerning me. My father was fallen. What did that make me?

Shaking off that thought, I walked outside and tried to screw on a smile. "Thanks for helping me with this." I handed Melissa a cup. Her auburn hair flowed past her shoulders, debris-free. "Your usual."

"Oh, you're a lifesaver." She swallowed a huge gulp, and I wondered how she didn't burn her mouth. (Were coffee drinkers just made different?) She nodded at the guy next to her. "Jayden. Molly. Molly. Jayden."

"Hi." I held my hand out, but he kept his fists buried deep in his bomber jacket's pockets. "I didn't know what to make you, but I can go back in and get you something really quick if you'd like."

He shook his head. "Coffee's not my thing."

"Mine either." I sipped my hot cocoa as we crossed the street. My house, which until recently I had thought was off the radar, had become a hub of activity. Letting go of negative energy before stepping inside wasn't as easy as it had been either. Melissa seemed nice enough, but Jayden… Well, I didn't know what to think about him at all. Why had he refused to shake my hand? Was it because of what I was? Or who I was? Could he see through my glamour?

"I need to get Schmendrick and my car keys." I stood on the threshold, wondering if I should invite them in or not.

"Car keys?" Jayden's thick blond eyebrows shot up. "I can't ride in your car."

Melissa set her hand on his forearm. "He needs as little contact with you as possible if he's going to track your mom."

"Oh." Some of my tension lifted, knowing that maybe his resistance was because of that and not because he hated me on sight. "I can try to create a portal. It's been a while. Would the garage work? I don't spend much time there. Otherwise, we can use the side yard and hope nobody's watching."

He strolled toward the driveway, not stepping too near the house. "The garage should be fine. Just air it out while you get your cat."

Chapter 16

"You got this, Molly." Schmendrick trotted toward the door to the garage with his tail pointing straight up into the air.

If having the wolves here bothered him, it didn't look like he was about to show it. "I hope so. I haven't opened a portal in what? 10 years? 15?" I wrapped my arms around my roiling stomach. "And it was an accident."

"It may have been." He walked in a figure eight through my legs, rubbing against them as he went. "But Caius never trapped you again."

Needing another second to ready myself, I bent down and scratched behind his ear. "You always know the right thing to say."

I straightened up, squared my shoulders, and strode into the garage. The car was parked on one side, and the other was empty. Jayden and Melissa stood in the driveway, facing away from the house.

The only other time I'd created a portal, I was fifteen. Caius had cornered me, and something that terrified me danced in his pale blue eyes. Then he'd lifted his hand, and an axe had appeared in it. "You're an embarrassment, Mahlia."

I'd cowered, searching for a way to escape him. I'd lifted my hands to block him, and magic had flared from them in a blinding flash. A shimmering portal had opened between us. I'd darted through, and it had slammed shut behind me.

Fear was a powerful motivator.

But standing in my garage, I wasn't scared. I lifted my hands and closed my eyes, trying to remember the way it had felt. I pulled on the spark of magic that pulsed in my chest, but nothing happened. I dropped my hands. "What am I doing wrong?"

"Shape it, Molly." Schmendrick rubbed against my leg, his presence comforting and his faith in me priceless.

I imagined Ravenwood Estates. The way it felt with magic pressing down on me, the smell of spring in the air, even though it was fall. I pictured the buildings, the roads, the grass, and the trees. Calling everything to memory.

Then I lifted my hands again, focusing on my desire to travel there.

Magic pulled through me, shooting from my fingers, and nearly toppling me. I sucked in a deep breath and released it.

My arms shook from the surge of power. When I opened my eyes, a shimmering portal stood in the garage.

I squatted in front of it, bracing my hand on the floor in front of me, and watched Melissa and Jayden.

Melissa was at least three inches taller than I was, and she only came up to Jayden's shoulder. He leaned toward her with his hands tucked in his jeans' pockets, pulling his jacket tight across his shoulders. His dark blond hair was cut in a mullet that was longer on the top than most of the ones I'd seen. A buzz cut would have made him intimidating and unapproachable, but this gave him a bit of a shaggy, no-need-to-be-afraid-of-me look.

The portal shimmered along the edges, and in the middle, Ravenwood Citadel towered over the surrounding houses. I shivered and realized it was the gryphons. I felt like they were watching me, judging me. Their gazes weighed heavily on my conscience. I knew that in their eyes I'd failed. I'd fled. I hadn't stood up for myself, and Mom had been taken.

I turned my back toward the portal, not wanting to face their verdict, and shoved my hands into my hoodie's pouch, so Jayden and Melissa couldn't see them shake. "Are you ready?"

"Are you?" Jayden tilted his head as he turned to face me. He strode toward me, scenting the air, making his nostrils flare. "You seem nervous."

Once they were both in my garage, I closed the door behind them. "I am." The truth shall set you free, right? Right? "I'm taking two wolves to Ravenwood. I'm hated there. You're hated there. I have to step into the house I ran away from and play nice with the man who abused me for years. Why wouldn't I be nervous?" My eyes widened, and I smacked my hand over my mouth, wondering why I had told him so much.

"Fair enough. I apologize for my brashness." Jayden flipped his hands up. "Working with sorcerers is new to me, and if he lays a hand on you, I'll rip it off. How does that sound?"

Schmendrick stepped out from behind my legs, appraising Jayden. "I never thought I would see the day."

"What's that, Buddy?" I had expected a snarky comment and suspected it was still to come.

His tail flicked from side to side, and he held his mouth open in that way cats do when they smell something unpleasant or new. "That I might respect a dog."

"Wolf," both Melissa and Jayden growled the word.

"You say tomato. I say dog." Schmendrick strolled through the portal.

I shrugged. "I asked him to play nice, but I can't control him."

"No one can control the fae." Jayden ducked as he stepped through the portal, followed by Melissa.

A fae? Was he? I was the first to admit I knew next to nothing about Schmendrick, but was he really fae? I'd always been told they were tricksters and would never do a favor without expecting something in return. I'd never heard anything good about them, but Schmendrick was my buddy. He was my only friend. He'd done plenty for me. *Jayden had to be wrong*. I decided as I stepped through the portal into Ravenwood.

My ears popped, and I closed my eyes for half a second while the world settled around me. While it felt like just a step, portals actually moved your body at extreme speeds. The longer the distance, the longer the disorientation lasted.

We stood on the sidewalk between the citadel and the manor. Birds fluttered in the nearby trees; their songs disrupted by our sudden presence. Sunbeams brushed against my cheeks. Everything seemed so normal, but I knew it for what it was.

Fake.

The weather, the animals, the smell that hovered in the air. I never could figure out what it was exactly, but I'd never smelled it anywhere except here. A little sweet, a little spicy, and surprisingly, quite comforting.

Everything was controlled by the cabal. If Mom didn't want snow, it didn't snow. I didn't know who was in charge now, but there wasn't a single cloud in the sky, and the trees were the lush green of a wet spring, not the colorful hues of fall.

Growing up, I hadn't known any better, but since I'd been away, I could feel the magic weighing on the air, pressing down on everyone here, and I wondered what it did to the sorcerers living beneath it.

I looked from the citadel to the manor, wondering where I should take the wolves. I didn't even realize Schmendrick had disappeared until I saw him trotting down the sidewalk in front of a frazzled-looking Caelan, who stopped toe-to-toe with me. "Don't ever send your demented cat after me again."

"I didn't." I stepped back, not because he was intimidating me but because he was in my personal space.

Jayden stood behind me and slightly to the side. "Is this him? The one whose hand I should rip off?"

"No." I felt like a Molly sandwich trapped between these two. "This is Caelan. Caelan, Jayden. He's here to see if he can track Mom. You already met Melissa." I nodded toward her. The silence that followed wasn't the least bit comfortable.

"Well…" I smacked my hands together, then pointed at Ravenwood Manor with both index fingers. "Let's get this over with."

Caelan latched onto my shoulder, and Jayden growled. (Like full-on growled.) The inhuman sound lifted the hairs on my neck. "Are you sure he's not the one?"

Chapter 17

*D*id Caelan's fingers tremble before he dropped his hand, or was it my imagination?

"Oh, he's definitely not *the one*." I hoped my comment might release some of the tension, but it was looking like nothing would do that.

"We don't rush into things," Caelan ground out through clenched teeth as he backed up a step. He looked toward me, but his hazel eyes, more green than brown at that moment, were focused somewhere behind me. "We take everything to the council. We work with them. We do what is agreed upon. It's not a solo-charge-into-everything kind of operation. There are procedures, and if you want to help find Seraphina, you *will* follow them."

I rolled my eyes at him. "Fine. Whatever. But the wolves are here out of the kindness of their hearts, so can we get this show on the road?"

"Look here, Mahlia." Caelan's hands clenched into fists. "I don't care what your last name is; I'm" —he stabbed his finger into his chest so hard that it had to hurt—"in charge of the Ancestral Guardians, and *you* will play by the rules." He stomped off. About halfway to the citadel, he turned around. "Well... do you need a personal invitation?"

"What a dick." I didn't think Melissa intended for me to hear her, but at her comment, a small chuckle escaped me.

"Technically," Schmendrick licked his paw and dragged it over his ear, "it's your house. Nobody could fault you for dropping your things off." He gave Melissa and Jayden a pointed glance.

"I'm kinda startin' to like the cat." One corner of Jayden's mouth hitched up.

"Caelan hates me enough." I sighed. "Let's just play by his rules... for now."

I trudged behind him for a few steps before realizing I didn't want to touch the door. I didn't want the gryphons to show me anything new. "Caelan, wait up!" When he didn't stop, I threw in a "please" for good measure.

His steps faltered before finally, reluctantly stuttering to a stop. "What now, Molly?"

"I get that you hate me." I didn't want to do this in front of an audience, but it needed to be done. "But we're going to have to work together. You can't get pissed off at me for things I don't know."

His gaze flicked toward me, then away again. "I don't hate you."

"Uh-huh." My head bobbed up and down.

"I don't." He shrugged. "I don't want you here. I don't like you at all. I don't trust you. I think you're selfish. You don't care who you hurt or how you do it." He dragged his hand down his face. "But I don't hate you. Hating you would take energy, and I have none to give you."

His words bit into my flesh, ripping and tearing it from my bones, leaving me feeling completely exposed. Tears burned my eyes, but I refused to let them fall. Not here. Not in front of him.

Either he didn't notice my reaction or, more likely, didn't care. "If you can keep your smart-ass comments and your superiority complex in check, I'll teach you our procedures and anything else I think you should know. But no combat training." He shot me an apologetic smile—that honestly shocked the hell out of me. "I can't guarantee your safety."

My eyebrows drew together, and I shook my head. I was totally not expecting that comment. "What's that supposed to mean?"

He held the door for Melissa, Jayden, and me, glaring at Schmendrick when he tried to follow us inside. "It means I might want to hurt you as much as you hurt me." He strode past us. "The council's waiting."

"That was tense." Melissa patted my back. "A run through the bushes with only the full moon and your instincts guiding you would do the two of you a lot of good." Her eyes twinkled as if remembering her latest romp through the woods.

"Last time she stood in front of us, she brought her *cat* in here." Caius stood in front of Mom's chair dressed in what was surely the most expensive suit created by the most prestigious designer, but a jewel-encrusted turd was still a turd. "And now she brings these *animals* here. She has no respect for the sanctity of these halls."

Melissa and Jayden stood so closely behind me that were my tail loose, it would flick against them. I turned and mouthed, *That's him.*

Jayden stepped up beside me. "I kinda want to rip his tongue out, too, now."

Siobhan stood. "The wolves are here to help track your wife." She turned toward Caius. "Caius, sit in *your* chair." She glared at him until he slid over.

"Caius is right." Alden stared down at us with his top lip curled and his eyes narrowed. "These beasts should never have been allowed to set foot into Ravenwood Estates, let alone inside our citadel." He waved his arms around. "Inside these hallowed chambers." He stroked his long, gray beard like I did Schmendrick when he curled on my chest, but as far as I knew, I was the only sorcerer in the cabal to have a familiar—if that was what Schmendrick truly was. "Every stone they touch is tainted... desecrated... by their evil."

Jayden's low growl lifted the hairs on the back of my neck.

They had come here to help, not to be discriminated against and insulted. They were here, surrounded by hostile sorcerers who were judging them. Yet the sorcerers felt like they were the superior beings.

"I, for one, think it's great they're here. This—" Thaddeus bowed toward us "—will be the catalyst that brings us into a new, brighter future."

"Fool!" Alden slammed his hand down on the arm of his chair. "You know good and well that she will bring about our downfall."

Thaddeus shook his head at the old man. "Oh, pish posh." His warm, brown eyes held an anger in them that belied his words.

I took a step toward the dais, but Caelan held his arm in front of me and stepped forward. "If you don't mind, I'll go with Molly and Nahvienne to let the wolves investigate Ravenwood Estates. Once that's done, we can start searching for Seraphina in earnest."

"They'll not step foot in my house without me present." Caius sprang to his feet, narrowing his eyes on me as if it had been my suggestion.

Schmendrick appeared, sitting on Mom's chair. "You're not hiding anything; are you, Cai?"

"Really like the cat." Jayden laughed, earning him a few glares of his own.

Schmendrick propped his front leg up on the arm of the chair like he was a person sitting there. "I see why you like it up here. You don't even have to lift your haughty nose to look down on them."

"Mahlia, get your damn cat out of here!" Caius' face made red delicious apples look like they were a dull, washed-out shade of pink.

Schmendrick jumped down. "You might want to remember that Ravenwood Estates belongs to Molly more so than you." He winked at me, then disappeared.

Chapter 18

"Egotism is the anesthetic that dulls the pain of stupidity."
-Frank Leahy

Caius strode to Ravenwood Manor in front of us, straight-backed and full of himself. I thought he looked like someone had shoved a broomstick up his butt, but I was sure he felt far superior to the rest of us.

The wrought-iron gate nearly slammed into my face when he let go of it. I held it open for Jayden, Melissa, Caelan, Nahvienne, and of course, Schmendrick.

The lawn was perfectly manicured with a black stone pathway winding through it, leading to the covered front porch of the house I had hoped to never step foot into again.

Raven-headed gargoyles watched from the rooftop. Their eyes flashed red. Their winged bodies looked ready to jump down at the first sign of trouble. More than once, I'd imagined them coming to my rescue, but they never had.

My foot hovered above the step, refusing to touch down.

"Breathe, Molly." Schmendrick hopped up the stairs, gazing at me from the shadowy porch.

Everything about this house was dark. From the deep gray stone exterior to the inside woodwork and burgundy accents. There weren't enough lights in the world to make it bright and cheery.

Jayden growled, pulling me out of my thoughts. I glanced around but saw nothing to warrant that reaction.

Melissa leaned in close to me. "You smell like prey."

"What?!" My eyes popped open wide, and I staggered back a step.

She covered her nose and mouth with her hand. "Your fear calls to the predator in us, urging us to hunt. It's harder for him to resist."

"Great. That's great." My hand trembled when I finally set it on the railing. "It's not really fear. Well, maybe it is, but it's not what you're thinking."

She patted my shoulder and gave me one of those oh-you-poor-thing smiles.

Normally, a smile like that would've pissed me off so much that I would have marched through the door and proven that I wasn't a wuss, but at that moment, it did nothing.

I'd vowed to never go back. I'd promised myself that nothing would make me return. I wouldn't be dragged back, and I wouldn't crawl back. Yet, there I was staring up at the house that I hated nearly as much as the man holding the massive wooden door open.

"Keep that annoying cat of yours outside." Caius glared down at Schmendrick as he stepped inside. "I don't want his filthy paws dirtying the rugs."

I patted my leg, and Schmendrick followed me without missing a beat. "That annoying cat was right." Pointing at my chest, I looked around the dark house. "This is mine, not yours, and I like him a helluva lot more than I like you."

Caius marched toward me, not stopping until his nose nearly touched mine. His magic slammed into me, pushing me back a step. "Do I need to remind you of your place?" The words scraped through his clenched teeth.

The little girl inside me who had wanted nothing more than a loving father cowered, but I wasn't her anymore. I hadn't been for a long time. She never would have escaped. She would have stayed and kept searching for a way to please the pathetic excuse for a man who stood in front of me. So, I rolled my eyes and donned a bored expression. "Why don't you wait outside while Jayden does his thing?" I turned my back on him, knowing full well that it would infuriate him, and waved Jayden up the sprawling staircase in front of me. "Maybe while you're out there, you can find the weed your gardener missed."

"Caius," Caelan's voice was soft but authoritative, "go outside. Let them track Seraphina."

"I will *not* be kicked out of my own home!"

I turned just in time to see him stalking toward me.

Melissa stepped between us. "If you lay a finger on her, just one lowly, little finger, we will end you. Right here. Right now."

The color drained from Caius' face, and he galumphed to the door.

I concentrated on the yard, focusing on what lay beneath the lush grass. Then I called on my magic to germinate the dandelion seeds, forcing them to grow rapidly. Really, it was the little things in life.

"Make it so two grow back every time one is pulled." Schmendrick's green eyes twinkled with the same delight I felt.

Nahvienne bent down and scratched his head, and surprisingly, he didn't pull away. "What is he talking about?" She brushed her azure curls over her shoulder as she straightened back up.

"I mighta just filled the yard with dandelions." I shrugged. "But it's been so long since I used my magic, I could've put real lions out there by mistake."

Chapter 19

A smile lit up Nahvienne's whole face, and she covered it with pink-painted fingernails. "Oh, that's too funny."

Schmendrick jumped up onto my shoulder, then curled himself around my neck like a floofy, little kitty scarf. His tail flicked against my chest in a rhythmic motion.

We were halfway up the massive staircase when a battle cry exploded out of Caius. "What the hell?"

"Must be flowers. I didn't hear any roars." I climbed the rest of the steps double-time with Melissa and Nahvienne keeping pace beside me.

Mom's office was the first door on the left. It wasn't cordoned off or blocked in any way. Anyone could have come and gone since she went missing, but hopefully, Jayden could find something to give us a lead.

While I stood in the hallway staring at the office that looked the same as it had four years ago, the front door slammed against the wall. "Mahlia! You will fix that before you leave here."

"Fix what?" I feigned innocence as my gaze continued to rove about the room. The only thing that seemed out of place was the overturned chair where Mom had surely been sitting before she was taken.

His steps thundered against the stairs. Every crash of his shoes against the wood made me wince. A deluge of memories flooded through me, taking me back to my youth.

Jayden growled, and Caius' steps quieted. "Don't come any closer." The werewolf somehow seemed bigger as he glared over my shoulder.

Caius slunk down the steps, mumbling the whole way. "You will not come into my home and ruin…" His words trailed off as he descended, finally halting when he went back outside, slamming the door behind him.

Caelan pried my fingers off the doorframe and moved me to the side. "We couldn't detect any traces of magic." He waved Jayden into the room. "We used several tracking spells, but our attempts were futile."

"So I see." Jayden lifted his head and scented the air. When he breathed in, he closed his amber eyes and parted his lips slightly. "You all left your stench everywhere, but there is something else." He walked the perimeter of the room, sniffing the bookcases, the wooden globe, and the edges of the burgundy-patterned rug. Ever so slowly, he moved toward the center of the room and the massive wooden desk.

How many times had I hidden there with Caelan? Did he ever think about those days, or had he resigned himself to hating me, never thinking about the good times?

"Getting a little off the topic there, aren't you?" Schmendrick's words pulled me from the memories. "A trip to Yesteryear won't help you find Seraphina."

I grabbed his tail and petted it while I breathed in and out, in and out, in and out. "It's hard to be here without losing myself to the past."

"Ask the dog what he found." Schmendrick smirked at Jayden.

If Jayden had been in canine form, I was sure his hackles would be standing straight up like a wannabe punk rocker's mohawk. "Watch it, pussy gato." He stood by Mom's overturned chair. "Whoever took her smells a lot like you." He turned toward me, shooting me one of those sorry-about-your-bad-luck smiles. "But it's much stronger. I'm guessing fullblown demon."

He kept talking, but his words blended into a humming background noise that I could make no sense of. My hands fell to my sides, and Schmendrick slipped, catching his claws on my shoulder to right himself.

Everyone stared at me while I tried to make sense of what Jayden had said. Did Mom consort with demons frequently, or had it been the sperm donor? And, if it was, what did he want with her?

"A demon." The words were barely a whisper, but my hand slid to my mouth to cover them. "My dad?"

I'd never seen the monster that fathered me—not a photo, not a glimpse, nothing in my twenty-two years—but I pictured him in Mom's office, standing behind her. His hands trailed down her arms, changing from human-looking ones to pitch-black scaly skin, tipped in sharp claws.

In my vision, he threw her over his shoulder and disappeared in a puff of ebony smoke. Her chair toppled to the ground, and someone watched from the doorway, shadowed and covered in a dark cloak.

"Can you tell who stood here?" I gestured to where I'd seen the person.

Jayden prowled toward the doorway, scenting the air with each step. He stopped in front of us, shaking his head. "Several sorcerers have been in here." He turned around and pulled off his shirt. Scars crisscrossed every square inch of his back. He kicked his shoes off and slipped out of his jeans before I realized what he was doing.

Light brown hair covered his body as his wolf exploded out of him. Maybe dire wolves had been this massive, but no canine—domestic or wild—came close to the size of Jayden. He made mastiffs look like cute, little puppies.

I took a step back, and Melissa chuckled. "First time seeing the shift." Candlelight danced in her golden-brown eyes.

"Yeah." I watched him sniff the floor and walls, amazed by how careful he was not to knock anything over, not to scratch the wooden boards with his claws. "First time seeing one of you up close and personal." I'd seen them racing me to the road, but without the protection of my car, this was different.

Nahvienne nodded, not taking her eyes off Jayden. "Me, too."

Caelan stood across the doorway from me, one shoulder leaning against the wall, a look of complete nonchalance on his face, but he couldn't keep the excitement out of his eyes. He stared at the grizzly-sized wolf, watching him canvas the room again. When Jayden finished, he stood next to his clothes.

"He wants you to know that he doesn't get dressed as quickly as he stripped." There was a definite grin in Melissa's voice. "If you want to watch, he doesn't mind, but he wanted me to give you fair warning."

Even though I wanted to witness his transformation, it didn't feel right to gawk at him while he was naked. Instead, I focused on Caelan. "Will you have time to work with me after this?"

"No. Find someone to train you in combat." His fists opened and closed multiple times.

I couldn't help but scoff. *How did he expect me to learn if he wouldn't teach me?* "Who do you recommend?"

"How 'bout me?" Nahvienne's voice was high-pitched with excitement. "I'm wicked good with a sword."

When I turned to look at her, Jayden was just sliding his feet into his shoes. "I can teach you hand-to-hand combat if lover boy over there doesn't mind." He tugged his fingers through his tousled blond hair.

"Lover boy?" I might have snorted. I glanced over my shoulder at Caelan. "Yeah, I think not. He hates me."

Jayden stared at Caelan for several seconds. "Okay, then." Jayden extended his hand to me. "Now that I've done my job, I can shake your hand."

"What'd you find out?" Caelan strolled into the room, walking between Jayden and me before I could shake his hand. Caelan picked up Mom's chair and pushed it up to the desk.

Jayden smirked and dropped his hand to his side. "Training tomorrow morning. Come to the castle." He took his time tying his shoes. "Seraphina was taken by a demon. That demon, whether your father or another one, was the only non-sorcerer that had been in this room until today. Caius and somebody who smells a lot like Caelan have been in here frequently."

"Probably my mom." Caelan held onto the back of the chair, very obviously not looking at me. "She's second in command of the Arcane Council and spends a lot of time here. Do you have any idea where Seraphina was taken?"

Jayden stood next to me and moved like he was going to wrap his arm around my shoulders, but instead, he petted Schmendrick's head before propping his hand on the doorframe behind me. "I can't say. The magic he used isn't anything I'm familiar with. I would assume, though I don't like to, that he used some sort of demon potion or teleportation spell to take her back to whatever hell he came from."

"Thank you for your time." Caelan strode past us, knocking his shoulder into Jayden's on his way to the stairs. When he was almost to the bottom, he turned around. "Nine o'clock tomorrow morning, meet me at the citadel for training."

Jayden dropped his arm and placed his hand on the small of my back. "He's got it bad for you."

"He hates me." I shook my head.

Melissa laughed, and I couldn't help but smile. "He sure does." She tapped her nose as she started down the steps. "But he wants you all the same."

Chapter 20

"One man alone can be pretty dumb sometimes, but for real bona fide stupidity, there ain't nothin' can beat teamwork." –Edward Abbey

Swords clashed together, and each time, I flinched. (Really? Who used swords in this day and age? Was I going to be walking down the street only to have some moron shout 'En garde' at me? Well, I'd be ready if they did.) My life as a sorceress was nothing like the barista lifestyle I'd been leading for the past four years. After portaling the wolves back to my house, I quickly changed before returning to meet Nahvienne for sword training.

The arena sat behind Ravenwood Citadel. The two-story walls were made of the same nearly black granite as the citadel. I entered through the north door. The hallway had massive arches every 150 feet that let in light and led to the sparring field.

From outside, the building didn't look any bigger than the surrounding houses, but once inside, it was the size of a football stadium. I walked at least halfway around before finding Nahvienne.

She stood by a plethora of swords hanging on the wall. Her blue hair cascaded over her shoulders like a rippling waterfall. As soon as she saw me, she waved me over.

"Geez, how many different kinds of swords are there?" My eyes widened, and panic squeezed my heart. "Do I have to learn how to use all of these?" My gaze trailed over the weapons. Some of them were tiny, and others were probably taller than me. Nobody could expect me to swing one of those. Could they? "And why not guns?"

Her laughter reminded me of the tinkling of wind chimes. "No. We'll figure out what your preference is and then mostly stick to that type." She reached for a slender sword but stopped, turning toward me. "Not everyone likes swords either. Who knows, maybe you're a crossbow person or something else even? But guns… they just aren't the best. They are ineffective against most non-humans. You can carry one, but you'll still have to train with more traditional weapons."

"So… how often do you need a weapon other than magic?" Nahvienne's excitement was not rubbing off on me. I just couldn't picture myself stabbing or shooting anyone but Caius. And only because he deserved it.

"Honestly. More often than you'd think." She shrugged at me before pulling a sword down. It wasn't as big as some or as small as others. "Magic takes energy. Once it's depleted… well, actually before it's depleted, it's best to change tactics or at least have a backup plan." She handed me the sword. "Hold this loosely at your side, and tell me how it feels."

I took it from her and tried to mimic the way she'd been holding it, but she'd looked so natural. I wondered if I would cut my tail off or something stupid like that. "I don't know what you mean. It feels like I'm holding a sword."

"Of course, it does." She unsheathed her sword. "When I'm done training you, it will feel like an extension of your body." She swung her blade in a series of graceful swipes that I was sure I'd never be able to imitate. "Okay. Hold your sword firmly but not too tight. Now, feet shoulder-width apart, one foot slightly forward, knees bent."

She walked around me, then stood by my side. "Okay, bring the sword overhead, keeping your elbow slightly bent."

I followed her instructions, holding the stance and hoping my arm would stop shaking. It wasn't like handing a cup of coffee to a customer after all.

"Good." She shot me a smile. "Now, you're going to use your legs, hips, and core… basically your entire body to generate power for the cut." She swung her blade down, smoothly returning to a relaxed stance. "Your turn."

I swung the sword nowhere near as gracefully as she had, staggering forward with its weight. "Oof."

Nahvienne's laugh tinkled as her hand slid under my elbow. "That wasn't bad."

"Sure." Warmth spread up my neck and onto my cheeks, and I was glad my dark skin would help hide my embarrassment.

"No, really." She patted my shoulder. "For a first swing, it wasn't bad at all. When you're ready, try again."

With each swing, the blade sliced the air a little cleaner. I lifted the sword above my head. "What happens next?"

"What do you mean?" Nahvienne's eyebrows pinched together, and her head tilted toward the side.

"Mom." I brought the sword down with a whoosh.

Hers followed. "Caelan will go to the Arcane Council with Jayden's findings. Then they will set the course." She watched my next strike, nodding when I brought the sword back up. "I imagine he'll have some information to share with you tomorrow when you meet with him."

I practiced my swing until my muscles ached. Lowering the sword's tip to the ground, I rubbed my shoulder, hoping to ease the pain a little.

Nahvienne grinned at me, an ornery look that let me know we weren't done. "Next arm."

"Ugh." I switched the sword to my left hand, but it felt awkward and off-balance. "This is going to be harder."

"Let's start with one." She switched hands and twirled the blade.

"Show off." I lifted the sword she'd given me and brought it down. The swing was weak and wobbled, but at least, I didn't stumble forward this time. Practicing with the other hand had at least taught me to balance myself. "Hold this a second." I handed her the sword and practiced the movement a few times without the blade. "Okay."

She sheathed her sword and stood with her toe tapping and finger pressed against her lips. Then, without a word, she turned and walked toward the weapons. She hung my sword on the wall and pulled down a smaller one. "Try this one instead. It's a stiletto dagger. I think it will help you with the movement until you strengthen your arm. Plus, you could learn to dual-wield along with the sword."

"One step at a time." I laughed. "First, I need to figure out how to swing a blade with my left hand, hopefully without killing myself." I took the dagger from her and repeated the downward cut until that shoulder also ached.

Then, of course, we moved on to upward cuts and horizontal cuts. "That's enough for today," she said when I could barely lift the dagger. "Take the short sword and stiletto with you. Practice those moves daily. You'll get stronger with time, and then we'll start working on the dance that is sword fighting."

"Great." I took the sheaths from her and strapped them on. "Dancing is so not my thing."

Chapter 21

The next morning, I could hardly get out of bed. My muscles screamed at me with every move I made. I thought that standing beneath a hot shower would help relax them, but no such luck.

I pulled on leggings and a sports bra before walking back into my room. My sweatshirt lay across my bed. I reached for it, whimpering with each millimeter I stretched my arm.

Schmendrick cracked his eye open and peeked up at me. "You could always call the dog and tell him your muscles are too sore to train. I'm sure he wouldn't bark at you for wasting his time."

"Ha." (Who knew a fake laugh could hurt your abs so much?) I slid my arms into my hoodie's sleeves and sucked in a deep breath, hoping I could pull it over my head without Schmendrick realizing how badly it hurt. "Are you coming along?" I hissed in a breath through clenched teeth.

"Why not?" He stood and stretched like only a cat can. "The puppies love me."

Castle Unicorn's gate opened before I pushed the buzzer. I looked up the driveway, wondering if somebody was leaving. "Head on up, Miss Ravenwood."

"Here goes nothing." I pulled up where I'd parked a couple days ago and looked over my shoulder at the swords lying on the backseat. Did I dare strap them on? Would the wolves think I was threatening them?

A knock on the hood made me jump and turn around. My elbow crashed into the steering wheel, and I clutched my funny bone.

Jayden grinned at me through the windshield. "I wondered if you'd come or if lover boy would find a reason for you to stay away."

"Caelan hates me." I shook my head and rolled up the window.

Schmendrick's whiskers curled forward. That action usually meant he was happy or wanted to say something.

"Spit it out." My hand was on the handle, but I waited, wondering what he had to say.

His ear twitched, but he didn't say a word.

I opened the door and tried not to show my discomfort when I stepped out, but I couldn't keep from cringing.

"Why don't you grab the sword and dagger out of the backseat?" Jayden's t-shirt clung to his body like a second skin, showing off his hardened muscles. "You can show me what Nahvienne taught you."

I reached for the back door and mumbled, "If I can even move."

His laughter startled me, making me jolt again. "A bit jumpy, are we?"

"Being thrown back into this world…" Mom needed rescued, but I didn't know if I'd ever be ready to be part of this world again. I shook my head. "Escaping kept me on edge, too. I kept waiting for Mom or Caius and his goons to drag me back."

Jayden led me to the backyard. I strapped on the swords, fumbling a little with the straps. Then I looked up at him.

"Show me what you got."

I pulled out both the sword and dagger, cringing at their weight in my hands. I lifted the sword above my head, trying my best to ignore my protesting muscles, and brought it down, then did the same with the dagger. My movements were slower than yesterday, but I repeated them until the pain wasn't so intense. Then I moved on to the upward cut before finishing with the horizontal cut.

Sheathing my weapons, I waited for him to say something. He stepped toward me, grabbed my arm, and swung me around so my back pressed against his chest. His other arm slid around my neck.

"Merely flexing my arm would crush your windpipe." His low growl raised the hairs on the back of my neck. "How're you going to escape?"

The middle of my chest tingled, intensifying until it felt like a current was flowing through me. I let it build until it felt like an electrical storm raged within me. Then I released the magic. A bright light flashed, and Jayden flew off of me, landing a few feet away, looking up at the sky from flat on his back.

I sashayed over and held my hand out to him. He took it with an evil grin and pulled me down on top of him. Quicker than I'd have thought possible, he rolled over, pinning me beneath him. "Now, what?"

Chapter 22

*F*or four years, I'd kept physical and emotional contact to a minimum. I dealt with the customers of Harvest Moon, the employees, and my boss. Schmendrick was my only real companion in the time since I left Ravenwood Estates.

I'd never felt provocative or sexy. After all, what would people think if they saw the real me? But this seemed like the time to channel my feminine side. I lifted my head and brushed my lips across Jayden's.

His eyes opened wide, and he started to pull away, but I bit down on his bottom lip, pulling it into my mouth. Gold flecks sparked in his amber eyes, making them look like flames were dancing in them, and his canines elongated.

You're playing with fire. Schmendrick's voice startled me. How'd he know what I was doing? Last I'd seen him, he was curled up on the passenger seat.

Maybe, I thought back to him, *but I'm immune to fire.* I deepened the kiss, and when Jayden's grip loosened, I pushed against him, knocking him off of me.

He jumped to his feet and strode away. He lifted his hand to his face, and his back muscles shuddered as he sucked in deep breaths and released them. When he turned back, his eyes were back to normal, and his teeth looked human again. "I can see that training you is going to be different from everything I've done before."

"Well, Jayden," I looked down at my fingernails, "I am one of a kind."

Laughter howled out of him. "That you are, Molly. That you are." He stepped toward me, and I backed up. Lifting his hand in a stop motion, he said, "We're done for the day. You need to meet with Caelan, and I need a cold shower."

"Sorry about that." I grinned at him. "I gotta use what I got."

He walked toward me, lifting his hand toward my face. "If you ever want to practice, don't hesitate to call."

Suddenly, it felt hotter outside. "If you knew what I looked like under this glamour, you wouldn't want anything to do with me."

"Darlin', I've shown you mine." He tucked his thumbs into his pockets and strolled toward my car. "You can show me yours anytime."

I knew he meant his wolf, but I couldn't help but picture him stripping down to nothing before he changed. "Shouldn't you buy me dinner first or something?" (What the hell? This was not the conversation I should be having. Flirting with the werewolf that was training me was a bad idea. A really bad idea.)

He snatched my phone out of my pocket and typed his number into it before handing it back. "I'll pick you up at 6:00."

I spent the whole drive to Ravenwood Estates wondering how I'd gotten myself into this position.

"You didn't listen, Molly." Schmendrick stood on the seat, looking out the window. "I warned you that you were playing with fire, but you just kept striking that match until you got burned." He turned toward me, shaking his head. "That dog thinks you know what you're doing."

"I know." I groaned. "But Nahvienne said to be careful about using magic because of its limitations, and I didn't know how else to get out from under him." I smacked my hand on the steering wheel. It'd been stupid, and I knew it. "It felt good being close to someone for once, though. It's been a long time."

Schmendrick settled his paw on my leg. "Molly, Nahvienne's magic is limited just like other sorcerers. Yours… not so much."

"What do you mean?" The car swerved onto the rumble strips when I turned to look at him. I got it under control and breathed in, trying to calm myself. "I know you know more about me than you let on. Can you tell me something... anything?"

He yawned, showing me every tooth in his pink mouth, then curled up on the seat. "Sorcerers are born with magic muscles. Always flexing, always trying to become stronger. Demons, now they've got it figured out. They pull energy from everywhere, all at once." He settled in a sunbeam, blinking up at me. "Energy is everywhere, all the time. No recharging needed."

"So—"

"It's nap time, Molly." He stretched his paw forward, extending his claws before retracting them. "Dwell to yourself."

The music in the car seemed to disappear as I focused on my thoughts, listening to the same line over and over again. *They pull energy from everywhere, all at once.*

Was I like a demon? Was that why I'd flooded my bedroom when my magic came in?

I turned into Ravenwood Estates and rubbed Schmendrick's head. I couldn't wait any longer. "Is that why holding my glamour doesn't make me tired? Is that why it doesn't leave traces of magic?"

"Molly," he looked up at me and shook his head, "if that was a glamour, don't you think they could've traced the magic?"

My head cocked seemingly of its own volition. "What do you mean?"

"You're not glamouring yourself. You haven't since you switched to this look." He settled his paw over his eyes. "You shape-shifted into this."

"But sorcerers can't shapeshift."

His tail slapped against the seat. "Precisely." He shot me a look that said, *You really can't be that dumb, can you?* "Demons can."

Chapter 23

"Think of how stupid the average person is, and realize half of them are stupider than that." -George Carlin

$\mathcal{F}$or the first time in my life, I climbed the stairs to Ravenwood Citadel without noticing the gryphons, without wondering where they came from and how they seemed to watch every step. When I got to the door, the image flickered, but I didn't notice what appeared there.

It swung open, and I stepped into the entryway. All of the light seemed to get sucked through the slowly closing door, leaving me wondering where I was supposed to meet Caelan. I looked up the staircases and down the dark halls. (For the life of me, I couldn't understand why Mom hadn't brightened this place up.) Finally, I decided that, since I was here to learn about council matters, the great hall was most likely where he meant for me to go.

Each clack of my heels echoed back to me, announcing my arrival to anyone within earshot. I pushed through the doors and stopped on the blue runner. The council was in session, and twelve sets of eyes glared down at me.

"What is the meaning of this?" Caius glowered at me, a look filled with more hatred than anyone should possess.

I focused on Siobhan. "I'm sorry. Caelan told me to meet him at the citadel, and I assumed he meant here."

"When will you stop playing the part of the tortured little girl and grow up?" Caius flicked what I suspected was an imaginary piece of lint off his pants. "For eighteen years, you could have studied our ways. Instead, you chose to run off, hide in the human world, and forsake your heritage. Now, you're back, and you still can't take the time to learn what happens in these hallowed halls."

My hands squeezed into fists, and I fought all the things I wanted to say to him. "Caelan told me to meet him for training today. He didn't say where, but since we were to discuss the procedures of the Arcane Council, I thought maybe he meant here." I took two steps backward. "I'm sorry to have intruded."

Lucian Marino stood and walked toward the edge of the dais. With his dark hair slicked back and his expensive suit, he looked like he belonged in the mafia. "Despite what Caius believes, there is no reason for you to apologize." He smiled at me, softening his features and giving him an almost playful look. "The Ancestral Guardians are as welcome within these walls as any member of the council." He shot Caius a disgusted look before striding toward his seat.

"She is not what she seems." Caius pointed his perfectly manicured finger at me, then waved his hand. "She hides the monster behind a glamour. Everything about her is a lie."

Siobhan stepped between the two of them. "Caius, every one of us knows that Molly is half-demon. We all know that Seraphina was tricked into having relations with Molly's father. We are all aware of the unfortunate circumstances surrounding Seraphina's involvement with Molly's father, and we have witnessed Molly's journey from childhood to the present." She looked at me, and I could see the sorrow in her eyes. "It pains me to acknowledge that we have allowed you to mistreat her simply because of her shadowborn nature. However, she is not just a shadowborn; she is a member of the Ancestral Guardians, and starting now, you will give her the respect she is due."

"She will be the end of us." Caius sprang to his feet. Rage contorted his face.

"Caius!" She spun around faster than I would have expected. "You will respect her, or you will step down."

He backed into his seat, and the hatred that had churned beneath his skin writhed and surged.

"Caelan is in his office," Siobhan said without taking her eyes off of Caius. "Take the hallway on the right. It's at the end of the hall on the left."

I backed out of the doors, refusing to turn my back on Caius. As soon as I was in the hall, I ran the length of it to Caelan's office, knocking before I entered.

"Come in." His voice was calm, kind even. He obviously didn't realize it was me.

I stepped inside, checking out the room as I did. Like every other room in Ravenwood Citadel, it was dark. Dark wood, dark carpet, dark drapes, dark furniture. Would it kill them to have a little light in the place? "Good morning, Caelan."

"Molly." His guard went up. "You're late." He sat behind an antique wood desk, scowling at me.

I shrugged. "Well, you didn't tell me where to meet you, so I got to have a lovely conversation with Caius."

"I'm sorry." (Surprisingly, he actually looked like he was.) He pointed at a chair. "Have a seat. This won't be exciting by any means, but you need to know our protocols."

Caelan started yammering on about the relationship between the council and the guardians. His voice droned like he was reading from a textbook written by a robot, and throughout it all, he wouldn't meet my gaze, so I stared over his shoulder at the bookcases that took up most of the wall. The shelves were filled with hardcovers bound in leather or faux leather with gold stamping on their spines. As far as I could tell, they were all to help Caelan become a better guardian. Their topics were the races of supernatural creatures, magic, bestiaries, ancient relics, ethics of magic, demonology, and healing, with one exception. A special edition of Alice's Adventures in Wonderland sat in front of a row of herbology books. The edges of the dust cover were worn like he'd read the book almost daily.

My heart clenched, and I pulled my focus back to Caelan. That was a rabbit hole—pun intended—I didn't want to go down at the moment.

When I stood to leave his office nearly three hours later, I could barely keep my eyes open, and my mind felt mushier than a bowl of soggy oatmeal.

"Molly." Caelan's voice stopped me at the door. "We have a meeting tonight with the Arcane Council. They wish to discuss how to move forward with your mother's investigation. Be here at 7:00, not a minute later."

"Well, shit." I wasn't sure how I felt about going on a date with Jayden, but I didn't like the idea of calling it off.

Caelan tilted his head to the side, and I said, "I had a date."

He shook his head and rolled his eyes. "This is more important than your sex life."

"Like I have one of those." I snorted. (Yep, actually snorted. Pathetic. I know.) "I've been too afraid to have a life, let alone a sex life."

He leaned forward, studying me like a sample under a microscope. "The council would like you to bring the wolves along if they're willing to come back."

Chapter 24

"We are all born ignorant, but one must work hard to remain stupid."
~Benjamin Franklin

"*H*ello," Jayden answered the phone on the first ring.

Seriously, who does that? No one! People don't answer their phones. They text to see if it's okay to talk and then don't. I sucked in a deep breath, hoping to calm my internal dialogue.

I needed more time to figure out what to say. I'd actually been hoping for the voicemail to pick up so I could leave a message and not have to tell him I was canceling.

"Hello," he said again.

Pinching my eyes closed, I said, "Hey, Jayden." My voice sounded meek and not at all like me.

He sighed. "You're canceling."

"No… rescheduling." Was that what I wanted, or was I saying it to spare him? "And, I have a favor to ask."

His sudden bark of laughter surprised me. "And what do I get in return for a favor?"

"To see me tonight." I sucked in a deep breath and started rambling before he had a chance to say anything. "That's not what I meant. I didn't mean to say it like that." I rubbed my forehead. "The Arcane Council would like you and Melissa to come back to Ravenwood Citadel tonight. I have to be there at 7:00, so I need to reschedule our dinner."

There was a long pause while I wondered how he would respond. "I'll pick you up at 5:00."

"O-okay." The shocked word stumbled out of my mouth, tripping all over itself. I couldn't believe he actually wanted to go out with me. "See you then." I hung up and plopped down on the couch harder than intended.

"You'd better shower and get ready." Schmendrick jumped up behind me. "The dog will be here before you know it."

After my shower, I stood in front of my closet, staring at my clothes. I basically owned sweatshirts. I pulled on a pair of skinny jeans before rummaging through my closet one more time. Toward the very back, there was a dressy black shirt that I couldn't remember seeing before. I tugged it on and admired myself in the mirror. The front dipped lower than I was used to, showing off the amethyst pendant that hung around my neck, and the back was a crisscross pattern of fabric that made me feel a little self-conscious.

"What the heck?" I pulled on a pair of black boots. "You only live once, right?"

I walked down the stairs just in time to answer the door. Under his brown, leather bomber jacket, Jayden was dressed in a tight-fitting black t-shirt and jeans. I looked from him to me. "I guess we match."

"No." He brushed the back of his hand against my cheek. "You are beauty, and I am but a beast."

I giggled. (Giggled! Like a silly schoolgirl.) "Something tells me you've used that line before."

"Maybe." A fox's grin spread across his face. "Are you ready?"

I grabbed my jacket and waved at Schmendrick as I stepped out into the cool evening. Kids in superhero, princess, and monster costumes ran down the sidewalks, followed by their parents. With everything that had been going on, it had totally slipped my mind that it was Halloween.

Jayden gestured toward his black truck in my driveway. "Your chariot awaits." He opened the door for me. With the height of the step, I was glad I had opted for pants and not a skirt. Once I was seated, he closed the door before walking around and climbing in next to me.

I fidgeted with the seatbelt and then my necklace before pulling my hair over my shoulder. The whole time I watched him through the corner of my eye.

He reached over and pulled my hand down. "No need to be nervous. I only bite when asked."

"I… uh," I swallowed over the lump in my throat and started again, "I really haven't ever been on a date."

I expected him to laugh or make a rude comment or something, anything other than what he did. "Then I am honored that you accepted my invitation."

I did laugh. "It's not because I was asked and chose not to go. It's because the other sorcerers could see through my glamour, and they feared me." I looked out the window while he pulled onto Locust Street and twisted my fingers together in my lap. "Caelan was the only one who didn't, but except for a kiss, we were never more than friends."

"You've been away from them for four years." Jayden gently stroked the back of my hand until my fingers relaxed.

I looked over at him, wondering where this was going and what I was doing with him. "I've been hiding." I bit my lip, facing the truth. "From them. From myself. I haven't been living at all."

"I won't do anything you're not comfortable with." He pulled in front of Buck Snort. "I'll be a perfect gentleman… right after I tell you something."

What was he going to say? Did I have something in my teeth? Had he been looking down my shirt the whole ride here?

He leaned close to me and smiled. "You don't kiss like someone who's never been on a date."

Before I had a chance to come up with a response, he was standing outside my door, opening it for me. He lifted his hand to me and helped me down. "It's not fancy, but since we're short on time, I figured this would be the best place to go tonight."

"It's great." I stood back and let him hold the door open for me. When I stepped past him, his hand gently pressed against my lower back, guiding me inside.

We ordered our food, then sat in a booth in the back. I drummed my fingers on the table and stared up at the shadows the giant moose head made on the ceiling.

Jayden's hand pressed down on mine. "Just be yourself. I've liked you since you came up to Castle Unicorn. Not many are brave enough to make that trek, especially on their own."

"Sorry." I didn't know what to say or how to act, so I picked up my glass and gulped down half of my pop. (Yes, I call it pop. I'm from the Midwest; you cannot expect me to call it soda. Not now. Not ever.) "Have you always lived here?"

His features darkened for a moment. "No. I'm a recent addition to the Loess Hills Pack."

"Do you like it?" I didn't want him to focus on whatever had made him upset, but I wanted to know more about him.

He waited while the waitress placed our orders in front of us. "Can I get you anything else?"

"No thanks." He smiled at her, and as soon as she walked away, he said, "I do. Garrett and Melissa are great. I think I've really found my place here."

"It's the first place that I've ever thought of as home." I took a bite of my burger.

He ripped a paper towel off the roll on the table and wiped his mouth. "For me, too."

I relaxed after that initial conversation and ended up enjoying eating with somebody besides Schmendrick.

Jayden's size made him intimidating, but on the inside, he was a teddy bear or at least a cuddly wolf. He waited politely while I finished my fries, not staring at me or making me uncomfortable while I ate. When I was done, he threw his napkin over his basket and motioned toward the door. "We'd better get going if we're going to be there by 7:00."

"Yeah." I slid out of the booth and nearly plummeted when I forgot about the step down to the main floor.

Jayden shot forward and grabbed my elbow, not letting go even after I was steady.

I shook my head and looked at the floor. "Thank you. I can't believe I did that."

"No worries." His fingers slid down my arm, then slipped to my lower back as he guided me outside. Once again, he opened the truck door for me. His phone buzzed, and he looked down at it before stepping away. "Melissa can't meet us. She has pack matters to deal with."

"Did somebody wolf down all the food instead of sharing?" Schmendrick sat on the backseat, licking his paw. "I'll bet she's having a howling good time managing the hairy situation."

Jayden sat behind the wheel and pulled his seatbelt on. "Ha-ha, kitty. I bet you're feline fine with those cat-chy puns."

"Oh, no." I covered my face with both hands. "Not you too."

Jayden shot me a shit-eating grin. "Oh, yeah. You know, just yesterday I told Melissa ten puns to see if I could make her laugh, but no pun in ten did."

"And I thought the worst thing about tonight was going to be dealing with Caius." I peeked through my fingers.

Jayden pulled onto Highway 34, and Schmendrick jumped onto the center console. "No, the biggest issue will be pussy-footing around why the two of you are showing up together."

"I'm paws-itive that won't be a problem." Jayden tapped his temple. "Several members of the Arcane Council believe

I've got nuttin' but fur 'tween my ears. They won't be surprised to see me leashed to her."

145

Chapter 25

"It is better to keep your mouth closed and let people think you are a fool than to open it and remove all doubt." -Mark Twain

Ravenwood Citadel loomed dark and foreboding under the afternoon sun. At night, its eerie presence intensified, making it downright spooky. Lights shone from underneath the gryphons, magnifying their imposing statures. With each step I took toward them, their eyes flickered between red and yellow, glowing from within, coming to life.

The only good thing about the ominous building in front of us was that Jayden and Schmendrick had finally stopped trying to outdo each other with their awful puns.

"If I didn't know any better," Schmendrick trotted along in front of us, "I'd say the cat's got the wolf's tongue, but then again, I always knew I was the cat's meow."

He just had to have the last word. I shook my head as I stepped up to the door, centering myself before gripping the handle. The runes burned my palm, and blue light flashed, then raced across the veins in the wood, shooting through the crest like a lightning strike. A new engraving formed. Wings sprouted from my back, more bat-like than bird-like. Claws tipped them. They were glorious.

I was glorious.

The blue light continued its trek, illuminating the gryphons. They bowed in front of me. And at my feet lay a demon. A sword pierced his heart.

"Is this what will come to pass?" Jayden's voice startled me, and the engraving disappeared, leaving only the Ravenwood crest behind.

I pushed the door open before the invitation to enter disappeared. "No." I tried to etch every detail into my memory, planning to dissect it later, to figure out exactly what it meant. "Sometimes it shows what has passed. Sometimes it shows our desires. And sometimes what it shows isn't clear until we look back on our lives and find its meaning."

"So, what's the point?" He walked so close to me that his hand brushed against mine.

I huffed out a laugh and ignored the warmth in his fingers. "That's the question. Isn't it?"

"Where'd Schmendrick go?" He turned, looking all over for the black cat that had slipped into the shadows and disappeared.

"Another good question." I nodded toward the door at the end of the hallway. "He'll show up when he's ready."

I stepped into the great hall with Jayden at my side. The other Ancestral Guardians had already gathered, but the dais was still empty.

"Cutting it close." Caelan's gaze flicked from my face to Jayden's hand next to mine.

I rolled my eyes. "I'm here on time. Did you want me here earlier so you could glare at me longer or what?"

"I want you to respect this position." The muscles in his jaw jumped as he clenched and unclenched his teeth. "Not show up here, holding hands with your *date.*"

I slipped my hand into Jayden's, twining our fingers. His were warm and gentler than I thought they would be. "For the record, this is what holding hands looks like."

The herald strode across the dais, stopping in front of Mom's chair. "Esteemed practitioners of the mystic arts, I beseech your attention! Behold, the distinguished Arcane Council." He waved his arms toward the side where they would enter, then stepped away before they came in.

Caius focused straight ahead, never glancing in the guardians' direction. I'd hoped he wouldn't show up at all.

The council members took their seats. Siobhan glanced at the others, then out at the guardians. Her eyes seemed to lock on Caelan's face before moving to my hand entwined with Jayden's.

Heat climbed my neck, and I tried to pull my fingers free, but Jayden tightened his grip, refusing to let go.

Siobhan stood and strode to the center of the stage. "Thank you for meeting here." Her voice carried through the room, echoing in the alcoves. "Jayden of the Loess Hills wolves was kind enough to search Seraphina's office. He believes a demon kidnapped her."

She paused, and I felt like she was waiting for that proverbial gasp, but nobody seemed surprised at all. Ravenwood had always been a place where secrets spread faster than wildfire.

"The demon seems to have used a spell or potion to take her without being noticed, so the trail dies where it began." She spun her ring around her finger, the only outward sign of her stress. "Little is known about the comings and goings of demons, and Seraphina was the only one of us with first-hand experience with them."

Lorelei stepped forward and glared at me. The wart on the side of her nose was covered in makeup but still quite visible. She turned back toward the dais and flipped her white-blonde hair over her shoulder. "What about the demon spawn?"

Jayden growled, and Lorelei's face paled. The shit-eating grin she'd been wearing disappeared quicker than slop thrown into a pigpen.

Siobhan's eyebrows pinched together, and her toes tapped against the stage, the clack echoing through the alcoves. "Lorelei, you will respect Molly, or you will be excused from the guardians."

"Y-you ca—" She cut herself off before digging her hole deeper. "Yes, ma'am." When Siobhan turned toward me, Lorelei shot me the death stare that I'd seen several times in my youth.

"Molly, do you have any idea where the demon may have taken your mother?" Siobhan looked like she was just seconds away from slipping over the edge and releasing holy hell on everyone around her.

I pulled my hand out of Jayden's and crossed my arms over my chest, a defensive position I'd grown accustomed to in my childhood. Why it made me feel safer was beyond me. "I don't. I know nothing about demons. I've never met my sperm donor, and Mom never talked to me about him at all."

A snort came from the stage. I assumed from Caius, but I refused to look at him.

Siobhan wiped her hands down her legs, brushing out the wrinkles in her skirt. "Caelan, you, Nahvienne, and Molly will continue researching to see if you can figure out where Seraphina might have been taken. Molly, continue with your training, and if you think of anything that could be helpful, make sure to let Caelan know." She returned to her seat. "If nobody else has anything to add, this meeting is adjourned."

I cleared my throat and stepped forward. "I would like to look around Mom's office again."

"Come back tomorrow." Caius ground out through his teeth.

Shaking my head, I turned toward him. "No. I don't think I will. I'm here now, and as Schmendrick pointed out to you, it is my home."

"You insolent—"

"Caius!" Siobhan stood and pointed her finger at him. "What is the council coming to? Name-calling? Really? I won't stand for it."

"I would like Jayden to look around with me again, and he is here now." I waved my hand toward the werewolf, then felt foolish. They could see him standing there. He stuck out like… well, like a wolf in a room full of sorcerers. I sucked in a deep breath, hoping it would steady me. "He is here now, and I'd rather not make him come back again if he doesn't want to."

Thaddeus nodded at me. "You may go now if you'd like. Caius will be here for some time still." Something about him gave me the impression that annoying Caius meant almost as much to him as it did to me.

"Thank you." I grinned at him, spun around, and grabbed Jayden's coat sleeve, tugging him along behind me. When we were out in the hall, I slowed down. "I want to be in and out before Caius shows up."

Chapter 26

*"Remember, when you are dead, you do not know you are dead. It is
only painful for others. The same applies when you are stupid."*
—Ricky Gervais

*S*chmendrick was standing near the gryphon statues
when I stepped outside. If I didn't know any better, and maybe
I didn't, I would say it looked like they were having a conversation. He trotted toward me; his tail pointed straight up at the
stars above him. "Are you ready to go home?"

"Oh, definitely, but first I'm going to take a look around
Mom's office." Ravenwood Manor wasn't quite as imposing as
the citadel, but it still looked dark and ominous, shadowed by
oak trees.

Jayden motioned for me to walk in front of him, and admit-
tedly, it was comforting knowing that he had my back. Climbing the steps was easier this time. I'd already gone back. I'd al-

ready broken my promise, so doing it again wasn't nearly as traumatizing.

The floor creaked when I stepped inside. I fumbled around for the light switch. The yellow light barely illuminated the stairs. Schmendrick walked in front of me. His ears flicked from side to side, making me wonder what he heard that I didn't.

"What are you looking for?"

I jumped at the sound of Jayden's voice and pressed my hand to my heart. When I got control of myself, I glanced at him over my shoulder. "I don't know, but this is the only place I'll find anything."

Mom's office had always been off-limits without her in it. I stood outside the door, looking in for a moment before crossing the threshold. As soon as I did, I winced and glanced over my shoulder, waiting to be caught, waiting to be punished for breaking the rules.

"Hey," Jayden's voice was low and carried a note of confusion, "you okay?"

I stepped farther into the room. Candles flickered in sconces along the walls and in the massive iron chandelier in the center of the room. I'd never seen them extinguished. "Just trying to banish old ghosts."

Mom had never been the sentimental type. There were no family photos, no heirlooms, nothing personal in the room. The only trinkets or baubles on the shelves were ones with magical value.

I pulled open her drawers, looking inside each of them without knowing what I was hoping to find. In the bottom one, there was a picture of her with a man. At least a thousand times,

I'd asked her what my sperm donor looked like. According to her, he'd been the spitting image of a god with his long, dark hair, rippling muscles, and come-hither eyes. Seriously, what girl wanted that description of her father?

When she'd woken the next morning, he showed himself to her as the demon he really was. Black, scaly skin, horns, red eyes with slitted pupils, fangs, and claws. Yep. The whole she-bang.

I stared at the picture, and anger burned in my chest. Even though he wasn't part of my life, I'd wanted to know something about him, something more to make me feel connected, to understand why he'd sired me and then left.

I was certain that the man in this photo, with his dark hair and smoldering eyes, had to be my father. All along, she'd had this, but she'd never cared enough to show me.

I plopped down in her chair and snatched the photo, staring at it, wondering what he was like and why Mom had kept his picture all this time. Had she cared about him?

"There's a whole section of demon books over here." Jayden's voice snapped me out of my thoughts. "Maybe we should take some of them with us, see if they'll help us figure out where she was taken."

Schmendrick jumped up on the desk, crinkling papers beneath his paws. "The eternal hemorrhoid will be returning soon. If you don't want to see him, you'd better grab what you want and get out of here." He glanced at the photo in my hand. "Leave the picture of Malachai. Demons can see through their images, and you don't want him watching you."

I dropped the photo back into the drawer, catching something unreadable scrawled across the back as I slammed it shut. Then I walked over to Jayden and created a portal into my living room. He handed me books that I stacked next to my couch.

"Last one." He tried to hand it to me, but I pulled my hand away. Darkness pulsed out of it, and for a moment, I contemplated whether or not I wanted it in my house. "Molly?"

I snatched it from his hand and tossed it on the pile. "That book's evil."

He looked from me to the tome and back again. "I didn't sense anything." He rubbed his jaw. "I wonder what's in it."

"I don't know." I stared at it as I closed the portal. Then I made one more pass through the room. The hairs on the back of my neck lifted, standing like soldiers at attention. I stopped and let my gaze rove over the bookcase. A dagger lay in front of the books. Intricate carvings of skulls covered the ivory-colored hilt. The blade was black and twisted, shimmering with a pearlescent sheen. It seemed to call to me, and even though I was repulsed by the malevolence emanating from it, my hand inched forward. "Schmen, what is that?"

"Don't touch it, Molly." He stretched up, placing his paws on the shelf it rested on. "Seraphina should not have that here. Dark magic is forbidden."

The front door opened, and a draft of cold air shot up the steps and into Mom's office. "We've overstayed our welcome." I picked up Schmendrick, and he squirmed in my arms until I set him down again.

He trotted out of the room and down the steps.

"My guess is that Schmendrick just cleared a path for us." I grinned at Jayden and waved my arm like I was directing traffic. "So now would be a good time to skedaddle."

Jayden strode toward me and pressed his palm against my lower back. "You could've made a portal to your car."

"Yeah." I snorted. *Gods, I hope he didn't notice that.* "I guess I could've."

Without commenting on my unladylike snort or my stupidity, he guided me down the stairs and outside. I hadn't paid attention to the yard on the way in, but with the moon high in the sky, I could make out the carpet of dandelions covering the ground. I couldn't help the laugh that escaped me as Jayden led me toward his truck.

He opened my door, waited until I was inside, and then closed it before hurrying around to the driver's side. He drummed his fingers on the steering wheel while pulling away from the curb. As he drove out of Ravenwood, he glanced at me but didn't say anything.

"What?" I asked the next time he turned my way.

He grinned. "Just trying to see if I can catch a glimpse of you under that glamour."

"Well, uh…" I chewed on my bottom lip. Everything about Jayden screamed trustworthy, but I'd been burned before. "I guess it's not a glamour, so you won't be able to."

Chapter 27

Jayden turned toward me. His eyebrows pinched together, and his lips pursed. "What do you mean? Is this the real you, then?"

"No. The real me is a monster with horns, fangs, and a tail." I stared out the window, not wanting to see his disappointment. I nearly jumped out of my skin when his index finger rubbed the back of my hand.

He chuckled, a rich, throaty sound that sent tingles through my body. "The real you sounds a lot like the real me." He kept tracing circles on my skin. "No horns for me, though."

"Schmendrick informed me that I no longer glamour myself." I sucked in a deep breath, then exhaled the rest of my words. "I shapeshift."

His finger stilled, and he looked at me for longer than I was comfortable with. "I didn't think sorcerers could do that."

"They can't." I pulled my hand away and crossed my arms over my chest, wondering why I couldn't just be normal. "Demons can."

He settled his hand on my shoulder, then nodded at my arms. "You don't have to do that with me. I'm not like them."

I relaxed a little, but I couldn't quite bring myself to completely lower my defenses. "Except for Schmendrick… and Caelan before I left, everyone who knows has treated me like I'm a pariah. It's not my fault, though." I tried to smile at him, but it felt like a grimace. "I didn't ask to be a cambion. I just wanted to be normal."

His fingers trailed down my arm, pulling my hand toward him. "Normal is overrated. Nobody normal ever did anything to be remembered by. Nobody normal made a difference in the world." His voice was soft but filled with conviction. "If you think inside the box, you spend your entire life caged within those walls without ever realizing that you're trapped."

"Thank you." Warmth spread through my chest, and this time when I smiled at him, it was genuine. I wasn't sure if even Caelan had accepted me this unconditionally.

He pulled his hand away, and I instantly missed its warmth and comfort. He flipped on his signal, and when he pulled into the turn lane, he reached over again, sliding his fingers through mine. "You don't need to thank me for not being a closed-minded prick." A comfortable silence settled between us. Omaha's and Bellevue's lights cast a pink glow over the western horizon.

Once we passed Google and Bunge, it was pitch-black to the east.

Fifteen minutes later, he pulled into my driveway and put his truck into park. "I know it wasn't the most romantic first date, but I enjoyed spending time with you."

"Me, too." As soon as the words were out of my mouth, I realized how stupid they sounded, but it was too late.

He opened his door. "Wait there." He jumped out and hustled around to my side.

I unbuckled my seatbelt while I waited for him to open the door for me. Then I took his hand and let him help me down. (It was a big step, but I could've jumped out like I did the first time.) "Thanks."

His hand slid to my lower back as he walked me to my door. I reached to pull my keys out of my pocket, but he turned me toward him and brushed a strand of hair back, tucking it behind my ear and making a shiver rush down my spine. He stared into my eyes. Gold flecked his irises. "Can I kiss you?" His gaze fell on my lips, and suddenly, he was closer. His breath caressed my face. His arms surrounded me.

"Yes." My voice was unrecognizable, low and throaty.

I didn't know what to expect. Would it be like the stolen kiss I'd shared with Caelan or like the passionate kisses I'd seen in movies and read about in books? My heart raced in anticipation, but I just stood there, waiting, unsure what to do.

Luckily, he wasn't afraid to take the initiative. He cupped my face, brushing his thumbs along my cheeks. Tingles trailed his touch. His gaze held mine as he lowered his mouth and hovered in front of me, waiting.

I nodded, hoping he just wanted to be reassured that I was okay with this.

The corner of his mouth turned up right before his lips pressed against mine, soft and warm. He inched away, but I clutched his shirt, pulling him toward me.

His eyes snapped open, and he searched my face. Whatever he saw in it seemed to be answer enough. His lips moved against mine, his teeth scraping against my skin. One of his hands slid down my neck, and the other moved to my lower back, pulling me closer.

I let go of his shirt, then explored the hard planes of his chest before moving onto his biceps. His muscles tightened beneath my touch. My fingers glided further up, stopping on his shoulders. I pushed up onto my toes and slipped my hands into his hair, tangling my fingers in the silky strands.

His tongue flicked against my lips, and I opened my mouth with a gasp. He lifted me like I weighed nothing and pressed me against the door. I wrapped my legs around his waist, pulling his body closer to mine.

I'd never felt so alive. Never known something could feel like this. I never wanted to stop.

"Are you going to open the door, Molly?" Schmendrick's voice snapped me out of the moment.

I loosened my legs, and Jayden set me on my feet.

"The cat got here on his own, but he can't get inside?" Jayden's voice was husky, and his eyes were almost completely his wolf's.

Schmendrick sat on the step and lifted his paw to his mouth. "Of course, I can get in, but I need my treats."

"Sure." Jayden lifted one eyebrow and nodded. Then he leaned forward and brushed his lips over mine. "Will I see you for training in the morning?"

"Yes."

Lying in bed, staring up at the ceiling, my thoughts bounced from that amazing kiss to the black horn on Mom's shelf. I closed my eyes, but I saw it. The way the light played on it, making it shimmer. Blue and purple danced along the onyx spike. This was not where I wanted my thoughts to turn. I wanted to remember Jayden's lips pressed against mine. I wanted to dream about his arms around me, pressing me into the door, but the spooky relic kept interfering.

I sighed and rolled onto my side. "What was that on Mom's bookcase?"

Schmendrick opened one green eye and stared up at me. "Cursed artifacts, forbidden magic, and the folly of mortals… my favorite bedtime subject." Like normal, he took up about three-fourths of the mattress, stretching diagonally on top of the comforter. I'd given up fighting him for half of it a long time ago.

"Would you rather help me dissect my feelings for Jayden?" I rubbed his paw, and he pulled it away.

He licked his foot furiously, glaring at me the whole time. "It is a unicorn horn, but before it was taken, the poor creature was tortured with black magic, turning it from something pure and good to a malevolent beast. When the horn was removed, the unicorn became a wraith, cursed to roam for eternity."

"The handle?" I wasn't sure if I wanted to know, but I needed to.

He nudged my hand, and taking the hint, I scratched behind his ears. "You do enjoy nightmares, don't you? The handle is bone, taken from a virgin, sacrificed on the blood moon. Her screams are trapped inside, along with her terror."

"Why is it in Mom's office?"

Schmendrick tipped his head to the side. "That is the question, isn't it?"

Chapter 28

*"Just because I stop arguing with you doesn't make you right.
It just means I remembered that you can't fix stupid." -Unknown*

J woke up, feeling absolutely exhausted. Evil unicorns and the screams of a child being slaughtered had filled my dreams. I'd imagined someone cutting her bone out while she struggled on an altar, an athame piercing her skin.

I staggered to the bathroom and splashed cold water on my face. Standing above the sink, I clutched the countertop. "Why did that knife affect me like this?"

Schmendrick jumped up, and I turned the water on. He stuck his paw beneath the flow, then licked it. "Do you realize how lucky you are to be able to drink more than a drop at a time?" He sat back on his haunches. "It must be divine."

I laughed. I couldn't help it. His perspective on the world was so different from mine. "Yeah, I have to admit it's nice not licking one drop off my finger at a time."

"In all actuality, it's quite simple." He jumped down and stood by the door, waiting for me to follow. "And at the same time, profoundly complex."

I shook my head at him. "I need a better answer than that if you want treats this morning." I followed him down the stairs and into the kitchen. "I didn't sleep well, and I don't think I can deal with riddles this morning."

"Dark magic leaves echoes. Think of it like the rumbling of distant thunder. Ancient storms, whispering tales of shadows and sorrows." He watched me drop a handful of treats onto his silver platter.

Like most cats, Schmendrick believed himself worthy of worship, but at moments like this, he seemed more like a little kid than a god.

"Your unique nature makes you a sensitive conduit to such energies. Your essence vibrates with the echoes of darkness these artifacts emit."

My heart dropped to my stomach so quickly that his dish fell from my hand. Treats scattered across the floor, and the platter tipped from one side to the other, warbling as it slowly fluttered to a halt.

Schmendrick moved from treat to treat, scarfing them up like he hadn't eaten in weeks. When he'd found the last one, he turned his back, looking anywhere but at me.

I'd witnessed his embarrassment before, and usually, it made me giggle, but not this time. This time, I was stuck inside my own head. I pulled out one of the chairs and sat at the table, holding my head in my hands. "So, because I'm evil, the darkness haunts me more?"

"No." Schmendrick jumped onto a chair and stared at me. "No. There's a delicate balance of light and dark within you. More so than most. The knife triggered the nightmares, hoping to tip you toward the shadows, to remind you of the storms raging in your subconscious mind."

I sat back in my chair, folding my arms over my chest. "I don't know what you're trying to tell me, Schmen. Is the demon taking over? Will I become evil?" I tightened the grip on my sides, trying to keep my hands from shaking. "I've fought against it for so long. Am I going to lose?"

"No, Molly, no." He jumped onto my lap and rubbed his head against my arm, loosening my grip and making me pet him. "Even the strongest can be affected by the shadows of our past. You must embrace the light within you."

"How?" My voice softened until even I could barely hear it. "How do I do that?"

"Draw strength from every good thing in your life. Let your demon ancestry burn the shadows that haunt your dreams." He flopped onto his back and stared up at me, a rare invitation for me to rub his belly. "You, Molly, are not defined by the darkness around you but by the light you choose to embrace."

I scratched his tummy for about three seconds before he jumped down. His tail flicked from side to side. "Now, we need to address the dog in the room."

"No." I stood and pushed my chair under the table. "I need to figure that situation out before you try to talk me out of it."

He left the room, trotting up the stairs in front of me. "If he is what you want, I will not hold you back. However—"

"No however."

He turned and narrowed his eyes at me. "Yes, however." He stared at me, making sure I was listening. "*However*, I don't know what you know about wolves." He shook his head, and his mouth hung open slightly, reminding me of the way people acted when they said duh. "They mate for life, and once they find their mate, they don't easily let go."

"Oh." I grabbed the banister and dropped to one knee. "You don't think…" I couldn't finish the thought. I liked Jayden, but how much, I didn't know yet. I'd been on one date in my life. I wasn't ready for a lifetime commitment.

Schmendrick looked down at me from the top of the stairs. "I only want you to know what you could be getting into." He lifted one leg in what seemed to be a shrug. "For a mangy mutt, he's actually not too bad."

I backed out of my driveway and sat with one hand on the gearshift and one on the steering wheel. I could just pull back into the garage, change clothes, and go to Harvest Moon. The other guardians would save Mom. I could pretend like Schmendrick had never told me about wolves and their mates. Pretend like that kiss—dear God, that kiss—had never happened.

But I couldn't hide anymore. They all knew where I was. And given the chance, every single one of them would drag me back.

Schmendrick watched me from his perch by the living room window. As soon as I put the car into gear, he jumped down, most likely to stretch out on my bed and nap. I drove to the stop sign and pulled onto Locust Street. At each corner, I debated turning back, but I continued, merging onto Highway 34. At the top of the hill, I took my foot off the gas but tightened my grip on the steering wheel, forcing myself to keep going.

As I drove down Mile Hill, I tried not to focus on all the things that could go wrong today. Just last week, the trees had been stunning in shades of gold, orange, purple, and red, but today most of their leaves covered the ground. Only the oaks refused to let go of theirs.

I turned onto the gravel road leading to Castle Unicorn. *What would Jayden be like today? Would he pretend he'd never kissed me? Or would he want to kiss me again?* Heat rushed to my core, and my heart fluttered. *Did I want him to?*

Chapter 29

"Never argue with stupid people, they will drag you down to their level and then beat you with experience." -Mark Twain

*S*itting at the bottom of the drive, I stared at the callbox. For some reason, I couldn't quite make my finger press the button. I reached down to shift the car into reverse when the speaker crackled. "Come on up, Molly." It sounded like Melissa, and there was laughter in her voice. "Jayden is waiting for you in the courtyard."

The gate opened, and I drove through the trees to the top of the hill. I was making too much of this. I knew I was, but I'd never been here before. The unknown was wreaking havoc on me.

Jayden leaned against the archway. His hands were tucked into his jeans pockets with his thumbs sticking out, and he would've looked perfectly relaxed had it not been for the way his shoulders bunched up.

As soon as I parked my car, he strode toward me. "Having second thoughts?" His voice sounded off, not nearly as confident as normal.

"I… uh." I cleared my throat, hoping to release the words that were caught there. "Just a little afraid that you might regret that kiss." *Or expect more.* A lot more.

He stood so close to me that I could feel the warmth wafting off his body. "Do you?"

Heat rushed to my cheeks, and I stared at his feet. The brown hiking boots he wore were scuffed and grass-stained, and I realized that I had no idea what he did for a living. I knew he was a wolf and could track, but there was obviously more to him than that.

He slid his thumb under my chin and lifted it so I was looking at him. "Do you?"

"No." The word squeaked out.

He leaned toward me. "Do you think I do?"

"No." Without his wolf senses, I doubt he would've heard the word, even standing as close as he was.

He bent down, never pulling his gaze from mine. The warmth from his breath caressed my lips. My mouth fell open with a gasp. His finger still pressed against my chin, but we weren't touching anywhere else, and yet this was the most intimate position I'd ever been in.

Every nerve in my body screamed at me to close the distance, to pull him against me. But I stood perfectly still, waiting to see what he would do.

His amber eyes brightened until they were gold. He leaned even closer, making my pulse ratchet. His mouth crashed against mine, and his tongue slipped through my lips. The brush of it sent fire racing through me.

A moan escaped me, and I melted into him, my body molding to his. I wrapped my arms around his neck and pressed onto my tiptoes, wanting to be closer still.

His hand moved from my chin, trailing down my side, and then slid to my lower back, slipping under my shirt. He traced circles on my skin while pulling me closer.

I'd never felt anything like it. Shivers raced through my body, and my head tipped back. His lips moved from my mouth, skimming along my chin, and then trailing up my neck. He nipped my earlobe, and his breath in my ear filled me with a warmth I'd never known. "No regrets," he whispered.

"None." Oh, my god. Was that my voice? It was sultry, and dare I say, sexy.

He backed away from me, and when he let go, I felt as unsteady as a newborn foal. "As much as I would like to do this all day, you need to train." He skimmed his finger from my temple to my chin. "Maybe we can pick up here afterward."

He turned away and took a couple of steps before stretching his hand out to me. I slid mine into it like it was the most natural thing in the world and then wondered if I should have.

Jayden led me through the archway and onto the grounds. Castle Unicorn was secluded, making it the perfect location for a pack of werewolves, but it also offered a view like no other. I could stand there all day staring into the distance. The Loess Hills stretched to the North and South, their slopes covered in cedar, oak, and cottonwood trees. Below them lay the Missouri River Valley.

"Sunsets from here must be amazing." I was grateful to hear that my voice sounded normal again.

"Mmhmm." His voice came out deeper than normal, and his thumb stroked mine. "Sunrises, too."

(Yeah, even I picked up on that innuendo.)

As soon as we stepped into the courtyard, Jayden spun me into him, putting me in a chokehold. I grabbed his arm. Electricity sparked on my fingers. I tried to hold back, but it was as if my internal self-defense mechanism had kicked in. The power surged inside me. "Let go." I pulled my hands off his arm, knowing he wouldn't listen, but I had to try to get him away from me before he got hurt.

The charge jumped from me to him.

His body locked up, tightening his grip on me. Then he toppled over backward, pulling me along with him. I landed on his chest, and the air whooshed out of my lungs. I fought to suck in a breath, but the oxygen refused to come.

We lay like that for an eternity or maybe only a few seconds before he shifted me to the side and shook his arm. "Damn, Molly."

"Sorry." I rolled over and stood. "If you'd teach me how to defend myself without using magic, I'd try." I sauntered away from him. "You might find the results shocking."

"Oh, ha-ha." He sat upright, still shaking his right arm.

I watched him, wondering if he was all right. "So, you and Schmendrick can make bad puns all night, but I'm not allowed one?"

He sprang to his feet and grabbed me around the waist, throwing me over his shoulder. He was a blur of movement that my mind could barely comprehend. His arm was wrapped around my knees, and my head dangled near his waist. (I did have a fantastic view of his ass from there, though.) "I think you're getting carried away." I could hear the grin in his voice. "Our puns weren't bad." He looked down at me. "Maybe just a little over your head."

I tightened my core muscles and pulled myself up—thank God for Pilates. Then I squirmed and flailed until he lost his grip on my legs. He dropped me, and I stumbled when my feet hit the ground. Somehow, I managed to hook my leg around his and pull him down with me.

He braced himself above me, his face just inches from mine. "After that shocking experience earlier, this was quite the let-down." He kissed the tip of my nose before springing up. I had to roll onto my side and use my arms and legs to pull myself off the ground. (Was it a wolf thing or an out-of-shape thing?)

Our training went the same way for the next hour or so. Sometimes, I used magic, and other times, I fought him off, but no matter what, he came up with a reason to kiss me or brush against me and cracked a stupid pun that made me smile.

And every time, I felt myself falling for him just a little more.

Lying on the ground next to him for what must have been the hundredth time, I lifted my hands in surrender. "I'm done."

"Me too. I've been down here far too many times today." He rubbed his shoulder. "You're making me look bad, you know? The boss's gonna be all over me for lying down on the job."

I groaned, but even though I'd say we were both holding back, neither of us wanting to hurt the other, inwardly, I felt like I'd given as much as I got. My magic came easier than it had the day before. He shot me a look that resurrected the butterflies in my stomach for the hundredth time. (Zombie butterflies?) "We need to talk."

I swore I saw fear dance in his eyes before he turned away. "Shoot."

"This… uh, thing between us—" I pointed from me to him, even though he wasn't watching me "—it's not because you think Caelan is interested in me. Is it?"

He turned his head toward me. Every time we'd lain on the ground like this, he'd been playful, but this time, anger flashed in his eyes. "First, I don't think he's interested in you."

I pinched my eyebrows together and jerked my head back, waiting for his explanation.

"I can smell it on him." He tapped his finger against his nose. "His desire. You hurt him when you left, and he's afraid to trust you again, but that doesn't mean he's not attracted to you."

I nodded, not sure what to say.

"Second, I don't play with women to make men jealous. That's wrong." His jaw clenched, and I realized I'd hurt him. (Apparently, I was good at hurting the men I cared about.)

"I'm sorry." I rolled onto my side and reached across the gap, trailing my finger along his arm. "I've seen so many men and women do that, and I just wanted to be sure." I swallowed the lump in my throat, hoping I hadn't managed to ruin every-thing. "Can I take you to dinner? I'd like to get to know you."

His eyelids fluttered shut. "You don't know me?"

"I know enough to know that I'd like to know you better."

"Dinner." He smiled, warm and genuine. "I'd like that."

Chapter 30

I sat cross-legged on my living room floor, leaning against the couch. Schmendrick was curled up on the brown cushion behind me. His soft snores accompanied me as I skimmed through all the books we'd found in Mom's office, but so far, I hadn't seen anything to help in the search for Mom.

One of the tomes seemed to be on demon genealogy. A few names were circled in it, and one was Malachai. (Had Mom used it to try to find the dead-beat after he'd fled?) Unfortunately, it didn't give me any idea where he might have taken her. The others told about demon types and summoning, exorcism, and demonology. None of them seemed helpful.

I put the book I'd been looking through to the side of me and stared at the last book. My stomach churned at the thought of touching it. I could feel its malevolence from here. That book was evil.

And my last chance.

Between that and the unicorn-horn dagger, I didn't know how Mom could stand to be in her office. She must have had the heebie-jeebies all the time.

I willed my hand to move toward the book, but it flat-out refused. Instead, as if it had a mind of its own, it petted Schmendrick's head. "Schmen, I'm going for a walk."

He cracked one eye open. "It's not going to get any easier to open that book."

"You're probably right." I sighed, and he shot me a look that clearly stated, "Probably?" I stood and stretched my arms over my head. "Okay, you're right, but I'm still going to put it off for a bit."

I grabbed some money out of the vase by the door, then stepped outside. The damp cold settled on me before soaking in and clinging to my bones. (Humidity didn't just suck when it was hot out.) I tucked my hands into my hoodie's pouch, fisting the material in them to keep them warm, and walked to Harvest Moon.

The bell above the door chimed, announcing my arrival. Simone sauntered to the counter, plastering a phony smile onto her face before even looking up. As soon as she realized it was me, she dropped it. "Did they find your mom? Are you coming back to work?" She sounded so hopeful that I hated to let her down.

"Not yet." I lifted my hands into the air, then dropped them again.

Her shoulders slumped, and she sighed. "Has anyone sent a ransom note or anything?"

"No." I shook my head, buying a few seconds while I figured out the best way to word things without lying. "The authorities"—I figured I could say that since I was an Ancestral Guardian. They might not have been authorities in the human world, but in the sorcerer one, they were—"have me going through some of her things to see if I can find anything that might help, but I needed a break and a hot cocoa."

"Right." She turned and grabbed a cup. Her golden ponytail swung to the side, revealing a small tattoo on the back of her neck. I couldn't make out what it was before her hair settled back into place. "Salted caramel, extra marshmallow?"

"Yeah, that's it." I was sure I sounded more than a little confused. She'd never made my drink before, and as far as I knew, she'd never paid much attention to me.

She smiled. "I notice things. It's my gift." She handed my drink to me without the lid. I always made it that way so it would cool down to drinking temperature quicker. "Isn't it weird that someone would… could kidnap Seraphina?"

The cup nearly fell out of my hands. "How do you know Mom's name? I never told you."

"No, you didn't." She wiped off the countertop, not even glancing at me. "And I probably never would have realized that Molly Wood was Mahlia Ravenwood if Caelan Thornheart hadn't sauntered through that door, looking for you."

I stared at her, utterly dumbfounded. "Who are you?"

"Simone Wright." Her features distorted, becoming more angular, and the pointed tips of her ears poked out through her hair. "It was smart of you to use parts of your name. Otherwise, I would have sensed the lie."

For four years, I'd worked alongside one of the fae without having a clue. "What are you doing here?"

"As far as I can tell, the same as you were." Her features morphed back until she looked like the Simone I was used to seeing. "You can drink that. I made it just the way you like."

I took a sip. Not because I'm stupid or gullible or anything like that, but because I can also sense lies. Another side effect of being a demon. "Tastes good. Th—" Okay, maybe I was a little stupid. I'd nearly thanked a fae, but how many times had I thanked her before I knew she was one? "That's just the way I like it." I set it on the counter and put the lid on it to keep more heat from escaping. "So, why are you telling me this now?"

"I know what you're thinking, and you aren't indebted to me. It only works if you know." She laughed and flipped her blonde hair over her shoulder. "You can relax. I've never seen sorcerers and wolves get along, but I see the way you treat them." She held her finger up before touching it to her headset. "Welcome to Harvest Moon. Order when you're ready." She punched the order into the computer, then busied herself making it. Once she handed the cup out the window and the person drove off, she turned to me again. "I think I can trust you, and it feels good to let someone in on my secret."

The bells over the door tinkled, and Simone stepped behind the register. "Let me know if I can do anything to help."

"Th—" I caught myself again. "This is going to be really hard."

She grinned at me, a fox's smile that promised mischief.

"I appreciate everything." The lump that formed in my throat surprised me. I'd left the cabal without looking back. I'd never considered that something could happen to Mom. She'd always been there, and I guess I'd convinced myself that she always would be.

I walked back to my house without noticing anything around me. The last few days had been filled with so many revelations, and something told me that there were more to come.

Chapter 31

"You can't argue with stupidity." ~Jermaine Jackson

When I reached for my doorknob, I heard Schmendrick's voice. "She's about to walk in the door right now."

I shook my head and patted my pockets. Empty. How was the stupid phone supposed to count my steps when I left it behind? I'd told him so many times to quit answering it. I wasn't sure if he did it out of boredom or mischief, but either way, it wasn't always easy or comfortable to explain away.

I opened the door, planning to reprimand him yet again. Instead, I stopped and stared at the scene in front of me. Siobhan, Thaddeus, Caelan, and Nahvienne were all crowded into my entry hall. Schmendrick stood in my living room doorway with his hackles raised and his tail at least twice its normal size.

I glanced at everyone standing there and seriously considered walking right back out.

"Hello, Molly." Nahvienne peeked around Siobhan, giving me a little finger wave. She wore leggings and a sports bra that showed off her sleek muscles. "I missed you at training this morning."

I tipped my head to the side, trying to remember if she'd mentioned training to me. "I'm sorry. I didn't know I was supposed to be there. I spent a couple hours training in self-defense."

Caelan snorted, and his mouth pulled up into a sneer that twisted his face until all traces of my childhood friend were gone. "With the wolf?"

"Yes, with *Jayden*." I set my cocoa on the table. "You refused. He volunteered. Remember?"

Caelan's eyes rolled back so far I wondered if they'd get stuck there. He strode, the few steps he could in my cramped hall, toward me, pumping his fists. "And I suppose his intentions are nothing but honorable."

"His *intentions* are none of your damn business." I stabbed my finger into his chest.

Siobhan grabbed Caelan's shoulder. Her fingers were adorned with rings, but the one on her thumb caught my attention. The band resembled locust thorns woven together, piercing a garnet heart at the center. She jerked him back, narrowing her eyes at him. "We came here because Caius filed a formal complaint against you." She glanced into the living room. "He says you stole books from his house."

"Oh. My. God!" I threw my hands into the air. "Does he not want Mom found? I took several books about demons from *my* house." I pointed toward the tomes strewn across the floor. "I've been going through them since I finished training."

Caelan tipped his head to the side and lifted one eyebrow. "Really?"

"So, I'm not allowed a break?" My hands shook. Not wanting anyone to notice, I shoved them into my pouch. "I needed fresh air, so I walked to Harvest Moon. Is that all right, or do I need to get permission from the head of the Ancestral Guardians? Do I need to let you know when I have to pee, too?"

"Molly is right about Caius and Ravenwood Manor." Thaddeus' voice was a soothing balm after Caelan's condescension and bitterness. "Since he came into Molly's life, he has consistently displayed his disapproval of her heritage, but where she and the werewolves are concerned, he has attempted to thwart their progress at every turn." He smiled at me. It was warm and made me let go of some of my anger. "It is crucial for the Arcane Council to remember that Ravenwood Manor and its contents belong to the Ravenwoods, not Caius."

Siobhan fingered the amber amulet that hung around her neck. Caelan had once told me that it protected her. I didn't know if that was true or not, but I'd never seen her without it. "It appears as though Caius is the one who is out of line. Molly is obviously doing everything we've asked of her, even if Caelan doesn't approve of the method." She looked at the books again. "Please inform us if you find anything of interest." She strode past me, stepping outside, followed by Thaddeus.

Nahvienne stopped next to me. "Will I see you for training in the morning?" She looked away from me, shuffling from foot to foot.

It had been so long since I'd spent time with people, except for taking their orders, that I wasn't sure I was reading her body language correctly. "Yeah, I'll be there." I wiped my hand over my mouth. "I'm sorry if you told me about training this morning. So much has been going on lately, I probably missed it."

"No worries!" She bounced up and down on her toes, and her excitement was genuine and contagious. "I'll see you then."

I picked up my cocoa, hoping to take it into the living room and finish it before it got too cold, but Caelan hadn't moved at all. "Please leave." I didn't have the energy to be angry with him anymore.

"He only wants one thing, Molly." He clenched his jaw.

I set the cup down and folded my arms over my chest. "Oh, yeah. What's that? To make sure I can protect myself?"

"No." He shook his head and prowled forward until he was standing toe to toe with me. Anger simmered in his hazel eyes, and I realized I genuinely missed the sparkle that used to be in them when he looked at me. "He just wants another notch in his bedpost."

I couldn't believe he went there. Anger built in my chest, begging to be released. "Get out, Caelan." I pointed at the door.

"I only want what's best for you." He dropped his chin to his chest and rubbed the back of his neck. "You hurt me, Molly. I still care about you, but I'm afraid to let you back into my life."

I stepped back. I needed space so I could breathe. "And yet, you came looking for me."

"Just trust me, okay?" He swallowed, making his Adam's Apple bob in his throat. "Stay away from the wolf."

Chapter 32

I paced from the living room door to the fireplace and back again, over and over, careful not to step on any of the books. What made Caelan think he had a right to interfere in my life? He was the one who refused to train me. He'd been nothing but an ass since he walked into Harvest Moon in his tight jeans. Did he really expect me to wait for him to trust me again?

"Yes." Schmendrick had plopped down on the back of the couch shortly after I'd returned to find my house invaded by sorcerers. It was probably a good vantage point to watch as the chaos unfurled. "He feels like you owe him that much."

I stopped pacing and stared at him. "First, did I say any of that out loud?"

"Not a peep," he stretched his front legs forward and lifted his butt as high in the air as possible, "or as loudly as you were thinking those thoughts a roar. You really should quiet your thoughts. You never know who's listening in on them." He started bathing while I tried to process what he said.

I shook my head. I couldn't worry about who else might be listening to my thoughts. (They'd probably have to dig through a lotta stupid shit before finding what they were looking for anyway.) "Did he really think he could treat me like crap for days, and when he stopped, things would go back to the way they were four years ago?"

Schmendrick lifted one shoulder in what I could only assume was a shrug and nodded.

"Seriously?" I paced a few steps away, then turned toward him again. "Seriously. What an idiot! What an absolute idiot!"

He curled into a tight ball and closed his eyes. "Once he figures out how close you and Jayden have gotten, you're going to have a full-on magical dogfight on your hands."

"You're kidding, right?" My heart felt like it was going to beat right out of my chest. Its frenetic pace stole my breath. I bent over trying to calm down, and that movement made me feel like I might throw up what little of my cocoa I drank. (Why couldn't I just have stayed hidden?) I straightened up to find Schmendrick staring at me like I'd lost my mind. "Right?!"

"No. Caelan will realize he messed up, and fearing he'll lose you forever, which I can only guess by your reaction that he has, he'll try to win you back. And as for Jayden—" Schmendrick shot me a toothy grin "—he won't give up unless he thinks it's what's best for you."

I sat on the couch and picked up my throw pillow, hugging it tightly to my chest. Caelan had been there for me when no one else was, but Jayden… I touched my fingers to my lips. Was I just taken in by his good looks and my hormones, or was there more to it? Maybe I should walk away.

A sharp pain pierced my heart at the thought. Pressing my hand to my chest, I sucked in a deep breath. "Men." I shook my head and slid onto the floor, reaching for the book. It might have been evil, but for whatever reason, it didn't scare me nearly as much as the possibility of Caelan and Jayden fighting over me.

Chapter 33

"I have studied many philosophers and many cats.
The wisdom of cats is infinitely more superior." -Hippolyte Taine

A few hours later, I closed the book, and it sounded more final than anything in my life ever had. I'd been gutted and left empty. Nothing mattered because everything I'd known, everything I'd been told was a lie.

Schmendrick plopped his head on my shoulder and purred softly. "What is it?"

"I don't think I was a mistake."

He licked the tear off my cheek. "I always knew you weren't."

"Oh, Schmen." I grabbed him and pressed him against me, hugging him tighter than he liked, bowing over him, needing him close, needing his comfort. For once, he didn't pull away. "Did you know?"

He resituated himself. "I did."

"Why didn't you tell me?" The words caught behind a sob, but I managed to force them out.

"There are rules I have to follow to stay with you, Molly." He nuzzled his face against mine, softly purring as he did. "Even when I don't want to."

The sound soothed me as it always did. "Why? And whose rules are they?"

"Why is the easier of the two. Fate and free will and all that jazz." He squirmed until he was free from my grasp. He resituated himself on my lap, looking up at me. "I can't tell you who. It's one of the rules." His green eyes begged me to believe him.

I rubbed his ear, and he turned his head this way and that to make sure I petted him everywhere. "What are some of these rules?"

"I must always be the smartest being in the room."

I lifted one eyebrow.

"Fine." He tilted his head like I do when I'm thinking. "I can't tell you unless you ask." The look he gave me told me there was something he wanted me to ask… but what?

I rolled my neck from side to side, trying to loosen the tension. "Does it have to do with D—" I couldn't bring myself to call him dad. He didn't deserve it. "—the demon who spawned me?"

"I'm sorry, but I need you to be more specific." Schmendrick stared up at me.

I tapped my finger against my lips. "Why did you choose me?"

"That is a question for a different day." He lifted his paw and licked it. "I need you to ask me the right question. That is the only one I can answer at this time." His ears were lowered in the most somber expression I'd ever seen on him.

"Hey, Buddy." I rubbed his head. "Don't worry about it. I'll think of better questions while I'm getting ready for my date."

I lied. I turned my brain off while I showered and changed. It was hard enough to accept what I read, but it hurt knowing that Schmendrick hadn't told me. *Not thinking,* I reminded my-self as I tugged on a purple sweater, a slightly different shade from my hair.

Jayden was waiting by the arch when I pulled up to Castle Unicorn. His hands were tucked into his jacket pockets, and one foot was crossed in front of the other. His smile resurrected the butterflies in my stomach. Their wings flapped like they were fighting a hurricane-force gale.

He sauntered to the passenger door, and I couldn't take my gaze off him. He sat in my car, and before he even pulled the door closed, he leaned over the center console and brushed his fingers along my cheek. "Hey, beautiful."

"Hey." (Seriously, what was up with my voice?) I cleared my throat, hoping I would sound more like myself. "I was thinking Romeo's. Are you okay with that?"

He pulled his seatbelt over his shoulder and clicked it into place. "I've never been, but if you're there, I'm sure I'll enjoy it."

Heat sparked in my belly, then climbed up my neck and onto my cheeks. I shifted the car into gear, and before I could pull my hand away, Jayden grabbed it, twining his fingers through mine.

"What do you want to know about me?" His thumb brushed along mine, and my thoughts scattered.

"Uh—" I bit my lip as I pulled onto Highway 34. "What do you do for a living?"

"I'm Garrett's beta, so I do whatever he asks." He flipped his other hand up into the air and chuckled. "Sometimes, I fix bikes."

I nodded my head as my phone call with Melissa clicked into place. "I didn't realize the wolves owned that."

"Yeah, the Loess Hills Pack owns several businesses." He stared out the windshield, and from the look on his face, I didn't think he was seeing anything here. It seemed like he was looking at a memory. "Most do."

"You okay?" I squeezed his hand.

He shook his head and turned toward me. His smile seemed a little off. "Not all wolves are like me or Garrett or Melissa. Some of them can never be around humans, and on top of that, it takes a lot of money to take care of the pack. The days leading up to the full moon, I stick around Castle Unicorn and do yard work and keep the others in line."

"That sounds a bit… intense." I glanced at him before focusing on the road again.

"It can be, but I'm pretty good at calming them." He angled his body in his seat to get a better look at me. "What about you? Do you enjoy making coffee?"

I tipped my head toward my shoulder. "Is it my dream job? No, but Viv's been great. She gave me a job when I needed one, and she's a caring, understanding person."

We crossed over the Missouri River into Nebraska, and Jayden's grip on my hand tightened. I glanced at him, replaying what I'd said, wondering if I'd done something to upset him. "Everything okay?"

"We're not in pack territory anymore." Everything about him was tense, on edge.

"I didn't know." My eyes rounded, and my breath hitched. There was so much I didn't know about his world, so much I needed to learn if I was going to be around him. What did it mean to be outside pack territory? Was I putting him in danger? Was I in danger? "You should have told me not to come here."

His thumb rubbed across mine in tiny circles. The motion seemed to calm him. "We should be fine. There are some lone wolves in Bellevue and Omaha, but the odds of running into one are slim."

Oh, goody. One more thing to worry about. I chewed on my lip, hoping to force my anxiety down. I would've closed my eyes and taken several deep breaths, but I couldn't do that while driving. "How long have you been part of the Loess Hills Pack?"

"Two years, three months, and twelve days." He had that look on his face again, the one where he was physically in the car with me, but he was reliving something in his past.

This time, I rubbed my thumb along his and forced a laugh. "That was awfully specific."

"You don't forget the day you escape your abusers."

"I left mine on my eighteenth birthday." I pulled into a parking space. "You sure you want to go in. We could always find someplace to eat in Council Bluffs or Glenwood."

He glanced around the lot. "No, this is fine." He reached for the handle. "I left mine on my twenty-first birthday."

Chapter 34

"One can fight evil, but against stupidity, one is helpless."
~Robbn Miller

"*W*elcome to Romeo's." The hostess flipped her long, black braid over her shoulder. "Two?"

"Yeah. Can we get a booth in the back?" I pointed to the area I meant.

She marked us on the seating chart, walked us back to the corner, and placed our menus on the table. "Your waitress will be right with you."

I slid onto the seat with my back to the wall. Instead of sitting across from me, Jayden slipped in next to me and reached across the table for his menu and his silverware. "I hope you don't mind. I don't like having my back to the door."

"Me either." I wondered if that was normal or if it was a side effect of the abuse we had both suffered.

"Mexican food and pizza?" Jayden turned the menu over. "Weird."

My menu lay on the table in front of me, untouched. I knew what I wanted. "Yeah, I've never tried the pizza, but I've heard it's not bad."

We watched the waitress make her way to us. "Hello, I'm Maria. I'll be your server today." A warm smile lifted her lips. "Can I get you started with drinks and an appetizer?" She looked at me.

"Can we get the beef quesadilla? And I'd like a Dr. Pepper."

Jayden pulled his ID out and showed it to her. "Blended margarita, please."

"Would you like a lime?" She held her pen still. When he nodded, she scribbled on her pad. "And salt on the rim?"

"Definitely." As the waitress walked away, Jayden folded his menu and stretched his arm along the back of the booth. "Dr. Pepper, huh?"

"Whenever Caius got really mean, he'd been drinking." I tried not to think about those nights, but they were always there, waiting to surface. "He's not my dad, and I'm not sure if alcohol would affect me the same way, but I haven't tried it."

His arm dropped down around my shoulders, and it was warmth and safety. "I won't drink if you don't want me to."

"No." I shook my head. "No, it's fine if you want to. I just don't."

His hand rubbed my arm, and I leaned into him. "If anything I do makes you uncomfortable, tell me, and I'll quit immediately."

I rested my head on his shoulder while he perused the menu. "No complaints so far."

Several minutes later, the waitress came back with our drinks. "Are you ready to order?"

I sat up. "I'll have the beef tacorito with more rice and fewer beans and sour cream on the side."

"I'll have the same." Jayden reached for my menu and handed them both to the waitress. When she walked away, he pulled his lime off the rim of his glass and squeezed it into his margarita. "You wondered if I was trying to make Caelan jealous. Are you?"

I looked at him for a long time, trying to figure out if he was serious or not. "No. I told you he hates me."

"And I told you he doesn't, not really." He pulled his arm back and took a drink of his margarita.

Schmendrick's words from earlier played on repeat through my head. (I really didn't know what to think, but everybody else thought Caelan still liked me.)

Jayden set his glass on the table. "That first day, I could tell you were attracted to him, but I think you like me, too."

I smoothed out my straw wrapper, then rolled it up, needing something to focus my attention on. "Caelan and I probably would be married by now if I hadn't left the cabal. He was my only friend, my protector, and my first and only kiss until you." I unrolled the wrapper and rolled it up again, over and over, focusing on it, refusing to look at Jayden until I was done talking. "When Caelan came back into my life, all the good memories and feelings came flooding back as if a dam had burst inside of me, but he… he didn't feel the same. He looked at me like I was something disgusting stuck to the bottom of his shoe. I didn't know if it was because I looked like this. But then I realized, it was because he felt I'd betrayed him, and he hated me."

The waitress came back with our quesadilla. I kept my head down until she walked away. Then I wiped my eyes before looking at Jayden. "I don't want him to be jealous. I didn't realize how hurt he'd be. I thought he would be happy for me. I thought he'd be glad I escaped. I should have told him what I was doing, but I figured they'd use him to find me. I was selfish."

"Was I selfish for escaping my old pack?" Jayden's voice was low, almost dangerously so.

I glanced at him through the corner of my eyes. He was staring at the table, not looking at me either. "No. Not if they were hurting you."

"Then you weren't either." He grabbed my chin and turned my face toward him. "Don't ever let somebody make you feel like getting away from abuse is selfish. Ever."

My hand trembled as I lifted it to his cheek. "Kiss me?"

His lips were on mine in an instant. He still held my chin in one hand, and the other slid along my thigh. His touch soothed the broken places inside of me, piecing them back together, letting me know I wasn't alone.

He pulled back, and I was reluctant to let him go. He wrapped his arm around my shoulders and pulled me to his side. "Something's bothering you."

"It can wait until our date's over." I reached for a slice of the quesadilla. Throughout the rest of the meal, we kept our conversation light.

Our waitress came back several times, refilling our drinks and checking to see if we had saved room for dessert.

"Can we get a bunuelo with chocolate sauce and two spoons?" Jayden's lips curved into a playful smile, making him look younger, softer.

When Maria brought the ice cream out, Jayden handed me a spoon. "Ladies first." He waved his at the dessert.

Even though I rarely saved room, I'd eaten a bunuelo before, but I felt so awkward eating his. I scraped off a small bite, and he shook his head at me.

"No, you need to get a bite of the shell on there, too. That's what makes it so good."

"I thought you'd never been here." I pointed my spoon at him.

He took that as an invitation to eat the ice cream off of it, and the grin he shot me was more foxlike than wolfish. "I haven't, but I've had a bunuelo before." He dug his spoon into the dessert and held up a bite for me.

My breath caught as I leaned forward and opened my mouth, allowing him to feed it to me, hoping that I didn't look like an absolute moron. As soon as he pulled the spoon away, he leaned forward and pressed a kiss to my lips.

Warmth flooded my body, and I shivered. Jayden's affection was unlike anything I'd ever experienced. I picked up my glass and drank most of my pop, hoping to break his intense stare, afraid that if he looked too hard, he wouldn't like what he saw. Setting my drink down, I picked up my spoon and broke the shell, making sure to get a little of everything on the bite.

He grinned before shoveling a bite into his mouth, then waved at me to eat more. With each spoonful, a little of my inhibitions disappeared.

When the ice cream was gone, Jayden pushed the empty plate away and reached for the ticket. I snatched it up before he did. "I asked you on a date. I'm paying."

He growled low enough that I doubted anyone else heard it, but I held my ground, stuffing it into my pocket. "Besides, you actually pay at the counter here."

"Fine." He scooted out and held his hand out to help me up.

We walked up to the bar, and I pulled the crumpled ticket out of my pocket. Jayden reached for his wallet, but I slapped cash on the bill before he could. "Keep the change." I smiled at the cashier.

"Thank you for dinner." Jayden slipped his hand into mine and led me to my car. He opened my door, and as I climbed into my seat, two big guys prowled over.

"Jayden Cane," the larger of the two shoved his fingers into Jayden's shoulder, "I told you what would happen if you came here again."

Jayden shot me an apologetic look. "Look, Devon, I'm on a date. Let's do this some other time."

"She looks like she could use a real man anyway." Devon leered at me. "I'm sure she'll be fine going home with me instead."

Rage pooled in my gut. *How dare he?* My insides vibrated with red-hot anger. I stepped out of my car and slammed the door.

Jayden looked at me like he was going to ask me to get back in, but I shook my head. "This asswipe just insulted me, and he's either going to apologize or eat his words."

"Okay." Jayden threw his hands up and took a step back.

Devon tossed his head back and laughed like it was the funniest thing he'd heard in a long time.

I strode toward him, and he looked at me like I was a kitten with no claws. What he didn't realize, though, was that electricity was dancing across my fingertips. As quick as a striking rattlesnake, I grabbed his arm and let go of my rage.

Devon's body locked up like Jayden's had that morning, but this time I was able to let go. Devon hit the ground with an impressive whoomph, and his friend lifted his hands into the air. "Get out of here, Jayden, and take the witch with you."

"I'm not a witch, but if you don't pick up your buddy, I'll back right over him."

Jayden opened my door for me again. As soon as I was in, he closed it. His gaze caught mine, heat searing in his eyes.

When he climbed in, he grabbed hold of my hand. "Okay, I'll admit it, that was hot."

"Well, he pissed me off."

Jayden leaned over and nipped my earlobe, ratcheting my heartbeat up about a hundred notches. "Remind me to never piss you off."

"Mmm." It was the only sound I could make. His breath in my ear did something to my insides that turned my brain into pudding.

He chuckled and leaned back in his seat. "Martin's carrying Devon off, so if you're okay to drive, we should get back to Iowa… soon."

"Yeah." I wiped my hands down my face and took a deep breath before backing out. The stoplight on Avery Road seemed like it would never change. I kept watching the rearview mirror to see if Devon and his buddy were going to show up, but luckily, they didn't. By the time I got to Highway 75, I was a little less concerned about them following us and finally began to relax.

Until… "So, what's bothering you?"

Chapter 35

*J*ayden set his hand on my thigh, and my brain turned to mush again. He chuckled softly, making me wonder what he smelled.

"Are you sure you want to talk about this now?" My voice was low and breathy.

He crossed his arms over his chest and nodded.

"I went through the books." I twisted my hands on the steering wheel, clutching it way too tightly. "I always thought I was a mistake." I pulled off onto the exit to Highway 34. My blinker filled the car with its rhythmic clicking. I sat at the stop sign, waiting for traffic to clear.

Jayden watched me, somehow knowing I had more to say.

"I think my d—" The word caught in my throat. "I think Malachai, the demon that seduced my mother, wants to sacrifice me." I pulled onto the highway. "Probably fairly soon. Supposedly, my blood will be most potent before I turn twenty-five."

Fur burst across Jayden's knuckles. "Pull over." His voice was something feral, something wild and angry. He took his seatbelt off, not waiting for me to pull onto the shoulder, and jumped out of the car before I brought it to a stop.

I flipped on my hazards and got out after him. He fought to unbutton his jeans, but the change took him, ripping his clothes to shreds. His wolf stared up at me. Then he opened his mouth, and a low, mournful howl filled the night air. The sound seemed to resonate inside of me, and for just a minute, I forgot about everything but listening to him.

When he finished his song, another wolf answered. Its call didn't have the same effect on me as Jayden's. I wondered if it was because of the distance. We stood on the side of the road next to the overpass. Cars zipped by beside and beneath us. The hills here hid the city lights, keeping passersby from seeing Jayden for what he was. The other wolf's song finished, and I opened the passenger door. "Get in. I'll drive you home."

He shook his head, and I realized he was right. He wasn't going to fit in the front, so I opened the back door, and he stretched out across the back seat. I gathered his clothes and threw them in the front before getting behind the wheel again.

"I think you can understand me." I pulled back onto the road and looked in the rearview mirror to see if he reacted at all. His golden gaze met mine, and I swore he nodded. "Caius is interfering with the investigation." I then told him everything that had happened between training and our date. "And now you're a wolf, and I can't even have a conversation with you."

There was a shuffling noise, and when I looked in the mirror again, Jayden was sitting on my backseat naked as the day he was born. "I didn't think you'd want me to shift back since I shredded my clothes." He dragged his hand through his hair. "Sorry about that, by the way. I haven't lost control since I was a pup."

"So why did you?" I glanced in the rearview mirror, meeting his eyes.

He looked away first, and I focused on the road, hoping no deer would jump out in front of me. "I've heard about it happening to other wolves." He shrugged. "It's probably just the adrenaline rush wearing off."

"Really?" I remembered the scars that covered every inch of his back. "You haven't had an adrenaline rush since you were a pup?" I shook my head and muttered, "Unbelievable."

"I have, but—" he shifted in his seat, looking more uncomfortable than I'd ever seen him "—I'm usually alone."

I turned onto Deacon Road and bounced over the gravel for about a mile. Then I pulled up to the gate.

"In my front pocket is a fob." Jayden's voice stopped me from hitting the call button. "You'll need to use that. I'm probably the only adult in human form right now."

As I dug through the shredded remnants of his jeans, I mumbled, "Lovely, just lovely. First, I'm a sacrifice, then I have a formal complaint made against me, then I get to deal with rogue wolves, then I'm a liability, and now I'm heading into a pack of wolves with a naked one in my backseat."

Jayden's low chuckle sent my butterflies into a near frenzy, and my reaction pissed me off. (Yeah, I know. I'm a mess. What can I say?) "I'm sorry it's been a rough day." He rubbed my shoulders as I drove to the castle. "Let me get dressed. Then we can talk to each other face to face."

His fingers kneaded my neck and shoulders, and I think I might have moaned a few times (but if he doesn't say anything about it, I'm gonna pretend it never happened).

As soon as I parked, a little girl ran down the path. Landscape lights lit her from below, making it impossible to tell what she looked like until she was next to the car. Her pigtails bounced against her shoulders as she stopped, holding clothes and boots. Guessing by her size, she was maybe six years old, but with wolves, who knew?

Jayden rolled his window down and took the pile from her. "Thank you, Amala." He ruffled her hair, and she skipped off. He tugged on his jeans and boots, then got out of my car.

I leaned against the car, trying not to stare, but my gaze felt pulled in his direction. I couldn't help but admire his chiseled chest and six-pack abs, though. (Yeah, I'd seen him shirtless in the backseat, but the lighting wasn't great, and I was driving, but this, the way his muscles flexed… It was awfully hot for a November evening.)

He grinned at me as he pulled his shirt on. Then he grabbed me around the waist and stepped so close that barely a breath of air remained between us. "Liked that? Did ya?" His husky voice sent a shiver through my body.

It would have been so easy to close the gap, to lose myself in him, in us, but I needed answers. I rested my hands on his chest for just a moment before pushing off. Shaking my head, I stepped to the side, putting distance between us. "I want to know what's going on. How'd the little girl know you needed clothes, and why'd you really change?"

"Amala knew I needed clothes because I told the pack what was happening when I howled." He prowled toward me, backing me up against my car, and braced his hands on either side of me. "And I lost control because I'm the beta. I'm supposed to protect, and one of my pack was threatened."

I shook my head. "I'm not a real member."

"You are." He leaned his forehead against mine and held my gaze with his. "You are."

Chapter 36

My heart swelled, and instead of focusing on his change, I suddenly realized how close we were, how warm he was. My pulse ratcheted up, and every nerve in my body suddenly sparked to life. I tipped my head back and brushed my lips over his.

He chuckled against my lips and wrapped his arms around me, drawing us closer together. Then his lips crashed down on mine.

I stood on my tiptoes, pressing closer to him, and twined my arms around his neck. He lifted me, and somehow, without me thinking about it, my legs wrapped around his waist.

And, oh, the kiss. It wasn't like any of the others. It was fire and passion. It felt like he was claiming me, but I didn't stop him. I didn't want to. Somehow, it was everything I needed and wanted.

"Are you just going to get down and dirty with the dog out here where everyone can see you?" Schmendrick's voice was the last one I expected to hear.

I unhooked my feet and slid down Jayden's legs. "Hey, Schmen." He was sitting on the roof of my car, looking at me with what I could only call disappointment. "What are you doing here?"

"That's not the question I'm waiting for you to ask." His eyes flicked from me to Jayden.

"What question is he waiting for?" Jayden draped his arm over my shoulders, and I slid my hand into his back pocket and snuggled against his side.

With everything else that had happened, I had totally forgotten about Schmendrick's riddle. "He can tell me something that he knows but only if I ask the right question." I reached up and scratched Schmendrick's head. He nestled into my hand and even let a purr slip out. "I asked if it had something to do with Malachai, but he said I needed to be more specific."

Jayden rubbed his chin, and his scruff sounded like sandpaper against his palm. "Maybe you can ask him if you're my soulmate." His lips tipped up, and I shook my head.

"Are you sure I have a soul?" A part of me didn't want to know what he'd say, but the other part… needed someone to reassure me that I did. "I am half demon after all."

His head snapped in my direction so quickly that I wondered if he got whiplash. "Of course, you have a soul."

"Schmendrick," I turned away from the intensity in Jayden's gaze, not wanting to dissect it right now, "do I have a soul?"

Schmendrick nipped at my fingers. "That's a stupid question, Molly. Of course, you have a soul. I wouldn't be with you if you didn't."

"Knew it." Jayden squeezed my shoulder. "If you don't want to ask him if you're my soulmate, maybe he knows where your mom is or how you can save her."

"The *dog*," Schmendrick smirked at Jayden, "just might be smarter than he looks, Molly. If he's house-trained, maybe you can keep him for a while."

I lifted my hand and twined my fingers through Jayden's, needing his support. "Do you know where Mom is?"

"Why, yes, Molly. I'm so glad you *finally* asked me." He stood and fluffed the roof of my car with his claws out, of course.

I cringed, but nothing I said or did would change him. He was a cat—or something like one—after all. "Can you take me to her?"

"Not tonight." He curled into a ball. "Places like the Abyss are best traveled in the light of day."

Chapter 37

"*Against stupidity, the very gods themselves contend in vain.*"
-Friedrich Schiller

$\mathcal{W}$hy did hearing that send shivers marching up my spine?

Standing beneath the stars usually made me feel like I belonged. The night comforted me, but that feeling vanished. Instead, the darkness closed in on me, trapping me beneath shadows and despair... and fear, turning the night menacing.

"Schmendrick." I waited for him to look at me, but he was either asleep or pretending to be. Either way, he wasn't going to be any help. "So, I guess I'm going to the Abyss."

Jayden grabbed my arm and spun me so that I was facing him. All color had drained from his face, and a vein throbbed in his neck. "Malachai wants to sacrifice you, and you're planning to go to him." He shook his head and laughed, not the one I was used to hearing from him, but something darker. "Hey, Dad. How's it going? I know you want to kill me, but let me take Mom home first."

"Really?!" I threw my hands in the air and stalked away from him. We'd been on two dates. He wasn't in charge of me. It was my life, and if I wanted to storm into the Abyss to save my mom, I had every right to. "What do you expect me to do?"

He dragged his hand down his face, drawing my attention to his fangs. He was on the verge of changing again because of me. (Seriously, his protective nature was a little much.) "I don't know." His voice was a harsh growl.

I walked over and placed my hand on his arm, hoping to calm him down. "I don't plan on rushing in without a plan, but the whole reason I got back into this world was to save Mom, and I'm not going to let her down."

"Okay." His arms trembled as he reached up to wrap them around me and pull me close. "Okay, but we do it together."

"You'll have to let the Arcane Council and the other Ancestral Guardians in on it, too." Schmendrick stood, stretched, and then disappeared like he was never there to begin with.

I looked up at Jayden and then back to where Schmendrick had been. "One of these days, I'll figure him out."

"I wouldn't count on that happening." He let go of me, backed away, lifted his head to the sky, and howled. It didn't sound quite like his wolf, but something about it still called to me. When he stopped, he grabbed my hand and led me through the archway on the same path Amala had disappeared down, following the landscape lights along the pond.

His fingers in mine felt so natural. His calluses brushed against my skin. I could feel the strength in his hand, but it held mine so gently. "What was that about?"

His voice was still shaky, but his skin had some color to it again. "I asked Garrett and Melissa to meet us on the patio."

"No need for phones in the wolf world, huh?" I waved my hand at the water. "The pond is beautiful with the lights reflecting off of it."

He tipped his head, and his brows pinched together. "Pond?"

"Yeah." We strode away from it toward the patio, and I pointed over my shoulder.

"That's the moat, and you're right, it is." He pulled out a chair and waited for me to sit in it. "To answer your question, only when we're in public." He sat next to me, and we waited.

A few minutes later, two ginormous wolves ran onto the patio. One of them made Jayden's wolf look like a puppy.

Amala opened the sliding glass door, and the wolves trotted inside. When they came back out a few minutes later, they were fully clothed humans. Melissa's auburn tresses were a tangled mess, and I couldn't help but wonder if that was why Garrett's dark hair was buzzed.

"Hello, Molly." Garrett pulled out Melissa's chair and waited for her to sit before taking the seat next to me. "What's going on?"

I trailed my finger along the edge of the table. "Schmendrick, my cat, said that Malachai has Mom in the Abyss. I need to go there to get her, but he wants to sacrifice me. Maybe today. Maybe three years from now. Either way, I'd like to avoid it." I sat back and folded my arms over my chest. "So, yeah, that about sums it up." I felt Jayden tense up next to me. "Oh, and the idea makes Jayden explode into a wolf like he hasn't done since he was just a pup."

Melissa pushed back from the table and stood with her hands on her hips, glaring at Jayden. "Does she know why? Have you told her?"

"He told me," I answered for him since he looked like he was fighting the change. "Apparently, he feels the need to protect me since I'm part of the pack." I rubbed his hand, but it didn't seem to do anything to relax him.

Melissa focused on him for so long that I wondered if they were having a silent conversation.

When she looked away, Garrett stared directly into Jayden's eyes, and Garrett's irises turned from blue to bright gold. "Get a hold of yourself. She doesn't need you changing. She needs you like this."

Jayden's head dipped, and the tension left his body. "You're right. I'm sorry, Molly."

"So, you just tell him something, and he has to do it?" I looked from Jayden to Garrett and back again. "So much for free will."

Garrett's growl raised goosebumps all over my body. "Free will has no place in a pack, but Jayden's strong enough that if he didn't want to do it, he'd fight my command."

"What about the rest of them?" I shoved my chair back and stood with my feet spread wide. I knew what it was like to be under somebody's thumb, and I never wanted to be held there again. "What about me? As an honorary pack member, you don't have that kind of power over me. Do you?" Maybe I should have tried to rein in my anger. I didn't know how many wolves were in the Loess Hills Pack for sure, but I knew most of them weren't even close to human at that moment.

Garrett tipped his head back and laughed. "I doubt there's a single person on this planet who could control you. You seem like the type of person who will do the opposite of whatever you're told just to prove that you can."

Even though I wasn't sure if that was supposed to be an insult or a compliment, some of the anger drained out of me, and I sat back down. "Okay, so, do any of you have any suggestions?"

Garrett rubbed his chin. "Did the book say what sacrificing you could accomplish?"

I focused on the table. "Just that my blood would be the most powerful the closer I came to my twenty-fifth birthday."

"Blood magic carries immense power." His eyes were mostly yellow, and his canines longer than just moments before. "It's ancient, primal, and dark. Whoever uses it becomes twisted by the evil they manifest. Its corruption consumes the wielder, unavoidable and unbreakable."

Tremors racked my body, and I wrapped my arms around myself as tightly as I could, trying to stop them.

Jayden slid closer, draping his arm over my shoulders and pulling me against his side. His warmth did little to stop the chill that had settled on me.

Remembering what Melissa had told me earlier about smelling like prey, I pushed my chair away from the table and stood. Their eyes followed me as I paced the patio, but I was able to shake some of my fear.

When I sat again, Garrett picked up the conversation. "Do you know any vamps?" He didn't wait for me to answer. "I believe they can enter the Abyss unnoticed."

"No. I can't say I've had the pleasure of meeting one yet." I shivered. Even to me—a half-demon—a vampire seemed like the epitome of creepiness. Dead. Feigning life by sucking the blood out of others. It was abhorrent. (And not even a little sexy. Sorry, not sorry.) "Schmendrick knows how to get me there." I ran my finger along the table, tracing the grain in the wood. "I guess I'm asking for a way to make it back out."

Melissa paced the length of the patio, then to the table again. She stood with her hands on her chair's back. "What do you know about the Abyss?"

"That it's the last place I'd ever want to go." A knot crept up my chest, lodging in my throat. "And one of the next places I'll be going."

Chapter 38

$\mathcal{J}$ayden's hand covered mine, warm and comforting. "I'm going with you."

"I imagine Nahvienne and Caelan will be, too." I was grateful that he seemed to have his wolf under control, one less thing for me to worry about. Like this, his presence calmed me.

Something brushed against my leg, and I jumped up, knocking my chair over. Garrett, Melissa, and Jayden all looked like they were about to transform into their wolves.

Schmendrick chuckled as he leapt onto the table.

"What are you doing here?" I practically shouted at him as I righted my chair.

His ears lay back, and his green eyes narrowed. "A fine welcome. I leave your comfortable bed to share my knowledge, and you bark at me as if you've turned into the company you keep."

Garrett's hands clenched into fists, and Melissa squeezed his shoulder, shaking her head.

"I'm sorry, Schmen." I sat, putting my feet on the edge of the seat and pulling my knees against my chest. "You scared the ever-lovin' outta me."

He positioned himself in the center of the table, sitting like the Sphinx and looking every bit as regal. "Apology accepted."

"So, *cat*," Garrett seemed to be having a little difficulty reeling in his rage, "tell us about the Abyss."

Schmendrick stared him straight in the eyes, and I about fell out of my chair when Garrett looked away first. I thought I'd seen Schmendrick appear smug before, but those expressions had nothing on this. He sat taller, looking as though he'd single-handedly rid the world of vermin and was regaling in the adoration he'd earned.

"The Abyss," his voice dropped to an ominous tone that I'd never heard from him before, "is where light and hope go to die. The ground crumbles beneath your every step. Nightmares stalk you, keeping you from knowing what's real and what's imagination. And the creatures that inhabit the infernal plane were too gruesome to be left in hell."

The night seemed to hold its breath while Schmendrick talked. The air grew heavy and still. Jayden scooted closer to me, wrapping his arm over my shoulders as if he felt it, too.

"Why would he take her there?" My voice sounded so small.

Schmendrick stretched. "Malachai is one of the lords of the Abyss." He looked at me like I should have known this somehow. "His castle is its crowning glory. The one building that hasn't fallen to ruin beneath the soul-crushing despair that resides there."

"So… how do I get in there and get out again without being sacrificed?" I settled my chin on my knees.

"We'll figure something out." Jayden rubbed my arm. Whether to soothe me or him or both of us, I wasn't sure.

Schmendrick lifted his leg. "I'm working on it. Give me a day or two." He licked his fur but didn't take his eyes off me.

"Okay then." I patted Jayden's hand. "I should go home." All of this was too much. I needed to think, to figure out how to save Mom and myself.

"Stay here tonight." He stepped in front of me. "After everything today, you shouldn't be alone."

Schmendrick quit biting his toenail long enough to say, "She hasn't been alone since she was knee-high to a grasshopper."

"I meant nothing by it." Jayden reached toward Schmendrick, but Schmendrick pulled his head back. "You can sleep in my room, Molly, and I'll take the couch." There was a desperate edge to his voice, but I just wanted to go home, to be in my space.

"I'll be fine." I pushed my chair back and stood up. "Thank you." I nodded at Garrett and Melissa.

Garrett dipped his head. "Why did you name the cat Schmendrick?"

"He came to me in my *Last Unicorn* phase." I scratched Schmendrick's head. "Had I known what it meant, I wouldn't have named him that."

Schmendrick smirked. "I rather fancy it. Much like calling a giant Tiny." He disappeared without another word.

"Only a cat." Garrett shook his head, and he and Melissa went inside.

Jayden held his hand out. "Can I at least walk you to your car?" He wiggled his fingers, and I slipped my hand into his. "I won't push you to stay here if you don't want to, but it's in my nature to try to protect you."

I rubbed my thumb along his. "So, am I going to look outside my window and see your wolf pacing underneath it?"

"I'll do my best not to." He grinned at me, and my heart fluttered in response. "But instincts are difficult to overcome."

We stood next to my car, and Jayden swept a strand of my hair back, tucking it behind my ear. "You could just invite me in." His voice was husky, inviting. He leaned in, his breath brushing across my face. "I could sleep in your spare room or curl up on the floor in my wolf form and guard your bed."

I lifted onto my toes, cupped his cheeks in my hands, and pressed my lips to his. "I promise I'll be fine." I trailed my fingers along his neck and to his shoulders.

"Will you be here for training tomorrow?" There was something in his eyes that I couldn't read, something that made him look almost sad.

My stomach sank in response, making me want to give in, but I was afraid that if I let him pressure me into staying with him, I would resent him for it. We'd only been on two dates, and

I wasn't ready for more, especially with everything that had already happened.

He stood in front of me, waiting for my answer. I shook myself out of my thoughts. "I have to train with Nahvienne first thing. Then, I can come here to work with you." I chewed on my lip. "Unless you think I should talk to them about going to the Abyss."

"You're going to have to decide that." He stared up at the night sky, and I wondered what was going through his head. "Don't tell them until you have a plan. The council, especially Caius, will send you to retrieve her whether you're ready or not."

Chapter 39

"Life is an endless journey through stupidity." -Eddie Griffin

 $\mathcal{N}$ ahvienne stood across from me in the training arena. The sun shone behind her, haloing her like a goddess on the battlefield. She held her sword like she actually might have slept last night. She practiced her strokes, moving with the grace of flowing water. "Rough night?" Laughter danced in her aqua eyes.

"Yeah." I dragged my hand through my tangled hair. The short sword dangled from my other one, the point nearly touching the grass beneath my feet. The thought of lifting it exhausted me. My alarm went off about twelve hours too early. Instead of sleeping, I'd lain in bed, staring up at the ceiling, wondering if I should've let Jayden come home with me, wondering what I should say to Caelan, and trying to figure out a way to make it out of the Abyss alive. (And, you know, I have to say that's a lot for one person to worry about. I mean, shouldn't there be a limit?) "I had way too much on my mind to sleep."

She tipped her head to the side, and her cobalt curls bounced against her shoulder. "Well, try to put on a good show. You're being watched today."

"Great." I glanced around, expecting to see the council standing behind me. It wasn't until I looked up that I found Caelan, Siobhan, Caius, and Thaddeus standing on the balcony of Ravenwood Citadel. They were all dressed to the nines, but for once, Siobhan's hair was loose. It fell in gentle waves that shimmered red in the sunlight. "They realize this is only my second day of training, right?" I turned around to find her waiting in guard position.

She nodded. "Just do like you did last time." She brought her sword down, and I repeated the motion.

I followed her lead until I could barely lift my arms. Instead of letting me be done, she pointed at the dagger lying on the bench. "Hold the dagger in your right hand and the sword in your left." She picked up hers. "We're going to start by swinging them together. Same direction, same speed."

My left arm lagged behind the right, and the dagger clashed against the blade of the sword. I cringed, hoping the council members had grown bored and gone inside.

Nahvienne noticed. "Switch hands. See what that does for you."

As I swapped, I snuck a peek at the balcony. They were still watching. (Of course, they were. Why would my humiliation just be for me?) My shoulders slumped for an instant before I followed her movements, but it wasn't much better. Using my left arm in this way was awkward and took so much more concentration than it should have.

"Mahlia is not fit to be a sorceress, let alone a guardian." Venom filled Caius' voice. "We need to cut our losses before she goes on a mission and gets somebody killed."

My blades hit each other with a loud clang that reverberated down my arms, and I couldn't help but cower, expecting his wrath and torment.

"Hatred has no place on the council." Siobhan's response allowed the tension in my shoulders to ease. "If you don't figure out how to accept *Molly*, I will move to have your position terminated."

I peeked up at the balcony just in time to see Thaddeus step forward, stopping slightly behind Siobhan. "And I will second the motion. How can we properly lead if we allow discrimination among our ranks?"

"Discrimination, bah." Caius waved his arm through the air, stopping with his finger pointing at me. "She is a monster, an abomination."

Siobhan placed her hands on her hips, and power radiated from her, making her seem to dwarf Caius. I was sure he would have loved to argue with her, but his mouth snapped shut as he stormed away.

Turning back to Nahvienne, I realized how stupid I'd been. For four years, I'd lived as a human. No magic. (Not even a hint of an abra, let alone a cadabra.) Where it had once been second nature, it was an afterthought these days.

I sent a burst of energy into my arms and swung the blades, no longer fumbling like a Nebraska quarterback. (Hey, I'm from Iowa; what do you expect?) The motions were controlled, smooth, and, much to my surprise, easy.

"Well, look who finally remembers who she is." Schmendrick's voice didn't surprise me like it had the night before. I'd actually been expecting him earlier when I was making a fool of myself.

I grinned at him but said nothing as I followed Nahvienne's lead, adding steps to the dance. All my worries took a backseat to the rhythm of the movements. Peace settled inside me for the first time since Caius had entered my life. The feeling was so foreign that I almost didn't recognize it for what it was.

After several more minutes, Nahvienne's voice pulled me out of my trance. "Wow, Molly. You did great." She bit her lip and rocked from foot to foot. "So… uh, what changed?" She lifted her hand, still gripping the smaller blade she'd used. Three of her fingers raised in what I could only guess was supposed to be a stop motion. "No offense."

"No." I laughed. "None taken. I remembered that I'm magic, and I used it."

She nodded toward the balcony, and I followed her gaze. "Well, you sure showed Caius. He left shortly after their argument."

Siobhan sat on the balcony railing, then turned so she was facing us. Stepping off, she floated to the ground like Mary Poppins but without the umbrella.

I couldn't stop watching. It wasn't a great feat of magic, but it was the first open display of it that I'd seen in a long time. When Siobhan landed, I turned toward Nahvienne and said,

"He's hated me all my life. That's not going to change, even if I bring Mom back from the Abyss."

Oh, shit. I said that. So much for keeping it to myself until I had a plan.

"Wait… what?" She spun toward me, and I stepped out of the way of her blades. "Seraphina is in the Abyss?!"

Chapter 40

"There is no sin except stupidity." –Oscar Wilde

 I shook my head. There was no way Siobhan and Caelan didn't hear that. "Uh, possibly. It's a theory I'm looking into." (I mean, there wasn't any proof really, just Schmendrick's word.)

"How long have you known?" Caelan marched over to me, stopping just inches away.

I took a step back and looked from him to the balcony, wondering when he'd gotten down here. "Late last night." I sheathed my swords, then crossed my arms. "My plan was to see what I could figure out today and bring it to the council when I had something more."

"You just can't be a team player, can you?" Caelan's hazel eyes were flinty as he stared at me, clenching and unclenching his fists.

I wasn't sure if I was more shocked or angry. My mouth dropped open, and heat filled my chest. "Why would I?" I rubbed my hand down my face. "As long as Caius is on it, I can't trust the council. You flat-out told me you want to hurt me." Siobhan opened her mouth to say something, but I lifted my hand, effectively shutting her up. "I had every intention of letting you in on it as soon as I figured out how to get in and out of the Abyss without being sacrificed."

I mentally slapped my forehead. Was I seriously going to tell them everything?

Siobhan grabbed my arm right above the elbow and started leading me toward the citadel. "This is something that should be discussed in private." She glanced around. "Even here, someone could be listening."

Thaddeus, Caelan, Nahvienne, and I followed Siobhan inside. She walked at a steady clip to her office. Like every other room here, it was dark, but she'd added little touches to brighten it. Plants sat on her windowsills, soaking up the sunlight streaming in. She waved at the beige chairs and sat behind her desk.

Thaddeus stepped behind her, leaning against the window frame. He propped one foot in front of the other, then folded his arms over his chest. As comforting as his presence had been earlier, his gaze made me want to squirm in my seat. I fought the urge and sat as straight as possible.

Siobhan fidgeted with her ring, watching it as she spun it around her finger. When she looked up, the stern woman was gone. Her eyes drooped, and she appeared to have aged at least ten years. "First, I need to say that I don't blame you for not trusting us. We," she waved her hand through the air, "all of the adults in the cabal, should have been there for you when you were growing up. The pain and betrayal that you felt…" Her hazel eyes glistened, and she pinched her lips together while shaking her head. "I can only imagine." She pressed her hand to her heart. "For my part, I am sorry."

Holy furballs! That was not what I'd expected her to say, and I had no idea how to respond, so I just nodded.

"Caius sits on the council at your mother's behest." Thaddeus rubbed his neatly trimmed beard and stared at the burgundy-patterned rug that Siobhan's desk sat on. "Though his callous ways resonate with several sorcerers, he does not have the influence he desires." His warm, brown eyes met mine, and in them, I saw what I believed to be honesty. "There are more worthy members of the council than not, and though I imagine the near impossibility of this request, I ask that you trust us."

My heart tightened, and a deep yearning filled me. I had wanted their sympathy and protection until four years ago. I would've cherished it, but who would I be if I had stayed? "I will do my best, but you also have to trust me." I looked each of them in the eyes, meeting Caelan's first. Once I would've trusted him with my life, but those days were gone. Nahvienne's aquamarine eyes gazed back at me. In them, I saw someone who could be a friend. Of the council members, Siobhan and Thaddeus seemed to be the most trustworthy, but trust was not freely given; it was earned. "You dragged me back into this world, and I have done everything you've asked of me. Yet, every time I turn around, one of you is second-guessing me." My shoulders slumped forward. "I just want to find Mom."

"I'm sorry." Caelan's elbows rested on his knees, and he held his head in his hands. "I've been an ass since you came back, but I'll do better."

Siobhan nodded and set her hands flat on her desk. The haggard look from earlier disappeared, and once again, she resembled a leader. "Each of us must work to earn the others' trust. Right now, it appears as though you have the most knowledge of Seraphina's whereabouts. Will you enlighten us?"

Schmen, what do I tell them?

The black cat appeared on my lap. He stretched his forelegs out in front of him. His claws slid over my jeans, but he was careful not to scratch me. *As little as you can, and nothing about the dog's involvement.*

"Hello, Schmendrick." Nahvienne leaned over and scratched behind his ear.

He tried to look haughty but failed epically. "Nahvienne."

"Schmendrick believes Malachai"—I didn't even bother trying to say Dad that time. There was no point in beating a dead horse or a deadbeat dad for that matter—"took Mom to the Abyss." I sucked in a deep breath while they shifted in their seats. "He knows a way to go there, but—" I stared up at the ceiling. Dark, carved wood panels made ominous shadows stretch out from the chandelier. "One of the books…"

Schmendrick rubbed his head against my hand, making me pet him without consciously thinking about it. "The demon is itching to sacrifice Molly for her power, so she'd like to figure out a way to survive a trek to her daddy's domain."

"He wants to sacrifice you?" Caelan stretched out each word like he couldn't believe what he'd heard, but why wouldn't he?

After all, my sperm donor was a demon. He'd never seen me. Never held me or rocked me to sleep. He'd kidnapped Mom. Why wouldn't he sacrifice me?

"Yeah." Not thinking, I wiped my hand down my face, then flicked cat fur off my hand. "Sorry. Anyway, that about sums it up. I wanted to figure out how to get back out before I came to you with this. I'm sure Caius would be more than happy to see me go and not return, so I didn't want him to know." A hair tickled the inside of my nose each time I breathed in, but since everybody's gaze was trained on me, I left it, hoping it would go away without me looking like a fool.

Caelan leaned forward so I could see him around Nahvienne. "You should've come to me, though."

"Why? So you could take it to the council, and Caius could send me to my death?" I stood, set Schmendrick on the chair, and turned my back on everyone, giving myself a chance to wipe the cat fur off my face. I moved behind my chair, gripping the back of it. "You know all that I do. If you don't mind, I need to leave. I have self-defense training to get to."

"With the wolf?" Caelan jumped up, nearly knocking his chair over. "I told you to stay away from him."

I shook my head. "I can't." My shoulder lifted in a gesture more nonchalant than I felt like giving him. "I'd be disobeying the council if I didn't get trained in self-defense." Before he could answer, I snatched up Schmendrick and strode out the door.

Chapter 41

"*I* wasn't sure you'd come." Jayden gripped the car door. I'd driven to Castle Unicorn with the windows down and the radio up, trying to stay awake. Jayden's hands kept me from rolling the window up. Deep bags surrounded his amber eyes. His hair was mussed, and he looked smaller somehow.

I settled my hand over his, and he relaxed slightly. "I told you I'd be here." I tried to push the door open, but he didn't seem willing to move away. "You look tired. I didn't notice you pacing the sidewalk in front of my house."

"No. I stayed here all night." He sniffed, then tilted his head. "Something's wrong."

"I didn't sleep last night." I shuddered before slumping back in my seat. I should've expected this. Of course, he would be able to tell that I was annoyed. "Then Nahvienne worked my butt off, and I let slip that Mom was in the Abyss, so yeah, they know now."

He reached through the open window and brushed my hair back, tucking it behind my ear. "You okay?"

"I hope so." I leaned into his touch. His thumb trailed along my cheek, and the motion helped relax me. "Why didn't you think I would show up?"

Suddenly, he reminded me of a forlorn child. He stood up and tucked his hands in his pockets. "After being out of control last night, I thought you might see me as nothing but a monster."

"Oh, Jayden, no." I pushed my door open and scrambled out of the car. I didn't even shut the door before wrapping my arms around his waist and laying my head on his chest, breathing in the scent of him, cedar and fresh air mixed with leather. "You're not a monster. You shifted into your wolf. You didn't try to attack me or anyone else."

He pulled his hands out of his pockets and settled one on the back of my head while the other trailed along my spine. "I don't deserve you, Molly."

I tilted my head back and met his gaze. He truly cared for me. I could see it in his eyes. I settled my head against his chest again. It was the most peaceful I'd felt in… ever, maybe. "Can we not train today?"

His hand stilled. "If you don't want to, you can go. I won't make you stay."

"I was thinking that maybe we could, uh…" My cheeks burned. "Maybe we could snuggle up together and watch a movie or something. You calm me, and I'm so tired."

He chuckled, and my head bounced in time to the noise. "Sure, Molly." Before I knew what he was doing, he slid his arms under my legs and lifted me. He jostled me a little before I heard the distinctive sound of my car door closing. Then he carried me toward the castle.

I stiffened at first, but then, as if this was something that happened every day, I relaxed against him.

Somehow, without setting me down, he opened the patio door. A television droned in the distance. "We can watch TV with the others, or I can take you to my room." He didn't let me answer before he added, "We can watch a movie in there without an audience."

"That'd be good." My voice sounded distant, like I was almost asleep in his arms.

He lay me down on a bed, then sat next to me. I didn't even bother opening my eyes. I just snuggled against him until he wrapped his arms around me. "Sleep, Molly. I'll watch over you." His fingers traced over my arm, leaving tingling trails in their wake.

I woke up curled on top of Jayden, and I couldn't remember ever sleeping better. I wondered if I could pretend like I was still napping. My hand—not having gotten the memo—ran along Jayden's chest.

"Hey." His voice was husky. "How'd you sleep?"

I kept tracing the lines of his body. "Better than ever. Can I just stay here awhile?"

"As long as you'd like." He brushed my hair back and tipped my chin so that I was looking at him. "Forever if you want." He kissed my forehead and skimmed his fingers along my arm.

I shivered and flexed my hands, tightening my grip on his chest, and that was when I noticed Schmendrick sitting on the edge of Jayden's dresser, staring at me.

Doesn't look like self-defense training to me. The rumbling purr that followed surprised me.

I pressed against Jayden's chest in an effort to sit up, but he held me there. "Not yet." His arms tightened. "Let me hold you a little longer."

"We have company," I said as I snuggled against him.

He wrapped one arm around my waist and one around my legs. "Schmendrick's been here since I brought you in."

"Someone had to make sure the dog didn't try to steal your virtue." Schmendrick rolled onto his side and licked his belly.

I raised an eyebrow at him. "We both know that's not about to happen."

"We do." I was surprised to hear Schmendrick agree. "But still, he carried you into his bedroom like a bride on her wedding night. I had to be sure."

This time, I did sit up. "I'm sorry, Jayden. I didn't mean to imply anything."

"Molly—"

"No." I scrubbed my hand down my face. "I don't want to lead you on. All of this is new to me."

He sat up and took hold of my hand. "I carried you in here because you were dead on your feet, and well… my intentions might not have been completely honorable."

I didn't know whether to feel concerned or flattered. "What's that supposed to mean?"

"Well, you see." His hand trailed up and down my arm. "The idea of having you snuggled up against me was something I couldn't pass on." He leaned in, brushing his nose along my jawline and tracing the side of my face until he nipped my earlobe. "And you trusted me enough to sleep in my arms." The words were whispered and sent a rush of desire through me, unlike anything I'd ever felt.

"Mmm." I squirmed in his embrace.

He chuckled, and his breath in my ear sent shivers racing through my body. "So, you must like me a little bit."

That killed my desire, squashed it like a bug, even. He didn't know I liked him? "I'm so sorry, Jayden."

"Sorry?" His chin tucked under, and he pulled back a little. "For what?"

I wiped my hands down my face. "I like you. Like a lot." I peeked at him through my fingers. "I thought you knew that. I never meant for you to feel like I didn't."

"Molly." He pulled my hands down and wrapped his around them. They dwarfed mine. "I know you like me. I was teasing you."

"Dog." Schmendrick stopped his licking, sat up, and stared at Jayden.

Jayden pinched his eyes closed for a moment. "I know you desire me. I *hoped* you liked me."

"There's a good puppy." Schmendrick spun in a few circles before lying down. His tail covered his eyes, but he didn't fool me. I knew he'd be watching and listening.

I scooted to the side of the four-poster bed that he wasn't on and stood up, taking notice of my surroundings for the first time since he carried me in there. The rug under my feet was plush, and even though the furnishings were dark wood with navy accents, it didn't feel foreboding like Ravenwood Manor. The light streaming in through the stained-glass windows and the brightness of the white walls made it feel happier.

There weren't any personal touches on the dresser, desk, bookcase, or nightstands, and for the first time, it hit me that Jayden was just like me. He had nothing worth returning to in his previous life. The only differences were that I had Schmendrick, and I had been dragged back into my past.

When my gaze landed on Jayden, I could almost sense his loneliness. "I can't let you follow me into the Abyss without showing you who I am."

Chapter 42

"Stupidity isn't punishable by death. If it was, there would be a hell of a population drop." -Laurell K. Hamilton

Now that I knew this form wasn't a glamour, I could tell in subtle ways. The tail that I'd always assumed was there wasn't. I didn't actually feel it moving through the air behind me, but I did feel it, a phantom trailing me. Something that was supposed to be but had been banished. How had I not realized?

"You don't have to do this." Jayden hopped off the bed and stood across from me. He stretched his hands forward to stop me.

I felt like I'd been sucker punched. The king-sized mattress seemed like an uncrossable chasm separating us. Did the idea of seeing me repulse him so much?

I could certainly understand why it might. It wasn't like I was something cute and fluffy. I was a demon, a creature of nightmares. "Don't you want to know?" I could hear the tears in my voice, so I was sure he could.

"Of course, I do." He shook his head. "I'm doing this all wrong. I said I wouldn't rush you, but you're making confessions you're not ready for, and now this." He gestured toward me, and if it was possible, my heart plummeted even further.

I turned toward the door, ready to leave, when I heard Schmendrick's voice in my head. *Listen to him, Molly.*

"I don't want you to do anything you don't want to. If you want to show me, believe me when I tell you I want to see you." A slight tremble edged his voice. "But if you're not ready, I can wait."

The pain in my chest lessened. I wiped my hands on my jeans and faced Jayden. He looked like someone who was about to break, staring at the bed like he hadn't seen it before. His mouth pulled down, and I swore his eyes were shinier than I'd ever seen them.

Before I could overthink it, I slipped my hands into my leggings, pushing the back of them down enough that they wouldn't get ripped. I let the change come over me. Horns spiraled from my head, and my tail burst through the air, whipping from side to side. "This is me." It was my turn to stare at the bed. "This is what the cabal fears, and if you want to walk away now, I'll completely understand."

"Why would I want to walk away?" The confusion in his voice caught me off guard, and I glanced up at him in time to see Schmendrick disappear.

"You're beautiful, Molly." His steps padded across the floor toward me. When he reached me, he tilted my face toward his, holding my gaze with his. "Awesome, fierce, and beautiful." Then he backed up, staying arm's length from me, taking in every detail of my monster. Reaching forward, he stopped short of touching me. "May I?"

I nodded, not ready for him to see my fangs.

His fingers grazed along my horns. "Amazing." His voice was a whisper. "Can you feel this?"

"No." I cleared my throat, trying to remove the emotions that had lodged themselves there. "They're like fingernails or hair… just tougher."

He moved closer to me, dragging his hands through my hair to the pointed tips of my ears. His touch was feather light.

I sucked in a shaky breath, holding perfectly still, waiting for him to finish, wondering when he'd decide he didn't want anything to do with me.

His fingers continued their path, skimming over my cheeks before brushing across my lips. He pressed down, and I opened my mouth.

"You do have fangs." His voice was low; dare I say reverent? His hands slid back to the sides of my face, and he leaned forward. "May I?"

Still afraid to scare him away, I tipped my head in a nearly imperceptible nod.

His thumbs brushed over my cheeks while his fingers skimmed across my neck and ears. All the while, his face inched closer, his gaze never moving from mine.

His mouth hovered in front of mine. His breath caressed my lips, the ghost of a kiss.

My heart raced, beating against my ribs like a caged bird fighting for freedom. I held my breath, waiting, wanting, anticipating.

His lips touched mine before he pulled away, and the grin that tugged at them told me he knew exactly what he was doing to me.

"Again?" He leaned in. This time, he didn't tease. His lips moved against mine, slowly, tenderly. His fingers still tracing my ears and neck.

I lifted my hands, cupping his cheeks, brushing my palms over his scruff. I stepped closer and wrapped my tail around his leg, drawing him toward me.

He jumped and glanced down, chuckling while he slid his hands to my back. He tugged my body against his. Then his mouth crashed down on mine again.

My doubt was erased by every swipe of his tongue, every caress as his hands roamed over my back. His teeth scraped my lip, and I knew that for the first time, somebody truly accepted me for who I was.

I twined my leg around his, and he lifted me, walking until he backed me up against the wall. His hand slid under my shirt, tracing circles across my lower back while his mouth explored mine.

Following his lead, I untucked his tee and slipped my hands beneath it. I trailed my fingers along his scars. One led to another and then another. His muscles bunched beneath my touch.

An overwhelming urge to keep him safe, to never let anything happen to him again, rose inside of me as I explored every inch of his back. With each ridge my fingers crested and valley they descended, I realized I'd do everything I could to keep him safe.

The realization tore a gasp from me.

Jayden jerked back. His eyes were bright, and his lips were red and swollen. (Holy smokes, he looked hotter than hell.) "Are you okay? Did I hurt you?"

"I'm fine." I swallowed a few times and tried to catch my breath.

He leaned his forehead against mine. "Molly, please, tell me what's wrong. Tell me what I did."

"Nothing's wrong." (Except I barely knew him, and I seemed to be falling hard. Was it just because he saw me and didn't run away?)

He held my upper arms and took a step back. "Is it my scars?"

"No." The word slipped out harsher than intended. I softened my voice. "No." My chest constricted. His insecurity was just another way that he was like me. "It's just overwhelming. I never thought somebody would accept me like this."

Schmendrick materialized on the bed. "Honestly, next time you decide to play tonsil hockey, a warning would be appreciated. I thought I was going to hack up a furball."

I shuffled my feet and wondered if it had been this hot in here all along.

"Expect it whenever we're together." Jayden scratched the base of Schmendrick's tail. "Then you won't be caught off guard."

Schmendrick tipped his head to the side and stared up at me. "Ah, love is in the air." He sniffed, holding his mouth open while he did. "Or maybe it's just werewolf musk."

I shifted back into the body I'd worn for the last four years and sat beside Schmendrick. "What's going on, Buddy? You wouldn't have come back without a reason."

Schmendrick settled on my lap. "Azaroth, your guide to the Abyss, will be waiting at the Black Angel Statue tonight." The Black Angel was the source of several local urban legends. If she guarded the entrance to the Abyss, I had to wonder how many were true.

"No." Jayden slammed his fist down on the top of the dresser, then stood next to it, clenching his hands. "She doesn't have a plan yet."

Flicking his ears back, Schmendrick glanced up at me. "If you'd leash your dog, Molly, I will explain the plan."

Jayden leaned against the dresser he'd just assaulted and shoved his hands into his pockets. Every muscle in his body looked tense, but I had to give him credit for trying. His jaw ticked, and he nodded his head. "Go on."

"Azaroth is a lesser demon, but he is skilled in concealing spells." Schmendrick flicked his tail, but I didn't bother asking him what was wrong. He would tell me if he felt I needed to know. "He'll guide you through the Abyss to Seraphina. He will conceal her, too, and then he'll get everyone back to this realm."

"Demons don't do anything out of the goodness of their hearts." Jayden looked at me and winced. "I didn't mean—"

I held my hand up, stopping him from sticking both feet into his mouth. "First, I'm not a demon. I'm a cambion. I have a lot in common with both sides of myself, but I strive to be good. Second, you don't need to walk on eggshells around me." I lifted my shoulder toward my ear. "Most of the time anyway."

"Good to know." He sauntered over and sat next to me, taking my hand in his. "What does Azaroth want in return?"

"The dagger." Schmendrick flicked his tail once.

Chapter 43

J slumped back on the bed and stared at Schmendrick, trying to wrap my brain around what he was saying. "H-how does he even know about that?"

"No idea." Schmendrick's voice held no inflection, like this wasn't a big deal at all.

I huffed out a long, overly dramatic sigh. "I guess I need to go back to Ravenwood Manor." (So much for never returning there. Apparently, I wasn't good at keeping promises.)

"You can't." Schmendrick's pupils were huge, and his ears flattened against his head. "You mustn't touch it, Molly."

Jayden set his hand on my shoulder and squeezed. "Get me in there, and I'll take it."

"Let Nahvienne or Caelan or whoever else may be tagging along deal with it." Schmendrick stuck his tongue out to begin cleaning himself again, but he stared at Jayden instead.

Jayden nodded like they'd had some unspoken conversation.

"Whatever is going on between you two, I don't think I want to know. Especially if it involves puns." I let out a long, overly dramatic sigh. "If we're going to the Abyss tonight, we'd better go tell the council."

Jayden nodded and stood. As soon as he opened his door, he went into tour guide mode. "The furniture in the castle was imported from Germany when it was built. Other than the TVs and electronics, everything is antique. Melissa and Garrett have warned all of us that if we roughhouse in here and break anything, they'll hang our hides on the walls."

I cocked my head, giving it a little shake. Was he telling me this to get my mind off our impending trip to the Abyss? If that was his plan, I figured I might as well play along. "So far, it looks like the threat has worked." The paintings and tapestries hanging in the hallway were all of unicorns. I didn't see a single wolf skin. "The art doesn't seem to fit the castle's residents."

He chuckled. "No, but Garrett and Melissa wanted to keep it authentic." He stopped before walking into the room at the end of the hall. From the sound of it, several people were in there. "There's a good chance you're about to catch some shit about being in my room." He raised his voice. "The pack's made up of a bunch of juvenile jerks. It'd be nice if, for once, they could prove me wrong."

As soon as we stepped through the doorway, ten heads turned in our direction. The room was bigger than my house, maybe my whole block. There was a massive dining room table with a marble top, a seating area, a fireplace, and a grand open staircase to one side. Suits of armor stood guard over the room, but what caught my attention was the wall made entirely of windows, overlooking the Loess Hills.

Several of the pack members lifted their noses and sniffed. Then they all started talking at once. "She decide she didn't want you?" "Sucks to be you." "Bummer, dude." "Tough break, man." "Need a little, blue pill, Buddy?" "Good choice, Molly."

My face grew hotter and hotter with every comment. I stepped so that I was just slightly behind Jayden and tightened my grip on his hand. Then it occurred to me that if this was how they acted when we didn't have sex, how would they act if we did?

"If he's not man enough, come see—"

"If you finish that sentence, I'll tear your head off." Jayden's eyes were gold, and fangs pressed against his lips.

I'd never seen the guy who made the comment before. He cowered, looking like a dog who'd been beaten. I could practically picture his tail tucked between his legs.

The room was tense for about thirty seconds. Then everybody but Jayden, the guy whom Jayden threatened, and I burst into laughter.

Chapter 44

"No matter how smart you are you can never convince someone stupid that they are stupid." -Unknown

Schmendrick was curled up on the passenger seat when we got to my car. Jayden shook his head. "Will I always have to take a backseat to the cat?"

"Always." Schmendrick's whiskers curled forward. "That way, when you stick your head out the window, you won't risk slobbering on anyone."

Jayden walked to my side and opened the door for me. Then he settled in behind me. (Definitely a keeper. Who else would do that to keep my cat happy?)

Clenching the steering wheel way too hard, I drove to Ravenwood Estates for the second time since waking up. I tapped my left foot against the floor mat, wondering when I'd become a glutton for punishment or stupid or maybe both. I parked in front of the citadel and stared at the imposing building.

Jayden reached over the seat and rubbed my shoulders. "Might as well get it over with."

"Yeah." I sighed and let my head fall forward. "I can't let Caelan know we're dating. I mean, he knows we went out once…" Did I just jump into a commitment that he hadn't asked for?

The car shook, then Jayden got out. He opened my door and held his hand out to me. "I'll do my best to keep him from finding out… for now."

"That's all I can ask." I pried my hands off the steering wheel. "Going to the Abyss is already going to be tense enough."

Schmendrick climbed over my lap and jumped out, landing at Jayden's feet. "She just told you she can't let them know you're dating. That means she can't hold your hand here, dog breath." He trotted along the sidewalk to the door. "You need to talk to Caelan before going to the council. He needs to know what you know."

"Why?" I trudged along behind him with Jayden so close behind me that I could hear his heartbeat. Sometimes demon senses were more than a little annoying.

Schmendrick glanced over his shoulder and shook his head. "He's the leader of the guardians. Do you really want to piss him off again?"

"No." I huffed. "But I don't want to talk to him either."

Jayden squeezed my shoulder. "Everything's going to be fine."

"I wish I had your faith." So many things could go wrong.

He smiled at me, and somehow, it made me feel a little lighter. "I'll sit out here with Schmendrick while you talk to Caelan."

"Fine." I strode the remaining few steps to the doors. The raven on the crest glared down at me, and my heart lodged in my throat. Wiping my hands down my jeans, I grasped the handle. The runes drew power from my touch, and the flash of blue struck the top of the door like lightning, following the path to the raven's talons. The image that formed took my breath away. The full moon brightened the night sky, and Castle Unicorn was silhouetted in front of it. I stood on the grounds as myself. A massive wolf stood on one side of me, a gryphon on the other.

Caelan and the other sorcerers might not know I was dating Jayden, but the arcane magic that guarded Ravenwood Citadel did.

"Do you think it's still a secret?" Jayden's voice was little more than a breath against my ear, sending shivers down my spine.

I sucked in a deep breath to push down the desire that overwhelmed me, and Jayden chuckled. How he hadn't known that I liked him was beyond me. "For now."

"Maybe you should stop by the restroom and splash some cold water on your face so it stays that way." Schmendrick stretched out in a beam of sunlight.

I pulled the door open and shook my head before stepping inside. I didn't need to do that to get a grip on my emotions. Being inside the citadel was enough.

Chapter 45

*"With all of the knowledge in the world at our fingertips,
why do people seem more stupid than ever?"-Mandi Oyster*

My footsteps echoed through the hallway, making me miss my athletic shoes more than ever. There was no way I'd ever be able to sneak up on anyone wearing hard-soled shoes.

Standing outside Caelan's office, I sucked in a deep breath and knocked, hoping the Caelan that didn't want to be an ass greeted me.

"Door's open."

I pushed on it and peeked inside. "Is it still?"

"Molly." He smiled at me, and for just a second, he looked like my memories. A pang of longing shot through me. I didn't miss the old days, just the old Caelan. "Have you found out anything else?"

Pointing at the chair in front of his desk, I walked in and took a seat. "I have admission into the Abyss tonight."

"Tonight?" Caelan's face went ashen. "Are you… Will you…" He stood up, walked to a cabinet in the corner, and grabbed a bottle of liquor and two glasses. Then he strode back to the desk, setting a glass in front of me and one in front of him. He reached across to fill mine, but I put my hand over the top of it.

"None for me."

He huffed a laugh. "You're twenty-three now. It's not like when we were sixteen and shouldn't have been drinking anyway."

"First, you're twenty-three. I'm twenty-two." I leaned back in my seat and stretched my legs out in front of me. "Second, you shouldn't either. We're going to the Abyss tonight, and it would be good to have your wits about you."

He put the lid back on the bottle and sat on the edge of the desk. "Do you have a plan to make it out alive?" His leg brushed against mine, and he didn't pull it away.

I sat up, tucking my feet beneath the chair, effectively pulling away from his touch. "I hope so." I spent the next several minutes relaying most of the information I had to him.

"So… Schmendrick doesn't want you to touch the dagger." He licked his finger and rubbed it around the rim of his glass, making it sing. "Why?"

I shifted into the real Molly, and Caelan didn't even flinch. "Did you forget who I am?"

"No." He slid off the desk and walked to the window. He pushed the thick drapes to the side and stared out into the growing darkness. "I waited for you to return. For a year, maybe more, I woke up every morning thinking, 'This is the day she'll come back for me.' Gods, I was so lost without you, Molly."

An invisible hand reached into my chest and squeezed my heart. I sucked in a deep breath, but the pain only worsened.

"Then they sent me to get you, and you were happy—" he spun around, not bothering to wipe the tears from his face "—without me."

A lump formed in my throat, and even if I could've talked, everything I thought of saying would have been inadequate.

Caelan strode to his desk and poured himself a drink. Then he knocked it back in one swift gulp. "So, no, Molly, I didn't forget who you are."

"I'm sorry." The tears slid out of my eyes. "I didn't mean to hurt you."

He held his hand up. "I know, but if you had stayed, we could've fought Caius together. I could've helped you get away from him… without leaving me."

I propped my elbows on my knees and held my head in my hands. "Schmendrick says I can't touch the dagger because it could corrupt this side of me." I shifted back into the Molly I was used to.

"Well, I guess we'd better call an emergency council meeting." His voice was back to its new norm. "When you explain everything, I'd suggest that you leave out the part where you're giving the dagger to a demon. Just tell them you need it."

I jerked my head up and stared at him. "Are you actually helping me?"

"I'd like us both to make it back safely." He looked at the whiskey bottle, then back at me. "Maybe after we bring your mom back, we can try to go back to what we were."

Shit. Shit. Shit. "One step at a time." Bile rose in my throat, but I'd been warned not to let him know I was dating Jayden, not before going to the Abyss, and I had to trust that Schmendrick knew what he was talking about.

I truly was a despicable creature.

Chapter 46

*S*iobhan paced across the dais. Silver specks on her midnight blue slacks shimmered with each step she took, reminding me of the stars. "Do we have any volunteers to go with Molly and Jayden into the Abyss?"

Nahvienne, Caelan, and Storm all stepped forward. I was surprised Storm volunteered. I hadn't talked to the Aussie since my first day back. His blue-gray gaze settled on me, and he winked. It was so unexpected that I couldn't help but smile at him.

"Very well." She nodded before looking from Jayden to me. "Is there anything else the two of you require?"

I'd hoped that she would ask Caelan or Schmendrick. I didn't want to give Caius another reason to glower at me;

bringing two outsiders into Ravenwood Citadel had been bad enough. "I need something out of Mom's office."

"Why must you enter *my* home again?" Caius glared down his nose at me like I was bubble gum stuck to the bottom of his shoe.

My hands clenched together behind my back, and I fought to keep from rolling my eyes. "As previously discussed, it's my home, and I need the dagger from Mom's office to get into the Abyss and retrieve Mom."

"Dagger?" He rubbed his chin, putting on quite a show for the council members and guardians who knew nothing about it. "There's no dagger in there."

I sucked in a deep breath, hoping it could squash the frustration that was clawing its way closer to the surface. "There was when I took the books about demons. If it's not there now, you need to find it and get it to me before midnight."

"My darling daughter, I believe all of this attention has made you delusional." He drummed his fingers on the arm of his chair and smirked at Alden. The old man's expression didn't change in the least. "Can you describe it to me? Maybe I'll be able to find it, but not tonight."

Siobhan spun around, pointing her finger at him. "Caius Shadowfall, you have attempted to derail this investigation at every turn." Rage distorted her features, making her appear powerful and dangerous. "If I didn't know better, I would suspect you had something to do with Seraphina's capture." She strode to Mom's chair and set her hand on the back of it. "For the last time, Caius, step up or step down."

"I can describe the dagger." A little of the anger inside me dissipated with Siobhan's outburst. "I can even tell you exactly what it's made of. Do you want me to?"

The way Caius' face paled answered that question for me. "No need to bother the council." He pushed down on the arms of his chair and stood. Bowing to the other council members, he said, "May I be excused to search for the dagger Mahlia needs?"

"Molly." Caelan practically growled my name and shocked the hell out of me. "Not Mahlia, not darling daughter, not daughter o' mine. Molly."

I couldn't stop the smile that fought through my remaining anger to settle across my face. It felt like the old days, Caelan and Molly versus the world, but it would never be that again, and it was wrong of me to encourage him. As soon as he found out I was dating Jayden, he'd never speak to me again.

"C'est la vie," I whispered.

"Those of you who are going to the Abyss go to the armory to get whatever weapons you'll be taking." Siobhan walked to the center of the dais again. "Then go to the war room to discuss your plans. Food will be sent there." She looked to the side, and I saw a shadowed figure run off. "I'll have Caius bring you the dagger there."

As we turned to leave, she said, "Those of you not going can resume your previous assignments."

Caelan pushed the heavy door open and held it for the rest of us. Resuming the lead, he strode toward the armory. Our heels clicking against the stone floor were the only sounds. The door opened again, slamming shut this time.

"Molly." Lorelei sounded desperate, but I didn't turn around, didn't quit walking.

Her footsteps pounded against the ground as she ran after me. "Please."

Jayden stepped behind me and growled, stopping her. Caelan, Nahvienne, and Storm continued down the hallway.

I turned around, folding my arms over my chest. "What do you want, Lorelei?"

"I'm sorry." Tears pooled in her eyes. "I've been awful to you for as long as I can remember, and I don't deserve your sympathy."

I shook my head. "No, you don't, and I've got a full plate tonight." I looked at my wrist like there was a watch there. "Can I schedule you in, ah, a week from never?"

"Please, Molly." She dropped to her knees and held her hands as if she were praying to me. "I was awful to you. I made your life miserable. And I have no right to ask you, but please—" a sob caught in her throat "—please make it go away." She touched the wart.

Folding my arms over my chest, I looked at her, really looked at her. Seeing past her flawless exterior for the first time, I realized she was like most bullies. She was insecure and picked on others to make herself feel better. "Why don't you make it go away?"

"Every time I do, it comes back nastier than before." The sob she'd been holding back tore out of her throat, and I genuinely felt for her. "I'm sorry. You had everything, and I-I was jealous, okay?"

My mouth hung open, and I pointed at my chest. "I had everything?"

"You were going to be the next archon, you lived in Ravenwood Manor, and Caelan"—she looked over my shoulder and gave an apologetic shrug. Apparently, we had an audience—"followed after you like a lost puppy dog. Then you left, and he pined for you."

I laughed, and it completely lacked humor. "Yeah, I had a stepdad who cut my tail and horns off. One who filed my teeth down and wanted to torture the demon out of me. I can see why you'd want everything I had."

Her eyes widened with every one of my words, and she clamped her hand over her mouth. "I-I-I didn't know."

I waved my hand, and the grotesque wart disappeared. "Like the dandelions in Caius' yard, if you bully anyone else, two will come back in its place. Do better. Be better."

Chapter 47

"Ignorance is the absence of knowledge. Stupidity is the refusal to acquire or accept it." -Unknown

Standing at the edge of a cemetery at midnight wasn't something that I would normally do. Who would want to? Despite what humans thought, ghosts typically didn't haunt graveyards. They usually stuck around the place they died or the places they lived or even sometimes with the people who had loved them or even wronged them, but worse creatures frequented cemeteries, feeding off the negative emotions of the mourning, strengthening themselves with guilt, anger, and hatred.

Not wanting to draw attention to ourselves, we were all dressed in black. Black long-sleeved shirts of one kind or another, black pants, and black boots. We had turned our phones' flashlights off as soon as we arrived at the base of the statue.

With my enhanced senses, I was still able to see the closest tombstones as I circled the Black Angel.

The eight-and-a-half-foot-tall statue stood on a pedestal above a ship's prow. One hand held a basin that water dripped out of in the warmer months, and the other was outstretched. Her wings extended from above her head to nearly her feet.

Schmendrick sat in front of the fountain and stared up at the Black Angel. "They say she flies off her pedestal at night, but it only happens when somebody enters the Abyss." He licked his paw. "They also say that if you look into her eyes at midnight or—heaven forbid—touch her, you'll be cursed, but most people who go to the Abyss are cursed."

"Or bloody stupid." Storm dragged a hand through his windswept hair, then checked his weapons for at least the tenth time since we'd arrived at the cemetery.

Nahvienne stood between Caelan and Jayden, keeping them from getting into a pissing contest, and since I didn't want either of them to think I was choosing sides, I walked around the statue for the third or fourth time, but I still didn't see anything to lead me to believe she was guarding a gateway.

Rustling sounded in the bushes. Caelan, Storm, and Nahvienne drew their swords, and fur burst from Jayden's knuckles, a precursor to his transformation.

I clutched my sword's pommel, but Schmendrick shook his head at me, letting me know this was who we were waiting for. The creature, a hideous amalgamation of human and beast, stepped onto the stone path. An oversized t-shirt covered his bony body. "I'm not short. I'm fun-sized," was scrawled in purple writing across the bright orange fabric that clashed with his wrinkly, celadon skin. The shirt hung past his knees, and knobby, bowed legs stuck out from beneath it.

I chuckled. At least the demon had a sense of humor. He was shorter than Jayden's wolf, but he looked more vicious than fun. Obsidian horns spiraled back from his forehead and over his skull. Scuffs and cracks marred them, showing that they were for more than decoration.

"Azaroth on time." His voice was high-pitched and torturous, reminding me of fingernails being dragged across a chalkboard, and when he opened his mouth, it was filled with rows of sharp, jagged teeth. "Azaroth take Schmenny and his friends to the Abyss, but Azaroth get paid first." His long fingers, tipped with sharp claws, stretched toward me. He opened and closed his fist. Extra knuckles made the motion unnatural and nauseating to watch. His glowing yellow eyes stared up at me expectantly.

Schmendrick blinked at Azaroth. "You will open the portal. You will cloak all of them." He walked in front of me, and he grew until he was the size of a tiger. "You will accompany them to the Abyss, and after they find Seraphina, you will cloak her. You will lead them back to this entrance. Once we are all safely standing here, Caelan will give you your reward."

Caelan stepped toward the demon. "Do you need to see it?"

Schmendrick glared over his shoulder at Caelan, but Caelan didn't pay any attention to him.

"Azaroth knows you bringed it." He folded his arms over his emaciated-looking chest, glared down the bony ridge on his face that served as a nose, and tapped his bare foot against the path. "Azaroth smells its misery and fear." A malevolent smirk twisted his face, transforming his humanoid features into something monstrous. "And Azaroth wants it."

"You sure ya want 'im to have it, mate?" Storm's gaze traveled from Caelan's face to Schmendrick's.

Nahvienne shook her head. "I'm not sure it's such a good idea."

"It's the only way to rescue Molly's mom." Jayden's voice was closer to a growl than it should've been in his human form.

Schmendrick roared, shutting everyone up. "Does Azaroth agree to the terms?"

"Azaroth agrees." The malevolence was gone, and he looked like a petulant kid.

Schmendrick lowered his head and growled. "Swear, Azaroth."

Azaroth narrowed his eyes at Schmendrick before slicing his claw through his palm. Black blood dripped onto the pathway. "Azaroth swears to the immortal kitty, Schmendrick, that Azaroth agrees to the terms." He wiped his hand across his shirt, smearing gore across the words. "Azaroth promises to kill the kitty if kitty does not gives Azaroth *MaunDagnir* blade."

"Agreed." Schmendrick shrank back into his normal house-cat form.

Energy traipsed across my skin, lifting the hair on the back of my neck. I didn't like this one bit, but I assumed Schmendrick knew what he was getting himself into.

"*MaunDagnir*?" Nahvienne sheathed her sword.

Schmendrick wove through my legs. "The dagger's name is Purity Slayer in English. *MaunDagnir* is Elvish."

Azaroth climbed into the empty pool and walked around the inside, dripping his blood while chanting something under his breath. He climbed over the dedication wall and continued his circle in the grass. When his blood connected both ends of the circle, there was a flash, and black flames burst from the ground.

Chapter 48

"When I said how stupid can you be, it wasn't a challenge." -Unknown

The Black Angel spread her wings. The sound was the unsheathing of swords followed by a crack of thunder. Her wingspan was seventeen feet wide, if it was a foot. The feathers, even though carved from bronze, fluttered in the gentle breeze.

She bent her knee, then sprang into the air. Dust billowed up from the ground, and my hair blew around my face. The others murmured something behind me, but I couldn't pull my gaze away from the massive statue. Somehow, she was graceful in flight.

Schmendrick hopped onto the ship's prow, and for the first time that I could remember, he looked uncertain. "I cannot follow you into the Abyss, Molly."

"Why?" A lump formed in my chest, causing a dull ache.

He lowered his head. "That is one of the questions I am not allowed to answer." He stretched his paw toward me, letting it hover in the air, and I picked him up, holding him against my chest and burying my face in his fur.

"Will you be here when I get back?" I fought the tears that pricked my eyes.

He rubbed his face against mine. "Always, Molly. Always."

I set Schmendrick down and sucked in a couple of deep breaths. Suddenly, a trip to the Abyss felt more ominous and treacherous than before.

"Molly." Jayden's voice in my ear startled me.

I stumbled, but he caught me, pulling me against his chest and allowing his hands to linger.

"You can let go of her, Wolf." Caelan took a step forward. The muscles in his jaw jumped as he clenched his teeth.

Jayden lifted his hands in the air and stepped back. "Just making sure she had her balance."

"Azaroth ready to go." The demon stood on the prow of the ship and looked at the platform where the angel had been. "Angel returns soon. Must go." He waved his hand, beckoning us forward. "Come. Come."

Jayden strode toward Azaroth, but Caelan stuck his arm out. "I'll go first. I am in charge."

"Yeah." Jayden huffed out a laugh. "If you think so."

Caelan walked past me. "Why exactly did the dog need to come?"

"He's a wolf, Caelan." I let out an exasperated sigh. "We went to them for help, remember? We wouldn't be this far without him, and he's going to see it through to the end." (Boys, am I right?)

He looked Jayden up and down before standing in front of Azaroth. "Is he even house-trained?"

"Of the two of you, who's being more of an arse?" Storm walked over. "Aren't we supposed to be cloaked before going in?"

"Azaroth waiting. Cloak you when you go by. Won't see others." He waved his hands, and Caelan disappeared.

I stepped up next. "How will we keep track of each other?"

"Azaroth lead. You follow." He shrugged like we didn't need to worry, but if the Abyss was the soul-sucking place we'd been warned about, I wanted more assurance than that.

"Caelan, if you're here, take my hand." His fingers slipped through mine, and I yelped. "Everyone, make a train. We'll hold hands. Only let go if there's danger. Got it?"

Jayden grabbed hold of my other hand. "And he thinks he's in charge."

"Stop fighting." I stomped my foot, letting my inner toddler out for a minute, just as Azaroth cloaked me. "We need to be a team."

I thought I would be able to see myself, but… nothing. Not even an outline. It was more than a little disconcerting.

Caelan moved forward but stopped when I didn't follow. "What's going on, Molly?"

"I…" Stone steps led into darkness, and I couldn't see to put my foot on the first stair. I wanted to reach out to grab the wall, but Jayden and Caelan clutched tighter when I tried to pull my hand away. "…can't."

I urged myself to step forward, but my feet were stuck to the ground. My heartbeat pounded at each of my pulse points, and my chest tightened. My gaze darted from one wall to the other, watching as they closed in, pulling the oxygen from the entrance.

Jayden wrapped his arm around me, dragging mine with it, and set his feet outside of mine. "With me," he whispered before kissing my ear.

I nodded. (Yeah, sometimes I truly am that stupid.) "Okay." My voice trembled.

He flattened his hand on my stomach, allowing me to let go and drag my fingers along the wall, giving me a semblance of control. We descended what seemed like twenty flights of stairs.

After the first few steps, my panic lessened, and I realized that besides not being able to see anyone, I couldn't hear them either. Not their breaths or heartbeats, not their steps. I didn't notice when we were outside with all the noises of nature, but in the stairwell, it was weird. I wondered if this was what the world sounded like to most people.

My spirits lifted a little. If Azaroth could keep me from seeing or hearing the others, maybe this would work.

Jayden backed up a little and moved his hand to my shoulder, kneading the muscle as we continued to the bottom.

"Azaroth musts open door." After only hearing his footsteps for what felt like hours, his high-pitched voice nearly broke my eardrums. "You stands here in middle." His feet clacked as they hit the ground, and he mumbled like he had when he opened the entrance.

Black flames shot up again. I pinched my eyes shut against the blinding light and prayed that I'd made the right decision.

Chapter 49

"The problem with the world is that the intelligent people are full of doubt, while the stupid people are full of confidence."
-Charles Bukowski

Something scraped against the ground, grating and rumbling. I opened my eyes to see a circular chamber. Shadows climbed the walls. No… smoke trails. They led my gaze to a stone slab in the ceiling. It rotated to the side, and as it did, stairs extended from the wall.

"Azaroth takes you out now." He stood at the base of the stairs. "You follows. Stays quiet, and no one knows you with Azaroth."

We climbed out of the opening and stood in a fountain. The thick air held an acrid smell that stung my nose and burned my eyes. I pressed my face against my shoulder, hoping I would get used to the odor soon. Once my eyes adjusted to the dim light, I turned, scanning the Abyss. Desolation and destruction surrounded me. Rocks jutted from the landscape like the bones of a fallen god. Ash coated everything.

Azaroth motioned us forward, and a crash shook the ground. I spun, tugging Jayden and Caelan along with me. An onyx demon landed where the opening had been. Bat-like wings folded against its back with a whoosh. My gaze dropped to his feet, and my heart plummeted at what I saw.

Feet that made me think of a dragon's blocked the way home. A thick tail curved above the ground behind him. Muscular legs were bent in a fight-ready stance. Skulls adorned his belt. The statue held a mace in one hand and a sword in the other. Thick horns spread over the top of his head, sloping down before swooping up again. His teeth were bared, and his eyes were narrowed.

This beast was the angel's opposite in every way.

When it was clear the statue had finished moving, we followed Azaroth. Fog crawled across the ground, tracking our movements. We walked along a path with a sheer cliff rising as high as we could see to one side and a deep chasm on the other. The blackened earth crumbled beneath our feet, and pebbles fell for countless seconds before hitting the bottom far below us.

We stepped off the slender path onto a field of boulders stacked by an ancient rockslide. A crimson glow emanated from some of the cracks. The unnatural light danced off the miasma, casting eerie shadows over the land.

I stepped over a gap in the rocks and stared down into the unending depths. Hoping to ease my fear, I swallowed. With my next step, a boulder shifted beneath my foot. I hopped off of it quickly, not wanting to fall victim to this treacherous terrain.

Distant moans and howls kept me on high alert. My eyes darted from side to side without seeing anything new, but something was out there. I could feel it watching us.

If only I didn't feel so alone…

If only I could see the others around me…

Wispy shadows glided toward us, almost as if blown by a gentle breeze. As they neared, their forms became clearer. They were almost humanoid with purple eyes that glowed with malevolence.

Azaroth held up his spindly arm, and white light shot from his hand. "Shadow wraiths bes gone!"

The creatures screamed when the light struck them. They didn't go away, but they didn't come any closer.

"Shadow wraiths drains peoples' lives." Azaroth climbed onto a boulder and then down the other side. "Then peoples bes shadow wraiths."

We walked for an eternity, scampering over boulders. Every shadow seemed to draw closer to us, and the moans and wails of the unknown had me turning my head and looking for whatever menacing creature lurked nearby.

My heart raced, and my breath came in short, panicked gasps. Something scurried along the rocks, and the hairs on the back of my neck rose even higher.

The *whoop whoop* of wings beating against the air drowned out all other sounds. Azaroth stopped walking and crouched behind a rock. A dragon flew toward us, darker than the depths of Tartarus. Where scales had been ripped from its body, a trail of molten red fissures glowed. Its wings were tattered and torn. As it flew over us, the ground buckled and grumbled. Rocks bounced loose, tumbling into the chasm.

One of my companions groaned, and Azaroth turned, glaring at us. "Azaroth leaves you to bes eaten by Abyssal Drake if you not shutted up." His voice was a mere hiss, but it carried to us.

Azaroth didn't move until the beating of the creature's wings could no longer be heard. "Move now. Stays shutted up." He crouched as he walked, staying lower to the ground. The Abyssal Drake seemed to have left him shaken.

My mind conjured hundreds of shadowy monsters creeping toward us. Each of them more terrifying than the last. I sucked in a deep breath and held it, but I couldn't shake the fear that gripped me.

Chapter 50

"Fear or stupidity has always been the basis of most human actions."
~Albert Einstein

A thousand spiders skittered up my spine, and I glanced around again. A flicker of movement caught my eye. Every muscle in my body tensed, and I stopped walking. Caelan jerked to a halt, and Jayden ran into my back, nearly knocking me over. Two more bumps against me let me know that Nahvienne and Storm ran into him also.

"Why'd ya stop?" Storm's voice was muffled by the fog.

A demon emerged from the gloom, prowling over the uneven surface. Shadows followed her steps, whispering secrets too softly for me to understand.

I wanted to keep moving, to follow Azaroth to wherever Malachai was holding Mom, but I couldn't take my eyes off the demon striding toward us. The air grew thicker, closing in around the demon and me. Neither Jayden nor Caelan held my hands, and Azaroth disappeared, lost somewhere in the suffocating haze.

The demon's boots crunched across the ground, and with each step, her features became clearer.

My breath caught in my throat. She wasn't just any demon. She was me.

But her face…

Her features were twisted by hatred, and her eyes were filled with revulsion. "Well," she looked around, and a wicked smile curled her lips, "look what the cat dragged in."

"Who? How?" I swallowed hard, forcing myself to meet her gaze.

The demon Molly laughed, a maniacal sound that sent shivers racing down my back. "Oh, I'm you, darling. Embrace your true nature." She lifted her hands to her head and trailed them along her body, making the motion look sensuous. "And you could be all of this."

"No." She was everything I'd fought against becoming. She was the me straight out of my nightmares. "No." Sparks danced over my fingers.

My doppelganger shook her head at me. "Oh, dear, sweet, Molly, is that really all you've got?" She lifted her hand and pulled the surrounding shadows toward her. "You could be powerful, unstoppable if you'd quit allowing others to control you."

"Nobody controls me," I said through gritted teeth. "Not anymore."

"Neither of them believes you can be on your own." Her voice came from all around me. Every patch of darkness carried her voice. "They want you for their own. Be your own woman. Kill them, Molly. Kill them both."

Rage rose inside of me, filling me like I'd never allowed it to before.

"You can be so much more without them." Demon Molly stepped out of her shadows long enough for me to see the malevolence she used to shield herself. "You could rule this place with your father. You could be the most powerful being in the Abyss and on Earth."

Wrath whispered in my ear, wanting vengeance, reminding me of the way Caelan had acted when he returned to my life, murmuring my fears about Jayden's controlling nature.

But upon thinking Jayden's name, something burned inside of me, brighter than the sun. It filled my heart and spread through my body. Jayden's acceptance of me fought against the hatred and fear.

"You could be me, Molly." Her shadows wrapped around her again. "You could be powerful. Strong enough to fight off your oppressors, instead of hiding from them."

I squinted my eyes, staring into the darkness, trying to make out her form, but I couldn't see her. "I don't want to be like you. Power is what Mom and Caius want, not me."

Darkness slithered toward me, like snakes crawling over the ground. "Why wouldn't you want to be me? I'm free." The shadows inched closer. "Think of all the times you've been hurt or betrayed. Think of the torture Caius put you through, just for being you. Think of running and hiding. Think of all the things you held back."

I dropped my hands and listened to the dull thud of my heart. She was right. The truth in her words was unexpected. I had always feared my demon side. The darkness and rage. The depravity and chaos. But seeing the confidence in her, I wondered why I'd never embraced it.

"No." I smacked my hands against the sides of my head. "No!" This wasn't just fear. It was a struggle for my soul. "Power isn't everything." I threw my hands out in front of me, and beams of light shot from my fingers.

Demon Molly let out a feral scream, and her shadows surged toward me like a tsunami.

They clashed with the luminous glow, and the Abyss trembled. Shadows skittered away from the onslaught, and when they cleared, demon Molly was gone.

The darkness that had weighed on me all of my life seemed to lift slightly.

Chapter 51

"**M**olly," Caelan and Jayden both called out my name.
I stumbled back, knocking against someone.

Arms wrapped around my waist. "Molly." Jayden's breath
caressed my ear. "What happened?"

"Azaroth says you must bes shutted up." The demon threw
his hands up in the air and stomped over to us. "Azaroth says it
is for they do not know about you. If Azaroth not wants *Maun-
Dagnir*, Azaroth would leaves." He started walking away.

I searched for Caelan's hand, and when he grabbed hold of
mine, we followed after Azaroth.

"No more talkings. No chasing nightmares. Only follows
Azaroth and stays shutted up." He looked over his shoulder,

and I wondered if he could see us through his cloaking spell. "Stupid peoples bes lucky if demons stays away now. Azaroth warns them, but stupid peoples never listens."

Azaroth's rants kept my mind from wandering, and his annoying voice drowned out the noises that had haunted me since we arrived here.

We stepped off the last boulder onto dry, cracked dirt, and the path curved around the mountain. Luckily, Azaroth stopped.

If he hadn't, everyone would've slammed into me again.

My jaw hung open, and I stared at the black granite castle in front of me. It appeared to have grown from the land. Unlike everything else in this hellhole, its tall, slender spires elegantly stretched through the dense, swirling fog, reaching for the gloom above. Smooth walls gleamed with an iridescent sheen. Muted light filtered through the stained-glass windows.

"Azaroth take you to Malachai." He waved his hand. "Come now."

My legs shook a little more with each step we took toward the castle. I gripped Caelan's and Jayden's hands tighter. Caelan's fingers wiggled, loosening my hold on them, and Jayden squeezed back.

I focused on the details of the castle, hoping to occupy my mind with something other than what was inside those walls. Intricately carved buttresses arched gracefully from the main castle to lofty towers.

Gargoyles perched along the battlements and roofs. Like the guardians of Ravenwood Citadel, they seemed to watch our every move. Polished ebony doors barred the entrance on the far end of the drawbridge, which was lowered over a wide moat. The castle's reflection shimmered in the dark water.

Instead of leading us over the drawbridge, Azaroth followed a path around the side of the castle. The ground was less brittle here. A few plants even poked up through cracks in the black rocks. Bioluminescent spiky, blue flowers emitted a strange glow that made Azaroth's orange shirt turn a putrid shade of brown.

Azaroth stepped off the path and walked at an angle down the bank to the moat's edge. Humanoid skeletons littered the shore, some still adorned with bits and pieces of armor. Luckily, no skin. They crunched under Azaroth's feet, but I tiptoed between them.

"Azaroth must stays on rocks." He looked over his shoulder at us like he thought we were too dumb to realize he meant for us to stay on them. "Azaroth musts not touch water. Azaroth no wants wake beasty."

Ah, shit. Somewhere between ten and fifteen boulders peeked through the water. A few were just the jagged tips of stones. One misstep by any of us… one slip could be the difference in making it to the far shore or becoming another pile of bones.

"Azaroth bes careful. Quiet and careful." Azaroth hopped onto the first rock, staying in the very center of it. "Azaroth never touches water."

When I stepped on the boulder, I couldn't help but stare into the moat. It was so weird to see everything around me reflecting on its surface but not see my image looking back up at me. Caelan tugged on my hand, letting me know I could step on the next stone. I had to jump to reach the one after that. It wobbled when I landed on it, but I managed to keep from touching the water.

Each jump or step was a calculated guess. It was nearly impossible to tell where my feet would land without being able to see them. Some, I was able to feel for, but others were a leap of faith.

The water splashed in front of me. "Dammit." Caelan's voice was muted by the thick, fog-filled air. Ripples spread across the surface, racing for the shore.

Azaroth watched them with wide, fearful eyes. "Run!" He darted across the remaining rocks. "Run. Beasty comes now!"

Chapter 52

The water churned violently, forming a massive maelstrom. It swelled, crashing over the boulders and shores. From the center of the whirlpool, five dragon-like heads broke the surface.

Caelan dropped my hand. Water splashed off the rocks in front of me, and I followed the path. Jumping and praying.

One of the beast's heads roared, and flames shot toward Azaroth. A glowing blue shield appeared in front of the demon. The inferno struck the barrier and curled around it.

"Sorcerer save-ed Azaroth." Azaroth stared blankly before darting off again.

The beast's heads swiveled in different directions, scanning for the source of the magic. All of them faced the stone pathway, and fire blasted from all five maws at once.

Another shield appeared, and I raced across the stones, not caring when my feet slid into the water.

A bolt of lightning struck the hydra's body, and thunder crashed, shaking rocks and skeletons loose from the moat's banks. "Nailed him!" Storm's voice howled with the wind.

The beast shook its heads, and all five of them released their wrath. Flames struck the barrier, shooting over the top of it and sizzling against the water's surface.

"Get over here!" Caelan sounded drained, and I realized he must've been the one shielding us.

Azaroth scampered to the castle wall, pounding his hands against the stone until he pressed something on the side of the castle, and a door that I wouldn't have ever found opened. "Azaroth always bes servant. Never bes guest." He ushered us inside, and the sea hydra slammed against the barrier. It flickered with each hit.

Azaroth slammed the door shut, and I prayed we'd all made it.

"All is here. Yes." Azaroth scurried along the wall until he was in front of me, and I assumed Caelan. "Yes?"

"Yes," Caelan said. "By the skin of my teeth," Jayden's answer made me grin as I responded with a simple, "Yeah." "Thank the heavens," Nahvienne replied at the same time Storm said, "By some bloody miracle."

"Azaroth bes quiet." He opened another door and stepped into a hallway. His steps echoed, the only sounds I could hear.

We followed behind him for an eternity or mere moments. I wasn't sure, but it was long enough for my racing heart to slow to normal and for my limbs to start shaking from my adrenaline crash.

Azaroth opened another door, and we stepped out of the servants' corridors and into a main hallway. A crimson runner muted Azaroth's steps. Runes carved into the walls emitted a flickering light, almost like flames. They surrounded tapestries woven with dark threads that would fit right in at Ravenwood Manor and portraits of demonic-looking beings whose eyes seemed to follow us on our journey.

Massive double doors, at least 15 feet tall, were set into the far wall. The ebony doors were inlaid with wrought iron, and thick metal bars crossed through the center and a couple feet from the top and the bottom.

"Azaroth sees Malachai." He spoke the words to some invisible sentinel.

The doors opened outward, making us step back to avoid being hit. I stood beside Caelan, and Jayden's arm brushed against mine as he moved next to me. The room beyond the entrance was massive with curved walls. Towering arches drew my eyes to the high, vaulted ceiling that disappeared in the shadows far above us.

As I stared into that darkness, the most unexpected feeling washed over me.

Peace.

I closed my eyes and basked in this most pleasant surprise.

It was like standing in the middle of a field, gazing at the stars. Life was so much bigger than me and my problems, and I realized that no matter what I did, no matter what I wanted, life would work out exactly as it was meant to.

All too soon, there was a tug on my hand as Caelan followed Azaroth. Azaroth stepped through the doors, and his reflection shone in the obsidian floor that had been polished until it gleamed.

The doors slammed shut, and the peaceful feeling that had overcome me disappeared. My gaze dropped, and I noticed that the room was filled with hundreds of statues. The gargoyle-like creatures stood between columns in rows of at least five deep, a hideous army ready to spring to life when their master called upon them.

We followed Azaroth deeper into the vast hall. A towering sculpture nearly sixty feet tall stood at the end of the antechamber. Instead of looking like a monster, this one reminded me of a god carved from black marble.

As we approached him, the smooth floor ended. Sigils were carved in a pattern that I couldn't follow. My foot touched the etchings, and magic jolted through me like a shock of electricity, turning me visible.

Chapter 53

"Stupidity is something unshakable; nothing attacks it without breaking itself against it; it is of the nature of granite, hard and resistant." -Gustave Flaubert

"Shit." The word had barely escaped my mouth when someone grabbed my arms. "What the hell?" I dropped Jayden's and Caelan's still-invisible hands, hoping that whoever had me didn't know about them. My arms were pulled behind my back, and my hands were bound together.

A deep, gravelly voice that sounded like boulders rolling over the top of each other said, "Move, Azaroth."

The small demon's eyes were wide. The white showing all around the yellow. "Azaroth sorry. Azaroth leaves? Yes."

"Azaroth, come here." The new voice was velvet and seemed to come from everywhere all at once.

A puddle formed between Azaroth's feet. "Master says comes. Azaroth musts come." The poor demon trembled as he trudged in front of me, tracking his pee with each step he took.

A massive hand wrapped around my arm. I stared down at it for far too long, trying to make sense of it. The fingers appeared to be carved from stone with sharp claws tipping them. My gaze trailed from the hand and up the arm. Aside from being chiseled from black stone, it looked perfectly normal. Until my gaze landed on its head. Statue man had a head like a grizzly bear but with bull horns.

I turned as much as I could in his grasp and looked back at the row of statues we'd passed. One pedestal was empty.

Statue man jerked on my arm, and I stumbled, nearly pulling my shoulder out of the socket when he didn't ease his grip. "You made a grave mistake thinking you could sneak into Taras Mor unseen." The gargoyle's steps were soundless instead of the loud crashing that I'd expected. "Malachai does not take kindly to those who intrude. Pray he grants you a swift end."

Malachai. Of course, who else would Azaroth's master be? My steps faltered, but statue man dragged me along.

I shouldn't've come here. I should've known something like this would happen. The worst thing was I'd brought everyone else with me. Without Azaroth, they couldn't leave the Abyss. They would be trapped here without him.

My breath caught in my throat when another, worse thought struck me. When Malachai killed the little demon, would everyone become visible, or would the cloaking spell continue concealing them?

I tried to pull away from statue man's hold, but he was too strong.

Suddenly, my body felt too heavy to take another step, and my throat thickened as tears threatened to fall. We were never going to get out of here. There was no way we could fight off all these gargoyles.

Statue man tugged me past the massive sculpture where an archway led into another room. It opened up in front of me. Archways curved around the edge of the room. Another imposing stone guardian stood underneath each of them.

An obsidian dais sat on the far side of the room. Sigils carved into the stone flickered like the embers of a dying fire.

Steps led to the throne where a demon sprawled. His ebony skin almost made him look like one of the statues, but something, I couldn't quite put my finger on what, gave him the spark of life they were missing.

He was magnetic. Once my gaze settled on him, I couldn't tear it away, so I took in every detail I could. Horns that were the twins of mine spiraled gracefully from the top of his head. They started just above deer-like ears. A bony ridge led to up-turned nostrils. Fangs jutted from lips that were pressed into a thin line. His eyes were the only color I could see on him. Blood red.

His arms and chest were massive. A black kilt with silver accents barely covered his nether regions. (Thank the gods for it because if I had to guess, I'd say this demon was my father.) He leaned on one arm of his throne with his leg flung over the other one. His feet reminded me of the statue that had allowed us entry into the Abyss, dragon-like with curved talons.

Azaroth fell to his knees in front of the dais, but Malachai didn't notice the little demon. His gaze was firmly on me.

He stood, and as he did, he transformed from the demon into the man who had seduced my mother. The kilt shrank to fit his new frame, and a black shirt and boots appeared on him. He bounded down the stairs, only stopping once he stood directly in front of me.

Malachai was everything Mom had said. He looked like a god, not a demon. No wonder people were so messed up. How could they not be when the bad guys looked like this? "Ah, my dulcet daughter." He spread his arms out as if expecting me to throw myself into them for a heart-warming hug. (Yeah, I don't think so.)

After a few seconds of me looking at him like he was a fool, he finally dropped them. "What? No hug for dear Papa?"

I scoffed. "You're not my father. You're a sperm donor gone wrong." I looked over his shoulder to avoid meeting his gaze.

The sigils on the dais flickered a brighter red, and something flashed on the throne, drawing my attention to it. Like everything else there, it was made from obsidian, but the arms were lined with black gemstones. They twinkled like stars against the backdrop of deepest night. Two massive wings were outstretched to make up the backrest. The talons that tipped them were made from the same sparkling gems.

"Well, isn't that a fine hello?" He flipped his long, black hair over his shoulder, and I was certain shampoo models everywhere sensed a disturbance in the hair-flinging force. "I plant the seeds of life inside your mother's womb, and I don't even rate a thank you."

I lifted my shoulder as much as I could with statue man still holding my arm. "Speaking of Mom, where is she?"

"No love for me, but the Wicked Witch of Ravenwood gets it?" He pressed his hands to his heart like I'd broken it, but I wasn't sure he even had one.

I ground my teeth together. "We are *not* witches. We're sorceresses, and I want her back."

He grinned, and I could understand why people were seduced by darkness. "At least you didn't say she's not wicked."

"Where. Is. She?" I stepped forward, holding his gaze, letting him know that he didn't intimidate me and that I wasn't here to play his stupid game. Statue man jerked on my arm when I tried to take another step.

Malachai waved his hand at a doorway behind him. "She's here somewhere. Wreaking havoc on my world and pretending to be queen."

His words pummeled against me, knocking the wind out of my sales. I opened my mouth to ask him to explain, but nothing came out. I tipped my head to the side, looking away from him, trying to make sense of what he'd said. "What do you mean?"

"She knows my name. My *true* name." His expression didn't change at all, but rage darkened his eyes, making his gray irises nearly black. "She commanded me to bring her here."

Chapter 54

*"What we really need is a crusade against Stupid.
That might actually make a difference." -Jim Butcher, Vignette*

Malachai reached forward and grabbed my chin. He tilted my face from side to side. "You figured out how to shapeshift." He said it like a proud father cooing at his baby. "Seraphina told me she'd never shown you a picture of me." He tipped my head again. "Yet, your skin tone and eyes look so much like my own."

He was right, but I didn't want him to know that I'd found it a bit uncanny, too, so I rolled my eyes at him. When I did, I noticed Azaroth still lying prostrate with his nose touching the stone floor.

Malachai followed my gaze. "Azaroth, how many sorcerers did you bring into Taras Mor?"

The demon pivoted around, keeping his nose to the floor until he was facing Malachai. Terror lurked behind his yellow eyes. "Azaroth n-n-not know."

"Why don't you know, Azaroth?" Malachai lowered his hand and turned his back on me.

The demon's gaze flicked to me for just a second before returning to Malachai. "Azaroth not knows what girl bes."

"Ah." Malachai nodded like he'd played this game with Azaroth before.

It wasn't what I'd expected at all. I thought Malachai would tear Azaroth apart. I thought his wrath would know no end. Was he putting on an act for my benefit, or was this the real him?

"How many sorcerers besides Molly," Malachai waved his hand in my direction, assumedly making sure Azaroth didn't intentionally misunderstand, "did you bring into Taras Mor?"

Azaroth planted his face against the floor. "Azaroth bringed three sorcerers."

"And…" Malachai tapped his foot, giving away his growing impatience.

Azaroth peeked up, then quickly buried his face again. "Azaroth bringed three sorcerers."

"Who else did you bring?" A hint of exasperation filled Malachai's voice.

Damn. I mentally slapped my forehead. I'd hoped Malachai wouldn't know about all of us.

This time, Azaroth looked at Malachai. "Azaroth bringed a werewolf."

"Is that so?" Malachai glanced over his shoulder at me. "You have a wolf ally? That, my dear, is impressive."

I shivered with disgust. "Enough with the pet names. You can call me Molly."

"But I do so like Mahlia." He turned toward me, and his eyes seemed to soften. "Your mother wanted you to have part of my name."

I shook my head. "Whatever."

He chuckled. "Azaroth, uncloak the others." He focused on the statues along the walls. "Intruders are about to be revealed."

Gargoyles stepped off their pedestals. No matter how many self-defense lessons I went to, I didn't think I would ever be prepared for something like this.

"Schmenny no gives Azaroth *MaunDagnir*." Azaroth sat up, fidgeting with his t-shirt as he did. "*MaunDagnir* no bes for Azaroth." He lifted his hands and began mumbling something I couldn't understand.

Part of me felt sorry for the little fella, but the rest of me wondered what he'd planned on using the dagger for anyway.

Azaroth finished chanting, and I was unsurprised to see Jayden standing right beside me. Somehow, even though I couldn't sense his presence, I knew he'd be there. The rest of my companions appeared behind us.

As soon as they became visible, the gargoyles bound their hands behind their backs.

Nahvienne squealed when she was grabbed from behind. "Hey, watch it, buddy."

"Go easy on the sheila, mate." Storm's voice boomed through the room.

With everyone free from Azaroth's cloaking spell, I felt more like myself. I could hear their heartbeats and breathing. I knew I wasn't alone. I hadn't wanted them to be discovered, but I actually felt like I could think again.

Two of the statue men held each of my companions. The marble creatures easily weighed a ton each and probably more. There was no chance we could fight them and win. I couldn't see any way out of this.

I nodded toward my companions. "So why didn't they become visible when they stepped on the sigils?"

"Demons can't sneak in here." Malachai shrugged. "If you hadn't come, they would've remained unseen." He rubbed his chin. "I'll have to remedy that."

My entire body slumped, like a helium balloon after most of the air had escaped. Caius had been right. The Arcane Council shouldn't have let me become a guardian. I single-handedly put everyone in danger.

"This isn't your fault." Jayden's voice was meant just for me, but I was sure everyone heard him and formed their own opinions.

"Take her friends over there." Malachai waved his hand toward the far end of the open area, then focused on me again. "I so hoped it would be you who came after your mother."

"Why?" I struggled against statue man, trying to get free of his grip. "So you can sacrifice me?"

Malachai's eyebrows pinched together, and he staggered back a step. "Oh gods, no. Why would you think that?"

"Just admit it." I shook my head. I couldn't sense a lie, but he couldn't be telling the truth, could he? "I found the book in Mom's library. I know what you're planning."

Malachai paced, rubbing his chin. "You found a book in Seraphina's library. Not mine." He sighed. "I'm doing this all wrong. I wanted you to come so I could meet you. I wanted to see the woman you've grown into. Seraphina hasn't allowed me near you since you were almost five years old."

"What?" I couldn't keep the disgust from my voice. "Mom said you left after conception and never came back."

A smirk pulled his lips up. "And you wonder why I call her the Wicked Witch." He waved his hand at statue man. "Let her go."

As soon as my hands were free, I pulled them in front of me and rubbed my wrists. "What about my friends?"

Statue man stayed right beside me as if waiting for Malachai to tell him to restrain me again.

"Ah, yes, your friends." He turned his gaze on them. "Three sorcerers and a werewolf. What an odd combination."

"Why?" I looked at Caelan, Nahvienne, Storm, and Jayden. Caelan and Jayden were the only ones who didn't seem to get along, and that was my fault.

Malachai huffed a laugh. "Yeah, I can see why your mom wouldn't want her cabal to know about that."

Storm dropped his blue-gray gaze to the floor. "Werewolves and sorcerers used to be mates." It was the first time I'd heard him sound subdued. The few times I'd talked to him before, he'd been so animated. "We stood against the fae when they tried to enslave humans."

Malachai strode over to me. "The sorcerers turned on the wolves, siding with the fae."

"Thousands of wolves carked it." Storm tipped his head at Jayden. "Sorry, mate."

Jayden lifted his shoulder. "The wolves took their revenge."

"So many lives lost." Nahvienne shook her head. "Pointless."

"And here you thought one side of you was good and one evil." Malachai lifted my hands, examining my wrists. "But which side is which?"

His touch was gentle. How many times had I faced the opposite at the hands of sorcerers? My chest tightened, and my thoughts seemed to freeze, stuck on that question. Yeah, he'd detained us, but we did sneak into his castle. I didn't know what to think.

Malachai pressed a kiss to the back of my hand. I wanted to jerk away from him, but at the same time, his affection made me soften. How many years had I yearned for Caius to treat me with even an ounce of kindness? Emotions swirled inside me, a cacophony that made me want to scream.

A growl tore out of Jayden's throat. "Let her go."

Malachai dropped my hands and strode over to Jayden, assessing him every step of the way. "You didn't just bring any wolf, did you?"

"He's the beta of the Loess Hills Pack." I watched as Jayden tried to back away from Malachai, but his guards held him firm.

Malachai snatched Jayden's jaw and leaned in, sniffing him. Then he turned toward me. "Your mate?"

Chapter 55

Mate? What the Hell? I looked at Jayden, and he lowered his gaze. He'd known. My mouth dropped open, and I stared at him. He'd known, and he hadn't told me. Why wouldn't he tell me?

"What the hell?" Caelan struggled against the statue holding him and glared at me. "Your mate! Him?"

I stabbed my finger through the air, pointing it at Caelan. "Don't you dare look at me like that, Caelan Thornheart. This is the first I've heard of it." I thrust an accusatory finger at Jayden. "And you?" I hated the slight crack in my voice. "Why didn't you tell me?"

"We barely know each other, Molly." Apparently, the sigil on the floor in front of Jayden was the most interesting thing in the room. He stared down at it, his blond fringe blocking his face from my view. "I wanted you to choose me because you wanted me, not because you knew and felt obligated." He glanced up at me, and the vulnerability in his eyes made my heart clench.

I didn't know what to say or how to react, and I didn't want to have this conversation in front of a bunch of people. (I mean really. How are you supposed to react when someone says, "Hey, babe, we've been on two dates, but you're mine forever"?) I wanted to give him some reassurance, but I didn't know how. I didn't know if I felt the same way. I didn't know anything.

Malachai tugged Jayden's chin, pulling Jayden's focus off of me and onto him. Then, without any warning, he pulled his other hand back and punched Jayden in the gut. Jayden's gold eyes narrowing was his only response. "How dare you lay claim to Mahlia!"

Heat blossomed in my chest, burning through my confusion, and my nostrils flared.

Malachai's fist slammed into Jayden's abs again. "She is *my* daughter, not some *wolf's* plaything!" He pulled his arm back, ready to throw another punch.

"Stop!" Magic blasted out of me unbidden, throwing statue man through the air. He landed with a loud boom and didn't move. I strode across the stone floor until daddy dearest was inches from me. "He is mine." The words escaped me in a growl that sounded nothing like my voice. They tore from my mouth before I could consider their meaning.

Malachai stepped back, and something flickered in his soulless eyes. It was gone too quickly for me to determine exactly what, but I thought it looked a little like delight.

Even though I was staring straight at the demon, I noticed Caelan's shoulders slump forward and heard the air whoosh out of his lungs, but I didn't have time to console him. Instead, I poked my finger into Malachai's chest. "I'm leaving here and taking my friends and Mom with me."

He lifted his hands in a surrender movement that shocked the hell out of me. Then, as quickly as a cobra striking, his thumb caressed my cheek. "I couldn't be prouder of you." He turned his head toward my friends. "Let them go, and bring Seraphina. Azaroth, you will lead Mahlia out of the Abyss."

The blazing inferno inside of me died down to a cozy fire. I wasn't about to let it burn out completely, not as long as I was here. I wasn't stupid enough to trust the demon in front of me. "Not just me." I shook my head and waved my arm at the others. "All of us."

"Yes, all of you." His hand slid to my shoulder, and he squeezed it. "You'll make a fine demon yet."

My heart seemed to skip a beat. I wanted to ask him what that was supposed to mean. He intended to sacrifice me. Didn't he?

Chapter 56

"You can fix a lot of things, but you cannot fix stupidity."
—Kenya Moore

"Molly!" Mom rushed into the room ahead of five gargoyles. Her heels clicked against the stones. Her sapphire, floor-length dress was elegant and emphasized her blue eyes, making them sparkle.

My gaze trailed over her, looking for any signs that she'd been mistreated, but she didn't look like someone who'd been held captive for two weeks. Her long, blonde hair bounced against her back with each step she took. It wasn't dirty or greasy. Her skin was like flawless porcelain, not bruised or marred in any way.

She looked more like someone who'd been visiting the spa, not trapped in the Abyss. Combined with her confidence and grace, she could've been in charge of this place. She stopped in front of me and pulled me into a hug. "You came for me."

I patted her back. "Of course I did."

"Of course you did?" She pulled away from me, shooting me a look that I interpreted as disappointment. "You disappeared four years ago, and I haven't seen hide nor hair of you since." Her voice took on a pouty edge, one she'd used to manipulate me several times through the years. "I've missed my baby girl."

Caelan trudged over, his normally perfect posture hunched. "Seraphina," he bowed slightly, "let's get out of the Abyss. Malachai has agreed to let Azaroth escort us home."

"Yes, Caelan, you're right. This isn't the place for this conversation." She grabbed my hand and squeezed it before walking off with the other sorcerers.

Jayden stayed a step behind me, and even though I didn't know what to think about him, his presence was a comfort.

"Mahlia," Malachai placed his hand on my shoulder, his gentleness catching me by surprise, "now that I have you back in my life, I'm not ready to let you go."

Jayden inched closer to me, and I felt his growl rumble over my skin.

My body tensed, and the hand that I thought of as gentle moments before felt constricting. "You said you'd let me go," I growled out between clenched teeth.

He blinked slowly, drawing my attention to irises nearly the same shade of gray that I'd chosen for my own. "What?" His shoulders slumped slightly. "I can see how you'd think I meant to keep you here."

Maybe it was sleep deprivation or the adrenaline wearing off, but it took me several seconds to make sense of his words. "You don't?"

"No." He shook his head.

Seraphina's heels clacked toward me at a rapid, aggressive pace. "Good." She grabbed my arm. "Then let's get out of here before he changes his mind."

Malachai suddenly looked tired, not sleepy but worn thin by all life had thrown at him. He pulled his hand away. "Go on."

"What were you going to say?" I tried to shake Mom's hand off my arm when she tugged me toward the massive statue where Nahvienne, Caelan, and Storm were waiting, but she wouldn't let go.

Jayden lifted her fingers off of me and stood between us.

Malachai's eyebrows rose, and he stood straighter. "Let me teach you to harness your powers."

My mind spun. This was the demon I'd been warned about, the one I'd pictured all these years was cruel and heartless. I studied his face, searching for a sign of deception, trying to reconcile the man from my imagination with the one standing in front of me.

His gaze caught mine, and the warmth I saw in his eyes was disarming. I wiped my palms on my leggings. He was a demon, born of darkness, but did he have the capacity for good?

His voice was a silken whisper, tempting. His eyes flickered toward Seraphina, a dark gleam in them. "I can teach you to defend yourself, to survive what lurks in the shadows. There are threats you can't fathom—"

"Molly," Mom whined, actually whined. "I've been here two weeks. I don't need to stay a moment longer."

"Let me hear him out." I snapped my head toward her, shaking it as I did.

Seraphina narrowed her eyes at Malachai. "The devil doesn't lure you to his side with threats and violence." Her voice was tinged with the weight of experience. "He gives you what you crave, and by the time you see the trap, it's already been sprang."

"Ah, Seraphina, always seeing deception where none exists." Malachai waved his hand, dismissing her. His voice softened when he focused his attention on me. "You know where you're going. You can make a portal to the base of the statue and save yourself from the hardships of the Abyss."

"Why can't I just portal home from here?" The thought of setting foot outside of Taras Mor sent dread skittering up my spine.

He placed his hand on my shoulder again, and I couldn't help but wonder how lonely his existence was. "Portals don't work between planes, only within them, but I can show you other ways to travel between."

He gave me a gentle squeeze before dropping his hand. "If you ever want to visit your old man, Azaroth will bring you." He turned toward the demon.

Azaroth looked like he'd been thoroughly defeated. "Azaroth dos what master says."

"Without expecting a boon." A bit of Malachai's demon slipped through, and Azaroth nodded while kicking at the sigil closest to his foot.

This whole day had been too much, and even with the nap I'd had in Jayden's room, it had been at least twenty-four hours since I'd slept. I was physically and emotionally exhausted. "Thanks."

I held my hands up, focusing my energy in front of me.

Malachai pointed toward the massive statue. "The wards will prevent you from—" He stood with his mouth hanging open when a portal appeared in front of me.

"You were saying?" I couldn't help but gloat.

"Huh… interesting." Malachai rubbed his chin as if trying to come up with a solution. "But you did use magic when I punched the wolf."

A possessive and hungry sneer tugged at Mom's lips as she stalked toward me. "I always knew my daughter was destined for greatness." She pushed Jayden to the side and wrapped her arm around my waist.

Pulling out of her unsettling grasp, I waved her and everyone else through the portal. Before I stepped into it, Malachai stopped me. "Remember where you found the book." Genuine concern seemed to flicker through his eyes, but could I believe him? "Seraphina is a lot of things, but trustworthy isn't one of them."

"And you are?" I stepped through the portal without waiting for his answer. *If he didn't want to sacrifice me, who did?*

Chapter 57

"Love makes you foolish. It makes you throw every bit of logic away. do stupid things, dangerous things." -Melissa Marr

After Azaroth opened the gateway beneath the demon statue, I created a portal to take us to the base of the Black Angel. Its walls had flickered, but it held until we were beneath the statue. Azaroth opened that gate. The night sky welcomed us. (Thankfully. What if we'd returned in the middle of the day?) And the angel hovered beneath the stars. I climbed the stairs, and the crisp, cool air slapped me in the face, waking me up a little.

When I stepped off the prow of the ship, I looked back at the others. "I won't be going to Ravenwood tonight or tomorrow."

"We'll have a debriefing meeting." Caelan wouldn't meet my eyes.

I walked toward my car. "I won't be there. I'm taking the rest of today and all of tomorrow off." I pressed the button on my fob to unlock the doors. "I'll be sleeping. I think I deserve it."

"You can use your bedroom at Ravenwood Manor." Mom's voice sounded hopeful, but there was no way in hell I'd sleep in the same house as Caius. Not now, not ever again.

I shook my head. "I'm going home. I'll see you all in a couple of days." I buckled myself in, then stared at Jayden. "You rode with me. Are you coming?" I wasn't sure if he or Caelan looked more defeated.

We'd brought Mom back and returned without me becoming a sacrifice. I counted our adventure as a win, but it was hard to tell that when looking at my companions. Nahvienne and Storm were the only ones who appeared content.

Before Jayden could get in, Schmendrick appeared on the passenger seat. "I was beginning to think I'd have to start buying my own treats." He stretched his leg over the console and rested it on my thigh.

"Me too, Buddy." I rubbed his head. "Me too."

He glanced out the window. "You and the dog need to talk. I'll be around if you need me." He disappeared, and Jayden opened the door but didn't get in.

"I can call Garrett." He held onto the door and the frame of the car, staring at the seat, looking lost and defeated.

Maybe I could've handled things better, but I still didn't know what to say or do. "Just get in, Jayden." As soon as the door closed, I put the car in gear and drove off.

"I—"

I lifted my hand in the air, cutting him off. "I don't want to talk about this in the car. We can talk about it when I drop you off or tomorrow, but right now, I need to focus on driving."

"Whatever you need, Molly." He folded his arms over his chest, making his muscles bulge and the veins surface.

I hated how broken he sounded, but I needed time to think. The drive was a blur, and all too soon, I was pulling up to Castle Unicorn. Jayden handed me his fob, making sure not to touch me, and my heart cracked a little more.

My car wound through the trees almost as if it were on autopilot. I parked in front of the iron gate, turned off the engine, and stepped outside. Jayden trudged over to my side and looked at me, waiting for me to say something. All the energy seemed to drain from my body, and I slid down the door until I was squatting in front of him. "Your"—I pointed at him, then turned my finger toward myself—"mate."

He knelt in front of me. "I knew you weren't ready." He rested his elbows on his knees and held his head in his hands. "I knew that first day, the moment I saw you." He looked at me through his fingers, and the pain that radiated from him threatened to crush me. "I hated that I couldn't touch you until I'd tracked your mom, and then I saw your reaction to Caelan and his to you." He dropped his hands and pressed his eyes shut for a moment. "I thought for sure I didn't have a chance in hell, but you gave me one and then another." He hesitated, reaching for my hand but pulling back before grabbing it. "I won't pressure you, and if you don't want me, I'll walk away."

I plopped down on the ground, not caring if my jeans got any dirtier. "Don't you get a choice? Am I even what you'd want?"

He sat at an angle in front of me and pulled my legs over his. "No choice, but Molly, you are everything I would've asked for." He ran his hand from my knee to my hip and back again, over and over. "You're smart, funny, caring, and strong. You're beautiful in this form and just as stunning in your true form."

I wanted to believe him. I wanted everything he said to be true, but how could it be? How could he believe any of it? I was a monster, a creature to be feared, to be tormented, and abused.

"Don't make up your mind about us yet." He trailed his finger from my temple to my jaw. "Get to know me, and then decide." He lifted my legs off of his, then stood and reached for my hand. "I won't rush you, and if you decide you don't want to be with me, I *will* walk away."

I let him help me to my feet. "What happens to you if I say no?"

"Some wolves eventually get another chance. Some don't." He shrugged like it was no big deal, but I could tell by the set of his shoulders that he didn't believe that. "All I ask is that you give me a chance."

I wanted what was between us to be real, not something Jayden was forced into.

"Can you do that?" Fear and hope mingled together in his eyes, and I could picture his wolf standing in front of me with his tail tucked between his legs and his ears down. Those golden eyes looking up at me, begging me for a chance.

I nodded, and he swooped me up, swinging me in the air. I couldn't stop the laugh that erupted out of me. His happiness was contagious and made me wonder if maybe his feelings were real.

"Thank you, Molly." His mouth crashed down on mine while I dangled in his embrace.

He was mine forever if I'd have him, and with one of his hands tangled in my hair and the other clutching my ass, I thought maybe forever wouldn't be long enough.

Chapter 58

$\mathcal{S}$chmendrick cleared his throat. "I see you and the dog have kissed and made up." He sat on the top of my car, staring at me. "So, you found out you're his mate, huh?"

"You knew?" My lips pressed together, and the muscles in my jaw jumped when I clenched my teeth too tightly.

"There's little I don't know." His ears flicked. "And even less I'm allowed to tell you."

Jayden set me down, and I settled my hands on his forearms. I filed Schmendrick's words away for the time being. I would drag them out and analyze them later—probably when I should be sleeping. "Of course, you knew. That was what you meant when you said he would only walk away if he thought it was best for me."

He licked his paw and rubbed it over his ear. "She can be taught." He smirked at me while he continued bathing. "I wouldn't go home if I were you."

My heart sank a little. "Why?"

"*MaunDagnir*." Schmendrick stood and stretched. "Malachai, Seraphina, Caius, and Azaroth all believe you have it. Stay here." He flicked his gaze to Jayden. "I'm sure the dog will be more than happy to share his bed with you."

Heat flared up my neck and over my cheeks. "I, uh, I'm not ready for that."

"No worries, Molly." Jayden wrapped his rugged hand around mine and led me to the castle. "I can curl up on the floor or hold you like I did yesterday."

My chest tightened. I couldn't stay. I just found out I was his mate. What would people think? What would he think? "I need a shower. I'm covered in Abyss, and I don't have anything to change into."

"I'll throw your clothes in the laundry, and you can sleep in one of my shirts." He squeezed my hand. "Relax, Molly. It's just one night."

Jayden took me in through the front door. As soon as we stepped inside, the smell of lasagna and garlic bread assaulted me. My stomach growled in response. When was the last time I'd eaten?

Jayden chuckled. "I'll fix you a plate while you shower. Just grab a shirt out of my dresser." He pointed me in the right direction, then headed the other way.

I found Jayden's room without running into anybody else, by the grace of God, and looked longingly at the bed. I just wanted to curl up and sleep, but I'd crawled around the Abyss, been splashed by that dark moat water, and I probably stunk. I opened up the second drawer of his dresser and pulled out the first shirt I found. Unsurprisingly, it was black.

When I finished my shower, I pulled on Jayden's t-shirt. It came to the middle of my thighs, but I felt naked in it anyway. I combed my fingers through my hair, then decided I'd procrastinated long enough.

Jayden was sitting at his desk with two plates piled with food in front of him. "Do you mind if I eat before I shower?" His eyes roved over me, and even though I knew he was admiring me, I squirmed under his gaze.

"No, go ahead." I held the bottom of the shirt while I sat, trying to keep it from riding up too much. I cut the lasagna into bite-sized pieces, then pushed it around on the plate. I'd eaten two meals with him, but this was too intimate. (Me sitting in his bedroom in nothing but his t-shirt, and him looking at me like I was a bunuelo that he was about to devour.)

He reached across the desk, his hand hovering over mine. "Molly, I promise I won't push you."

"I," I cleared my throat and stared at my plate, "I don't know what to do or think. I don't want to lead you on. I don't want to be that girl."

Jayden's expression softened. "I know you're not being that girl." He leaned closer, his amber gaze never leaving mine. "You don't have to figure it out right now, but, Molly, I want you to know that what I feel for you is real."

"How do you know?" My heart raced, and I looked down at his hand. Nicks and scars crisscrossed his tan skin. Veins stood out, hinting at his strength, but I knew, deep down, *I knew* that he would never use that strength against me. "I've spent so long hiding from people, and I'm not used to this."

His fingers twitched, but he left his hand above mine. I wondered if he was waiting for me to bridge the gap. "To what, Molly?"

"Any of this." I hesitated, not knowing how to answer. When I looked into his eyes, the sincerity and tenderness I saw in them were almost overwhelming. "To your kindness. You heard Lorelei and Caius."

A tear slipped down my cheek, followed by another. "I want to trust you. I want to try," I lifted my hand, twining my fingers through his, "but I don't know how."

"A chance is all I'm asking for." He squeezed my fingers, then looked at my plate. "Lasagna is Melissa's specialty. You'd better eat up."

Jayden strode into the room wearing nothing but a pair of loose-hanging athletic shorts. His wet hair was tousled. A drop of water clung to his collarbone. With his next step, it was jarred loose and trailed over his pecs and abs until soaking into the top of his shorts.

Warmth flooded my body, and I wanted to touch him, to run my fingers over his skin, to trace the path the droplet had followed.

He chuckled. "As soon as I cool down, I'll shift and sleep on the rug." He sat next to me on the edge of the bed, and I stuffed my hands under the covers. When my fingers touched my thighs, shivers tingled over my skin.

Jayden's pupils dilated, and his nostrils flared. (Me, here, in his room with him was a bad idea.) "Do you need anything?" His voice was husky, and warmth flashed through me.

"You don't have to sleep on the floor." My face heated until it matched the fire burning inside of me. *What are you doing?* I screamed at myself inside my head.

My hands itched with the need to run over every inch of his exposed skin, but I couldn't do that to him, not if I was going to eventually turn down his offer.

He brushed my hair back and tucked it behind my ear. "Thanks for the offer, but I'll be fine." He kissed my forehead. "Goodnight, Molly."

The morning sun streamed in through the stained-glass window. Colorful beams of light danced over every surface, and I woke up snuggled against Jayden. My head was on his chest, and his arms were wrapped around me. I tried to move away, but his grip tightened.

"You were having nightmares." I shouldn't have been surprised to hear Schmendrick, but I was. "You were thrashing and crying out, but as soon as he climbed into bed and pulled you to his side, you stopped." He walked over the top of me and settled on Jayden's stomach. "He soothes you."

I scratched behind Schmendrick's ear while I tried to remember what I'd dreamt about. I was sure it had to do with the Abyss or *MaunDagnir*, but whatever it was, the memory was gone. "He does."

Chapter 59

"What really bothers me—and what I think is the height of arrogance and stupidity—is when one group believes their way is the only way."
—Leslie Jordan

"**W**hy does everyone think I have *MaunDagnir*?" It hadn't occurred to me last night, but driving down Castle Unicorn's long driveway with Schmendrick curled on the passenger seat, I realized it made no sense. "Azaroth knew Caelan had it."

Schmendrick peeked up at me. "Caelan doesn't know what *MaunDagnir* is. He doesn't know the risks of having it, so I made them see him give it to you." He curled his tail over his face. "I knew the dog would keep you safe."

Dust from a passing car filled the air. I waited for it to clear before pulling onto the gravel road. "Caelan will give it to Mom.

He has an overdeveloped sense of responsibility, and he'll think it's the right thing to do."

"Which is why you must talk to him first."

Talking to Caelan was one of the last things I wanted to do. After hearing Malachai state that Jayden and I were mates, Caelan would probably like Mom or Malachai or Caius—or whoever wanted it most—to sacrifice me. "Great." As much as I didn't want to go to Ravenwood, I knew I needed to, though. (Damn conscience.)

Schmendrick was snoring softly by the time I pulled onto I-29. The gentle sound allowed my mind to wander.

Why would Mom have asked Malachai to drag her to the Abyss, and how often did they talk anyway? Why had she tolerated him being part of my life until I was five? Why not after, and why couldn't I remember him?

Was it just a coincidence that the book and MaunDagnir were in Mom's office? Was she trying to keep them out of somebody else's hands, or did she plan on using them?

And Jayden…

"No." I smacked my hands on the steering wheel. I needed to think about Jayden, about being his mate and all that meant, but not while I was driving to Ravenwood Estates.

I drove past Bunge and MidAmerican Energy. Trying to keep my thoughts on the road, but the growl of the tires reminded me of Jayden's protectiveness in the Abyss. He cared about me, whether I was his choice or not, but was he the one for me?

A smile crept across my lips when I remembered how good it felt to wake up in his arms, how right.

I shook my head and turned the radio up, trying to drown my thoughts beneath the music.

Schmendrick's ears flicked back. "I'm trying to sleep here."

"Sorry, Buddy." I bounced my shoulders to the music. "I'm trying not to think."

"About whom?"

I turned the volume down a little. "Jayden."

"Do you like him?" Schmendrick sat up and stared at me in that way that cats do, where it seems like they're looking into your soul.

I nodded. "Maybe more than I should for how little I know him."

"And how would you feel if you never saw him again?" His eyes narrowed with a knowing glint as he basked in his own superiority.

My heart clenched, and the anguish that consumed me caught me off guard. How had he become so important to me so quickly?

"That's answer enough." His gaze was a blend of aloofness and smugness that only a cat could perfect.

I stood in front of Ravenwood Citadel, wishing there was a way to enter without seeing whatever the guardians wanted to show me. Unfortunately, my magic didn't care what I wished. I grasped the handle, and the runes burned against my palm as blue light flared. It followed the veins, drawing an image from two sides.

I squinted, trying to figure out what was forming. Finally, the sea hydra exploded from the moat. Water sprayed up around the beast, and Taras Mor rose behind it. Even seeing it on the door made my pulse race and my hands tremble.

"Thanks." I rolled my eyes and shook my head. "Couldn't you have warned me ahead of time?"

I pulled the door open and stepped inside. The hallway to Caelan's office seemed never-ending, yet somehow, I arrived too soon. I stared at the door for several seconds before lifting my hand to knock.

"Come in." Caelan's voice was muffled by the thick wood.

I stood with my hand on the knob, debating whether or not to turn and walk down the hall, for long enough that he repeated himself louder. I twisted the handle and pushed the door open slowly.

His hazel gaze hardened as it traveled from the top of my head to my feet. "Guess you didn't go home." His lip curled up in disgust. "Spend the night with your mate, did ya?"

"Don't be an ass, Cae." I flopped down in the chair across from his desk, not waiting for an invitation. "I didn't know until D—" I huffed. "Malachai said it, and I don't know what to think about it. I've been on two dates in my entire life."

He folded his arms over his chest and narrowed his gaze on me. "If you didn't stay with him, why are you in yesterday's clothes?"

I sucked in a deep breath and held it for a few seconds. Anger wouldn't help. "I stayed at Castle Unicorn because Schmendrick warned me not to go home because of *MaunDagnir*."

He stood, walked past the bookcase to the cabinet in the corner, grabbed a bottle of whiskey, and poured himself a shot.

"It's a bit early for that, isn't it?" It wasn't even lunchtime yet.

He glared at me as he slammed it back, then poured himself another. "What does that even mean? What does *MaunDagnir* have to do with anything?" He walked to his window without looking at me.

"It's dangerous, and everyone believes I have it." Even though he was pissed at me, I decided to trust him. I explained what I knew of the dagger and told him about the book I'd found in Mom's office and even what Malachai had said to me. "You can't give it to Mom."

The entire time I'd been talking, he'd been staring outside. He finally spun around, and his eyes were wide. "I gave it to Seraphina as soon as we were alone."

My stomach dropped. "I knew you would. I told Schmendrick you would."

"You should've told me!" He slammed his hand down on the windowsill and knocked his lowball glass off. It hit the floor and shattered, scattering pieces of broken glass across the room. "You should've trusted me." He stomped to the corner, pulled a shot glass from the cabinet, and filled it.

I jumped to my feet, tossing my hands in the air as I did. "When? There wasn't much point when I thought Azaroth would end up with it. Once I realized he wasn't going to, you weren't exactly talking to me or even looking at me." I dragged a shaky hand through my hair.

"You don't…" He sat in his desk chair, looking deflated. "I'm sorry, Molly. For everything." He stared past my shoulder. "You don't think Seraphina wants to sacrifice you." He shook his head like the thought was too absurd to even be considered. Then he looked at me. "Do you?"

I plopped down on the edge of his desk. "I don't know what to think." I huffed out a laugh. "I think instead of the Abyss, we made a trip to Wonderland." I remembered the times Caelan had read Alice's Adventures in Wonderland to me while I hid from Caius. I remembered all the times we thought it would be a better place to be. All the times we'd talked about running away to Wonderland. Never realizing what a confusing mess it would be.

"'If I had a world of my own, everything would be nonsense. Nothing would be what it is because everything would be what it isn't.'" He dragged one hand backward and one forward, spinning the shot glass between his palms. "It is all a mess, isn't it?" He slammed down his shot before looking up at me. "What are you going to do about the wolf?"

I lifted my shoulder. "For now…" This was so not the conversation I wanted to have with Caelan. "…give him a chance, I guess."

He poured another shot, and I left him to drown in his bottle.

Chapter 60

"We live in a time where intelligent people are being silenced so that stupid people won't be offended." -Unknown

Schmendrick waited for me in the hallway. "I should have kept an eye on him." He walked with his body low to the ground, and the tip of his tail nearly dragged on the floor.

"We'll figure it out, Schmen." I stepped outside into the unnatural weather. It was November, but in Ravenwood Estates, it felt more like April.

When I opened the gate to Ravenwood Manor, I couldn't help but laugh. The yard was filled with dandelions gone to seed. Their fluffy heads stretched to the cloudless, blue sky. Thousands upon thousands of wishes waiting to come true.

"Miss Mahlia." I turned in a circle, searching for the high-pitched voice that had called out to me.

A swath of dandelions undulated in a path heading straight toward me.

"Get inside, Molly." Schmendrick arched his back, and the fur along his spine stood up. His tail was fluffed out to nearly three times its normal size.

I made it about five steps before a lizard rushed out of the dandelions and onto the pathway in front of me.

Schmendrick hissed and swatted his paw at the creature.

"It's just a lizard, Schmen." I bent to pick him up, to pull him away from the poor thing, and I realized the lizard wasn't just a lizard.

It lifted onto its hind legs, standing about knee-high to me. A tiny loin cloth was wrapped around its… his waist, and a scabbard was strapped to his chest. Weapons stuck out above his shoulders. He whipped a hat off his head and bowed with a flourish that would've made Jack Sparrow proud. "Miss Mahlia, if it pleases you, can you make the dandelions disappear?" He opened his eyes wide, the pupils taking up most of them, making him look innocent and helpless. (How do animals do that? And why can't I?)

Schmendrick stood rigid between us. Low growls emanated from him, and his agitation made the hairs on the back of my neck rise. I couldn't remember a time when he'd been so upset. His modus operandi was to resort to snarky comments and nonchalance.

"Why don't you want them here?" I petted Schmendrick's head, trying to understand why this creature aggravated him so much.

The lizard waved his arm, encompassing the entire yard. "They're everywhere." He looked up at me like he was afraid he might have offended me or something. "They're quite lovely, but no matter what we do, they come back, choking out the grass and flowers. Please, Miss Mahlia, help us."

Schmendrick sat on his haunches and licked his paw. He had an air of disinterest about him, but his eyes were still fixated on the lizard. "Caius hired kobolds to be his gardeners." He rubbed his paw over his ear. "That should've been Seraphina's first clue to rid herself of him."

"You're the gardener?" I knelt on one knee to get a better look at him.

He nodded and squeezed the brim of his hat with both hands. "Name's Vak, Miss Mahlia."

"Please call me Molly." I stood and looked around at the wishes waiting to be made. How I would've loved a yard full of them as a child. "All right." I closed my eyes and tried to remember how I'd planted the dandelions to begin with. It felt like it had been ages ago, but it had only been a few days. So much had happened since being dragged back into this world of magic and monsters, and for the first time, I realized I wasn't ready to give it up.

With my eyes closed, I felt the thrum of magic around me and the dandelions receding into the soil. I focused next on the grass, strengthening its roots and undoing any damage the dandelions might have caused.

When I opened my eyes, Vak tossed his hat in the air and did a little happy dance that made my heart sing. "The Raven-wood Warren of Kobolds is forever indebted to you, Miss Mahli—Molly." He put his hat back on, dropped to all four feet, and dashed off through the yard.

"What the hell was that about, Schmen?" I looked down at the cat still bathing at my feet. "Why didn't you want me to talk to him?"

Schmendrick stood and trotted off, his tail flicking haughtily through the air. "Kobolds are notoriously evil."

"Okay, well, Vak didn't seem evil." I knocked once on the door, not waiting for an answer before swinging it open.

He trotted inside and looked over his shoulder at me. "Looks can be deceiving. Don't forget that." He gazed up the staircase. "Especially now."

Chapter 61

*"The very powerful and the very stupid have one thing in common.
They don't alter their views to fit the facts.
They alter the facts to fit their views." -Doctor Who*

*T*hese walls had ears, and I didn't want to risk being over-heard as we trudged up the steps to Mom's office. *Why now? What do you know?*

Everything, Molly. He scoffed. *But nothing that I can share at this time.*

Mom sat at her desk so focused on whatever she was look-ing at that she didn't notice me standing there. Her blonde hair was pulled into a severe bun, and her charcoal suit had to have cost a small fortune. I knocked on the wood trim around the door and stepped inside.

When she looked up and saw it was me, her eyes widened, and I swore some of the color drained from her face, but it could've just been the candlelight flickering. She stood, setting whatever she'd been looking at face down on her desk.

She needn't have bothered. I recognized it from when I'd searched her office. The photo of Malachai had something scrawled across the back in a language I didn't know. I should've asked Schmendrick about it before, but I'd been a little freaked out by the prospect that Malachai could see through his image.

"Mahlia!" She rushed toward me with her arms spread wide. "I didn't expect to see you today." She wrapped me in a hug, then held me at arm's length, looking me over with a smidge of disgust or disappointment. I wasn't sure which. "You really should dress nicer when you're here."

I lifted one shoulder to my ear and took a step back. Knowing it would irritate her nearly as badly as my wardrobe, I said, "No, y'all"—yes, here in the southwest corner of Iowa, we say y'all—"should learn to accept me for who I am. I ain't about to change."

"So, you plan on sticking around?" Hope and a bit of hurt mixed in her voice.

I walked around her office, looking at the shelves, wondering what she had done with *MaunDagnir*. "I don't have a choice, do I? I pledged myself as a guardian so I could save you. From what I understand, that's a life sentence."

"Oh, Mahlia," she shook her head, "you've always been so difficult when it comes to magic and responsibility. I fear I spoiled you far too much."

There was so much I wanted to say, so many things I wanted to remind her of, but it wouldn't do any good. She would never see her faults, so I smirked at her and bit my tongue.

Schmendrick rubbed against my leg, letting me know I wasn't alone. Without him, I never would have survived long enough to flee.

I walked the entire perimeter of the room, but I didn't see or feel *MaunDagnir*. "Did you really ask Malachai to take you to the Abyss?"

"Is that what he told you?" Her perfectly plucked eyebrows pinched together, and she pressed her hand to her chest. "Oh, honey, why would I do that?"

She returned to her desk. As soon as she sat, she picked up a book and started flipping through the pages. "I will have Maureen change your sheets and clean your room. It'll be spotless by the time you return with your things." She glanced up at me. "I'll appoint a sorcerer to train you in self-defense. There's no need for you to keep spending time with that mangy wolf now that I'm back."

"I won't be staying here, and Jayden is the wolf's name." She'd find out soon enough—if she didn't know already—that I was his mate but not from me. "He risked his life to rescue you, and he's going to continue my training."

She widened her eyes and tipped her head to the side. "What can I do to make you see how much I love you, that I only want what's best for you?"

"That ship sailed, Mom." My hands clenched at my sides, but I tried to keep a saccharine edge to my voice. "I'm going back to work at the coffee shop, to live the life I made for myself, but I'll be here for meetings, missions, and sword training with Nahvienne."

She slammed the book against the desk. "You can't just leave the cabal! This is your home. It's your birthright."

"It was my prison." I strode toward the door. "But, no more. I'll be here for training tomorrow. I still plan on taking today off."

I bounded down the steps with Schmendrick on my heels. When I stepped outside, I lifted my head and breathed in the fresh air. There was still so much I needed to do, but first, I needed a day off.

"That won't be the end of it." Schmendrick trotted down the path.

I followed after him. Mom had never been good at taking no for an answer. She would try everything to drag me back, but, for better or for worse, I wasn't the same Molly she remembered. I smiled at Schmendrick as I opened my car door. "I'm sure it won't be, but it's a good start."

The best way to help an author or to thank them for writing a book that captivated you is to leave a review.

If you enjoyed this book or even if you didn't,
please go online and leave a review.

Reviews sell books.

Without them, authors struggle to gain traction.

Author Notes

Schmendrick is an amalgamation of all my kitties. If I could understand what they're saying to me, I'm sure most of it would relate to giving them treats, and the rest would be telling me how stupid I am for not being able to understand them.

When Schmendrick first comes into Molly's life, he bites her belly. That is what Galadriel does if she's sitting on you and you're not giving her the attention she rightly deserves. Schmendrick's embarrassment is also one of her traits. I've never had a cat that gets embarrassed before, but she does, and it is so cute.

In one part of the book, Schmendrick holds his paw up in the air, reaching for Molly. That is Bella. When she wants my husband to pet her, she reaches for him and holds her paw up until he does.

From Merida, Schmendrick gets his purr that sounds like a frog. Sometimes, she is so loud that her purr is all you can hear, and she sounds just like the tree frogs that hang out around our pond. He also gets his desire to only have his belly rubbed three times from her.

Westley is my buddy. He always wants to be near me and to help me with everything. He loves catnip and cat mint, and if one of my kitties was going to help drive a car, it would be him.

I started writing *Shadowborn Sorceress* shortly after Mom was diagnosed with breast cancer. Mom fought hard, always focusing on what she would do once she beat it, always planning to go back to volunteering as an EMT. Shortly after beating breast cancer, she was elected as the Assistant Chief for the Malvern Volunteer Rescue, Inc.

Then she was diagnosed with leukemia in December of 2023 and passed away April 18, 2024.

My mom, Vicki Drews, was nothing like Molly's mom in this book. My mom was a hero who saved many lives and impacted so many more. Losing her was the hardest thing that's ever happened to me, and I miss her every day.

Acknowledgements

When it comes to writing the acknowledgements, I feel utterly inadequate. It's not that I'm not grateful for anyone. It's not that nobody helped me. It's that I might forget to mention somebody, so if you're that person, I am truly sorry.

Thank you, Jeff, for always being there and never leaving me behind. Thank you for reading this book so many times that you're sick of it and for helping me figure out the places in it that were rushed or neglected. And, most of all, thank you for loving me unconditionally.

Thank you, Jami and Jesse, for always encouraging me, for understanding when I work on my book when we're together, and for being my biggest cheerleaders.

Thank you, Mom and Dad, for giving me wings so that I can fly.

My beta readers, Jenny Sandiford and Miri Cosette, are amazing authors, and when you finish reading this, you should check out their books.

My ARC readers and everyone who helped me promote my book on social media are the best! You have no idea what your support means to me.

I'd like to give a special shout-out to M.H. Woodscourt for taking time out of her busy schedule to read my book. You really should check out her novels. All of them are fantastic.

Most importantly, I'd like to thank you, my readers, for picking up this book and giving it a chance.

Thank You!

Thank you to everyone who sent me your coffee order:

Jeff Oyster and Jesse Oyster (Caelan's drink)

Jason Drews (Jason's drink)

Melissa Wadsworth, Sophia Alessandrini,
and Benjamin Davidson (Molly's drink)

Ashley W. Slaughter (Simone's drink)

Chuck Raymer (Chuckles' drink)

Darley Collins (Melissa's drink)

Kayla Griffith (Kayla's drink)

Mariruth Gruis

Dana Firkins

Cateline Isely

Analisa Krahmer

Valerie Garner

Michelle Timmins

Christine Elaine

J.C. Seal

Laura Quinn

Diane E. Samson

Jennifer Jones

I'm planning two more books in this series, so your order
might still show up in one of them.

If you liked this story, you can join my mailing list.
Drop by my website MandiOyster.com
or if you have any comments,
shoot me a note at mandi@mandioyster.com.
I am always happy to hear from people who've read my work.
I try to answer every email I receive.

Facebook – https://www.facebook.com/MandiOysterAuthor
Instagram – https://www.instagram.com/mandioyster/
My web page – MandiOyster.com

About the Author

Mandi Oyster lives in Southwest Iowa in the middle of an enchanted forest where unicorns, fairies, and dragons abound. At least, that's what she assumes when she looks out into the trees. Her husband, two kids (when they're not away at college), four cats, and two chinchillas share the house with her.

Besides being an author, she also runs her own editing business and works full-time as a digital prepress technician for a local printshop.

You can find her online at:
https://www.MandiOyster.com
https://www.facebook.com/MandiOysterAuthor
https://instagram.com/MandiOyster/